CHASING BENEDICT

The Gentleman Courtesans Book 5

VICTORIA VALE

PROLOGUE

ETON COLLEGE, 1797

The frigid air of a November evening permeated the bedchamber like an invisible, smothering fog, making every hair on Benedict Sterling's body stand on end. As he lay shivering beneath a pile of thin, scratchy blankets, he imagined himself surrounded by the comforts of home. A warm fire and his heavy, damask counterpane, his hound Caesar laid across his feet. His father had boxed his ears on more than one occasion for sneaking the dog into his bed, but it was never enough to deter him. Viscount Sterling was abominable as father's went. Still, Benedict would gladly have endured the man's dismissal and harsh punishments in exchange for rooms warmed by blazing fires, and the decadent warmth of a cup of chocolate heating his belly.

Curling his knees into his chest, he willed sleep to claim him. Once exhaustion pushed him into unconsciousness, the cold would no longer matter.

Mrs. Culpepper—the dame over the boardinghouse he inhabited with twelve other boys—was as stingy with coal and tapers as she was with smiles or kindness. The lives of some lads could be made easier by the generous allowances. Those who came from families with deep pockets had the blunt to afford such niceties that could lessen the discomforts of life at Eton. However, while Benedict came from a family with an illustrious name and several fruitful estates, his father's parsimony rivaled Dame Culpepper's. The viscount believed that the rigors of school life were part of what made a boy into a man. In his day, he had endured the same sparse accommodations, grueling schedule, and harsh physical punishments—and he expected his sons to do the same without complaint.

Benedict suffered in silence, determined that his father be given no further ammunition toward his scorn. Viscount Sterling was a hard, uncompromising man, but proved doubly so regarding his youngest son. For years, Benedict had thought it simply the matter of being neither the heir nor the spare, but time had proven otherwise. It was as if Benedict's father could sense something was wrong with him—something that should be crushed and obliterated to make him into the sort of man a father could be proud of.

That his mother doted on him to compensate for cruel treat-ment only made matters worse. The viscount hated what he saw as 'coddling,' and did everything he could to come between Benedict and the one person in the world who loved him without condition or requirement. The viscount had insisted that once his sons were placed in the care of a tutor rather than a governess, the time for cosseting was over. Only a man could make boys into men, and the early years of suckling at the viscountess's teat were behind them.

The viscountess had done her duty by providing sons, and she was now meant to step aside and allow the father to mold them into gentlemen. But Agatha Sterling had been the first friend Benedict had ever known, the only one to accept him without condition. For that, she had Benedict's devotion, and there was nothing his father could do to break it.

Slipping one hand beneath his lumpy pillow, Benedict

fingered the edges of the letters he kept there. On the pages were the viscountess' words, written with love and care. He only needed to survive the next six weeks before the term ended and he could travel home for Christmas. While there, he might at least pretend he would never have to return to this hellish place ever again.

He conjured his mother's image—soft and pretty with dark blonde hair and velvety brown eyes that shined with the light of a jubilant soul. Benedict had never been brave enough to ask his mother if the viscount made her happy, but then, he was certain he already knew the answer. Her light was dimmed whenever the viscount was near, as if the candle of her soul had been blown out. She became silent and docile, eyes lowered, voice soft.

She'd been a coveted debutante her first Season, pursued by all manner of titled, upstanding men. Marriage to his father had been practical, a good match by the conventions of society. She was the consummate viscountess, upholding the image of a titled family as she had been bred to. But she was most happy when painting, dressed in an old gown and smock, fingers dyed from her watercolors, hair in a haphazard knot. Benedict loved to sit and watch her paint, wanting to absorb the moments of peace and serenity she was allowed when immersed in her art. She would often pause in the midst of her work and smile at him, lighting up the entire room.

"Come and help me?" she would ask, inclining her head to beckon him over.

Her tinkling laughter always made him smile as she used her smock to wipe the paint splatter from his chin.

"You're a work of art all on your own," she would croon, kissing his nose. "You need no enhancement."

Benedict stiffened at the sound of scuffling, trying to determine if he heard footsteps or the scurry of mice. Or perhaps it was one of his roommates going to use the chamber pot. Both assumptions were proven wrong when the blankets were snatched away, exposing him to the cold and dark. Benedict thrashed and swung his fists, determined to fight off the hands that accosted him. There were multiple boys, strong fingers tightening around arms and legs to stretch him taut as something coarse and heavy fell over his head. His breath came in panicked gasps, this form of darkness far more frightening than that of the room itself. It suffocated him, making it difficult to fight as he rolled off the bed and crashed to the rough floorboards.

Jerked to his feet, his wrists were bound behind his back even as he struggled fruitlessly. Then, a kick in his rear propelled him forward. Chuckles and low, boyish whispers came muffled through what he assumed was a gunny sack.

Benedict had no choice but to go along with whatever prank was being played. He knew from experience that calling for Dame Culpepper—the old shrew—would only get him a verbal tongue lashing before the guilty parties cornered him at an opportune moment to deliver retaliation. Whatever this might be about, it was best to go along with it and let the other lads have a laugh at his expense.

The pounding of several pairs of boots would have been enough to wake the dead, though everyone knew the dame wouldn't stir if the entire house fell down around them. Her love of gin ensured she went jug-bitten to her bed every night. Benedict's stockinged, frozen toes ached with every step, and the clench of the binding around his wrists made his fingers throb.

He visualized each part of the house as they passed through it—the corridor and stairs, the entrance hall, then out the front door. The air outside was only slightly worse than in his room, but the ground was damp from this afternoon's rain, soaking through Benedict's stockings. His abductors became rowdier the farther they drew from the house, laughing and joking in voices he could hardly tell apart.

"Where are you taking me?" he demanded.

An elbow jabbed him in the ribs as he renewed his struggles, causing him to trip and stub his toe on a stone.

"Don't worry, Benny," a voice taunted in his left ear. "Nothing to worry about. We have a nice surprise waiting for you."

"Yes … a nice … warm and wet surprise," another boy quipped, producing more laughter.

"Come along, Benny-boy!" someone said from his right. "Step lightly! Jolly Jemima won't wait for you all night!"

Dread curled low in Benedict's gut as he realized what was happening. "Jolly" Jemima Thacker was the daughter of a local tavern owner, notorious among the boys of Eton. By day and early evening, she worked as a barmaid in her father's establishment, but when the old man had turned in for the night, and all within the village went quiet, she plied a different trade. Having just passed his fourteenth birthday, it was Benedict's turn to have a taste of Jolly Jemima—courtesy of the other boys who had already drank from that coveted, overused well.

The stench of horses and manure infiltrated his senses, and the prick of hay through his stockings told him they'd entered a stable. Shivering and seething, he was brought to an abrupt halt, then the sack was yanked away. Benedict blinked against the sudden burst of light from a lantern hanging on a nail. He stood in a—thankfully clean—stall surrounded by mounds of hay.

There was much murmuring and jostling as the other boys fought for a clear view. Benedict's eyes flared wide at the sight of Jemima Thacker, hands braced on her hips as she stood before him wearing nothing but a thin chemise, stockings, and a pair of worn shoes.

"'Bout time you lot showed up," she grumbled while hitching up her hem. "I'm freezing my bloody dugs off. But you'll make me nice an' warm in no time, won't you, lad?"

Benedict could only stare, numb with disbelief as she disrobed without a modicum of shame. She was a petite woman, with an unremarkable face and a head of stringy, lifeless hair. However, everything south of her neck made her popular among the young men—her wide hips and heavy breasts, the thick bush of dark hair between her thighs.

Morbid fascination gripped him, as he had never before seen a nude woman in person. His schoolmates traded books and bawdy prints, and Benedict had glanced over them all in a quest to understand the fascination of other boys with the opposite sex. While he could certainly appreciate a pretty face or the efforts of a well-dressed lady, he wasn't nearly as obsessed with body parts and erotic functions as the others. It seemed yet another thing that wasn't quite right about him, but the depth and meaning of it escaped him whenever he dwelled on it.

"Well? C'mon then," she prodded when he failed to act on her indecent display. "Night's already paid for, an' time's waistin'!"

Benedict stumbled when he was pushed farther into the stall, his heart thudding wildly against his breastbone. He had never given much thought to the inevitability of tupping his first woman, but certainly didn't relish doing away with his virginity in a stable with a gang of other boys looking on. Jemima advanced, but he backed away as if recoiling from the strike of a venomous snake.

"No," he protested, bumping against the wall of boys blocking his only way out. "Let me go."

"What's the matter, Benny-boy?" someone taunted, poking at his spine with a bony finger. "There's nothing to be frightened of. She doesn't bite."

"Not unless he wants me to," Jemima quipped, prompting more laughter. She grinned, showing a black gap where one of her front teeth ought to be.

"I said no," Benedict snapped, fighting to keep his voice from wavering as he spun to face the others. "Stand aside."

Among them stood his most hated foe, Lionel Blackburn. Like Benedict, he was larger than the other boys—tall and wide through the shoulders. His face was composed of arrogant lines and harsh edges, with dark, menacing eyes that showed his disdain for anyone he thought beneath him. Benedict, he had decided upon their first meeting, was perfect prey for teasing, insults, and cruelty.

"Now, now," Lionel chided with a sneer. "We went through all this trouble for you. The least you could do is say thank you."

Benedict ground his teeth, fists clenched at his sides as he stared at Lionel. He had never wanted to plant someone a facer as badly as he did Lionel.

"*No*, thank you," he growled. "Get out of my way."

"Here now!" Jemima exclaimed. "You told me the little shit was eager to 'ave me!"

Lionel inclined his head, as the other boys elbowed one another and grinned. "He ought to be ... unless there's some reason our friend Benny doesn't fancy a willing woman."

Benedict scoffed. "I'm not putting my prick anywhere yours has been."

A palm slammed into Benedict's chest, throwing him off his feet. With the wind knocked from him, he was helpless to avoid the hands of half a dozen boys divesting him of his meager clothing.

"He's just a little shy," someone bellowed as he was stripped of first one stocking, then the other.

"Nothing to be afraid of," another added. "Just lie there. Jemima will do all the work."

Laughter and ribald jokes floated through the air as Benedict scuttled away from his assailants, stark naked and freezing.

"Sod off, the lot of you," he snarled.

Lionel grinned, raking Benedict's nude body with a knowing gaze. "Something the matter? You're as limp as a dead fish!"

Humiliation washed over him as the other boys took in the evidence of his disinterest. He hadn't so much as stirred at the sight of Jemima.

"It's bloody freezing," he countered. "And I've already told you, I'm not interested. Now get out of my way!"

Crossing his arms over his chest, Lionel laughed. "I told you there was something wrong with him. He's backwards ... broken."

"I'll break *you* if you don't stand aside," Benedict roared, his face flushing hot. Fingernails digging into his palms, he shook with rage.

"You ungrateful little shit," the boy to Lionel's left spat.

Everything happened so fast that it was nearly over before Benedict could make sense of it. Lionel's fist slammed into his gut, making him double over. Another blow snapped his head back, and he lost his balance.

"The little cunt thinks he's too good for the likes of Jemima," one of the boys joked as they all converged on him at once, fists and feet swinging with vicious intent. "It is our duty to defend her honor."

Benedict curled into himself, gritting his teeth to keep from crying out as he was assaulted from all sides. Back, belly, legs, face ... none were safe as the boys went at him with the ferocity of a pack of wolves. He could only cup his hands around his privates to protect them and pray for it to end.

"What's the matter, Benny?" Lionel taunted, his voice booming over the jeers of the other lads. "If Jemima wasn't what you wanted, you should have simply said so ... I would have happily arranged a renter for you instead."

Benedict reared to his feet, rage boiling up from his gut to scorch his throat, making him feel as if he could spew fire. His fury lent him strength as he lunged through the phalanx of boys trying to pummel him, sights set on Lionel. He chuckled and kneed Benedict in the groin, throwing him back to the wolves.

"Now, now," he chided with a click of his tongue. "I am flattered you wish to throw yourself at me, but poor Jemima's freezing and needs someone to warm her up. Since you aren't man enough ..."

Benedict slumped onto a mound of hay, his attackers' interest in him waning as Lionel strutted toward the waiting prostitute like a preening rooster. Benedict's entire body ached, and the trickle of blood into one eye obscured his vision. Swallowing past the urge to vomit, he looked away from the unpalatable sight of Lionel lowering his breeches and sprawling over the waiting Jemima.

Swiping blood out of his eyes and crawling toward his discarded nightshirt, Ben did his best to avoid drawing attention back to himself. He quietly slipped into the garment, wincing at the throbbing in his ribs. Raising his arms caused enough pain to nearly render him unconscious, but Benedict remained on his feet, determined to make his escape.

He stumbled out into the night with both arms wrapped around his middle, the world around him narrowing to a single pinpoint. Staying alert felt essential to his survival, so he placed one foot in front of the other, refusing to give Lionel and the others the satisfaction of finding him unconscious in the mud. Dame Culpepper's house loomed just ahead, and the notion that he would survive if he could only get inside gripped him tight.

The dame's snores echoed through the corridors as he trudged up the stairs, his blood-soaked stockings staining the carpet as he went. He was bleeding from several places—his lip, his brow. His nose gushed like a geyser, making his nightshirt and stockings unsettlingly warm and sticky.

That he reached his bed felt like some sort of miracle, and relief swept over him as he fell face-first onto the mattress and lost consciousness.

When Benedict trudged into the kitchen the next morning—the only place in the house he was privileged to experience a warm fire—Dame Culpepper dropped a teacup and saucer at the sight of him. It took every ounce of his strength to stand tall and accept her wide-eyed perusal, along with that of ten other boys. Lionel gave Benedict a smug smirk from where he sat between two of the lads who had taken part in last night's abduction and beating. Snickers and whispers passed between them as the dame approached, hands braced on her hips.

"All right then. Which of them did this to you?"

Benedict fairly trembled with the strain of remaining upright. The binding he had improvised from an old shirt torn into strips did little to support his ribs, which ached with every breath. He was aware that he looked ghastly, one eye swollen shut and purple, lip split and fattened like a ripe cherry. Beneath his clothes, he was a tapestry of mottled purple, red, and green— a depiction of violence and scorn.

"I don't know what you mean," Benedict replied, rolling one shoulder nonchalantly and biting back a scream at the pain it sent stabbing through his chest. "No one did anything to me."

Lionel's smirk spread into a grin as his companions traded confused glances. Benedict glared at them, clenching his hands so tight his fingernails gouged his palms. He would be damned if they accused him of being a milksop as well as a molly. Telling Dame Culpepper what they'd done would earn him another beating, and piss in his shoes every morning for the rest of the term.

"No one, you say," the dame huffed, rolling her eyes. "And I suppose a ghost or demon pummeled you in your sleep?"

Benedict smiled, the split in his lip opening and sending a trickle of blood down his chin. He wiped it away with the back of one hand. "I fell out of bed last night."

Sputters and guffaws filled the room.

"You fell ... out of bed?" Dame Culpepper asked, pursing her lips. She narrowed suspicious eyes, taking inventory of his battered state.

"That's right," he said.

"You would have me believe that a tumble off the bed is responsible for the state of your face?"

"Benny sleeps like nothing I've ever seen, ma'am," Lionel spoke up, taking a large bite of his toast. "Such tossing and turning about. One wonders why he doesn't sleep on the floor and have done with it."

There was much nudging with elbows and whispers from the table, a handful of boys chiming in to lend truth to Lionel's claim. Benedict pulled a sheepish expression, though it did little to ease the dame's suspicion.

Throwing her hands up, she bustled off to clean up the shattered porcelain, commanding Benedict to clean himself up at the basin before sitting at her table. All the while, she muttered under her breath about the stupidity of boys.

It hurt his jaw to chew, but Benedict wouldn't let the others see it. He stared at Lionel from across the table as he nibbled on burned toast and swilled weak tea. Lionel wasn't bigger or stronger than Benedict—the sod had simply caught him unawares, with a veritable army of other boys. Man to man, Benedict could pound him into mincemeat and intended to at the first opportunity.

He chose to bide his time for the rest of the week, allowing his battered body to begin healing. Lionel seemed to sense that a storm was brewing, lines of consternation creasing his brow whenever he caught Benedict staring at him with unflinching resolve. Surprisingly, Lionel ceased his usual jibes and derision—as if he understood what he had done with his little stunt. But Benedict wasn't content with Lionel's silence, or the possibility that his foe now understood that he was not to be trifled with. The message needed to be delivered loud and clear, leaving no room for doubt.

So, ten days after he was dragged from his bed to be humiliated, Benedict found himself alone with his tormentor. By chance, they happened to return to their bedchamber before the three other boys they bunked with returned from their classes. Pausing on the threshold of the room, Benedict found Lionel crouched over a trunk he kept at the foot of his bed, oblivious that he was no longer alone.

There was no gentleman's code to be adhered to, no reason

to alert Lionel to what was coming. After all, the attack against Benedict had been unexpected and unprovoked—and so would his vengeance.

He was across the room in a few rapid strides, taking a handful of Lionel's hair. A shocked gurgle preceded a sharp cry as Benedict slammed Lionel's head into the trunk. Once Lionel fell to his back, groaning and pressing a hand to his bleeding forehead, Benedict attacked. Trapping the boy between his knees, Benedict delivered blow after blow. His fists produced spurts of blood, then the satisfying crunch of Lionel's broken nose. Attempts at self-defense were ineffectual in the face of Benedict's unchecked rage. By the time the other boys arrived, Lionel's face was a dappled mess of blood, swelling, and discoloration.

Benedict reared away from the hands wrenching him off his enemy, chest heaving as he snorted like a bull. Two boys stared at him in wide-eyed shock and horror as the other helped a sniveling Lionel to his feet. His knuckles throbbed like the devil, and he could taste the blood that had speckled his face, but the triumph swelling within him couldn't be denied. No one said a word to chastise him as he swiped a sleeve across his mouth before staggering to the washstand to clean himself up. By the time he'd finished, Lionel and his friends had vacated the room.

Benedict flopped onto his bed and clasped his hands behind his head. There was no chance Dame Culpepper wouldn't take one look at Lionel and know what had occurred. The woman might be a drunk, but she wasn't a fool. There would be harsh repercussions for what he'd just done, with Lionel likely going unpunished. It paid well to be the son of an earl who made hefty donations to the school. Benedict's status as a viscount's cast-off, one who was so obviously unlike the other boys, made him vulnerable.

However, he couldn't bring himself to care about the whipping the headmaster would inflict on him; not when he had finally done the thing he'd been fantasizing about the entire term. Benedict had been concerned with angering his father and worrying his mother. He'd wanted to prove himself a gentleman his father wouldn't have to be ashamed of. But one glance at the sparse accommodations he suffered compared to his bunkmates demonstrated that the viscount didn't give a bloody damn about him. His father saw him much the way Lionel did—broken, backward, wrong. A lost cause who would never be his heir. What did it matter if he was a gentleman in deed as well as in name? Trying to adhere to such strictures had won him nothing. Perhaps, what he'd just done to Lionel would earn him some peace of mind and the safety to sleep through the night without being accosted.

Staring up at the ceiling, Benedict grinned and decided that if it wasn't enough, he'd happily pummel every boy in this house. If that was the way to build a reputation as someone to be feared, then so be it. They would never dig deep enough to unearth what it was that made Benedict so unlike them if they feared him. Their avoidance of him and his fists would keep him safe.

CHAPTER 1

LONDON, 1820

22 YEARS LATER...

As Lord Alexander Osborne, Earl of Vautrey, descended into the underbelly of a public house known as The White Cock, he couldn't help but wonder just what he had landed himself in. Upon leaving Kent for London with one singular mission in mind, he never supposed he might find himself slinking into darkened basements reeking of sweat, blood, and ale, filled with the cacophony of men's roaring voices. He was a peer of the realm, not some rowdy young pup fresh from university. His days of occupying such spaces in search of a thrill were far behind him.

However, his determination couldn't be assuaged from the matter at hand. Nearly four years ago, he had made the worst mistake of his life and intended to correct it. There was nothing he wouldn't do, no place he wouldn't go, no lengths he would avoid to win back the love of his life. If lowering himself to attending illegal bare-knuckle brawls in public house basements brought him closer to his goal, so be it.

Alex shouldered his way through the sea of bodies surrounding the spectacle taking place in the center of the bare, dimly-lit basement. Everyone shifted to allow him through, his height and breadth of shoulders showing a physical advantage over those who dared block his path, and his immaculate mode of dress denoting someone of importance. The crowd represented a hodgepodge of people from every level of the social hierarchy—tradesmen and factory workers standing shoulder-to-shoulder with gentlemen of means. The occasional woman could be found here and there—Haymarket whores and bedraggled laundresses a sharp contrast to the well-dressed ladies clinging to their gentlemen and eying the brawl with wide-eyed fascination.

The White Cock's position outside London kept them safe from discovery, as well as scrutiny. This was not the orderly tradition of a legitimate pugilist match; this was a melee, plain and simple, with the potential for only one man to come out on top. And anyone who was anyone already knew who that man would be.

Alex spotted said man, his bright blond head standing out like a beacon. Alex's breath caught in his chest, and despite wishing to be anywhere but here, he was completely captivated. Grime and sweat covered a broad, naked back rippling with powerful muscles, and tufts of unruly, overlong hair swept the thick column of his neck. Sinews in his arms bulged and stretched taut as he threw powerful blows at the opponent before him with massive fists. The clearing amid the crowd was filled with brawling men, each fighting to be the one still on his feet when the dust cleared.

A cheer went up from the crowd when one of the competitors fell beneath the ferocity of the blond beast, out cold. Stumbling past three men grappling with one another for dominance, the beast accepted a small pint offered to him by a man standing on the fringes of the audience. Alex watched in disbelief as half the bottle was drained in a few gulps, then tossed carelessly aside. Sucking in his breath, Alex nearly bellowed a warning just before a stodgy man brought his joined fists down across the blond man's broad, naked back. With an annoyed snarl he whirled, bringing his knee up between the other man's legs, then throwing him to his back with a quick uppercut. As the attacker went down, Alex was graced with the full potency of Benedict Sterling.

Hair fallen into his eyes and lips peeled back into a feral sneer, he was alluring in his ferocity, as magnetic as he was frightening. There was so little of the young man Alex had befriended at Eton, though some things about him would never change. He was larger than before, wider through the shoulders with slabs of muscle bulging in his chest. The changes of time made him seem like some otherworldly creature —an avenging archangel breathing fire, smoke, and ash. Alex couldn't look away, hypnotized by the display of raw power as Ben tore through every man who stepped into his path with powerful right hooks and sharp uppercuts, his knuckles red and raw.

This was the same man who had pummeled every lad at Eton who dared to cross him, who'd learned that the skill of his fists could earn him the money to better his circumstances.

When Alex had been moved into Dame Culpepper's house in place of Lionel Blackburn, Ben became one of his roommates. It hadn't taken him long to realize why the change had been made. Lionel was seen sporting a swollen eye and broken nose, and Ben looked no better. What Alex had not expected was to watch Ben beat nearly every other boy under Dame Culpepper's roof over the subsequent fortnight.

One would think such mercilessness would be enough to warn other boys away, yet Alex had observed an opposite effect. Every lad seemed compelled to test their mettle against Ben, only to be sent limping away with bloodied lips and blackened eyes. Seeing this as an opportunity of sorts, Ben had begun placing bets on his own fights, which prompted others to do the same. By the middle of the following term, Ben had decked out his corner of their room with the comforts afforded by his winnings, and Saturday night fights became regular events.

Ben endured the harsh punishments of the headmaster without flinching. He'd thrown the scathing letters of his father into the fire before continuing as he pleased. He had always struck Alex as such a compelling figure—alone and willing to take on the entire world in a fight.

Alex wanted to believe that nothing had changed—Ben was as determined and independent as ever. Only, anyone who knew Ben well could see how time had altered him. There was an unrelenting hardness to him now, one that had obliterated any trace of vulnerability.

It was all Alex's fault; he knew that. He had done this to Ben with his cowardice and fear. This drunken man staggering about the basement of a public house as the crowd egged him on was not the one Alex had come to love all those years ago. Yet, he was unshaken in his determination. As long as there was breath in his body, Alex would fight for what he wanted. And what he wanted was Ben, for the rest of his life. The parts of Ben that had called to him in their youth were still there. Alex could see them as clearly as he could Ben's blue eyes and white-gold hair. It was those things Alex would have to appeal to if he wanted to gain back what he'd lost—Ben's hidden vulnerability, his courage, his strength.

There was only one problem, and it made itself apparent as Ben delivered a final blow to the last man standing, claiming his victory. As he stood over the poor, unconscious lout at his feet, Ben raised his head and caught Alex's gaze. The impact of fiery, bright blue eyes stabbed through him like a heated fireplace poker. Those sapphire depths glittered with malice and disdain, and years' worth of secrets held between them. Alex suppressed a shudder in the face of a truth he could no longer run from.

Alex still loved him as much as ever—had never stopped loving him—yet there was nothing in Ben's eyes now but hatred.

And rightfully so.

Raising his chin, Alex returned Ben's stare without flinching. He had weapons of his own in this battle of wills, and didn't intend to back down.

Ben's nostrils flared, and his jaw clenched and undulated as if he ground his teeth. A ripple of desire overwhelmed Alex, even now, in this undesirable place. But Ben was here, and that made Alex content to remain, no matter how unwanted he might be. If he had his way, the icy tension between them would soon abate, and the wounds of the past could be healed.

As Ben finally turned away, receiving handshakes, congratulations, and a heavy-looking purse containing his winnings, a sliver of doubt niggled the back of Alex's mind. Had too much time passed? Had he wounded Ben to the point of no return?

No, he refused to believe it was too late. From the moment they met, their paths had become intertwined. Though Alex's had deviated for a time, it had led him right back to Ben. Alex had a feeling it would always be that way. He was a hopeless romantic, and in their earlier years, Ben had been, too.

Alex hoped that part of Ben still lived, even if it happened to be locked away in some deep recess of his heart. It was the only hope Alex had left.

ALEX WAITED ONLY AN HOUR BEFORE DEMANDING ENTRANCE to the room where Ben disappeared to recover following his fight. He paid a barmaid a few shillings to apprise him of Ben's location, a room where he was wont to linger for beefsteak and a drink after a fight. Instead of charging to the abovestairs, Alex had settled at the bar for a whiskey, ruminating over what he would say once he was alone with Ben for the second time in as many days.

Their first encounter had not gone well, though Alex would have been a fool to expect otherwise. He *had* been foolish last night, forgetting his carefully calculated plan to remain in control and not to do anything stupid. Alex had done well at first. Having landed on Ben's doorstep immediately after arriving in London, he blustered his way past the butler to lie in wait. Alex had expected Ben to be furious at his intrusion into a life that had not included him for some time now—yet, hope was a strange and potent phenomenon.

Hope was what had driven him to try to plead his case, and when that didn't work, he'd done something reckless. Staring down into his half-empty glass, Alex relived the moment—as he had over and over throughout the succeeding day—when he had realized winning Ben back was more than a deep desire; it was an inescapable imperative.

"Hello, Ben," Alex said when he appeared on the threshold of the darkened study.

Beams of moonlight filtered through the windows to illuminate that shock of bright blond hair and the brilliant white of shirtsleeves exposed by Ben's lack of coat. Alex had waited over an hour for him to return home, but would have endured an eternity beyond that if necessary.

The door rattled in the frame when Ben slammed it.

"What ... the bloody fuck ... are you doing here?" he demanded. His slitted eyes were locked on Alex with the intensity of the blazing sun.

Alex knew that expression well, could see the flex of Ben's jaw that indicated he was clenching his teeth. His fists trembled at his sides as if he wished to thrash Alex within an inch of his life. But if there was one thing Alex had never been frightened of, it was Ben's fists. Ben only harmed those who attempted to harm him first—or, it would seem, those willing to step into the ring with him. Alex was in no danger here.

"I should think that was obvious," he replied, slowly approaching Ben from his side of the room. Surely you've heard the news. Katherine, she ... died."

His throat constricted on the last words, grief twisting violently in his belly and clutching at his heart. Alex had been aware of his inclination toward men since boyhood, and that had never changed. His marriage was one of convenience and necessity, but his wife had been the best of women. Katherine might not have appealed to him in a carnal way, but she had been his friend, his confidant, his solace after being forced to give Ben up. Her death had been a devastating blow.

Ben sneered at the mention of Alex's late wife. "So I have heard. You have my most sincere condolences, though I fail to understand why her death would bring you to my doorstep."

Alex couldn't help a smile, hearing the strain in Ben's voice. He took no delight in the other man's anger or pain, but knowing he felt anything at all boded well for Alex. "Oh, Ben ... you were never any good at hiding your emotions."

"I've changed. You'd know that if you hadn't run off to Kent with your blushing bride."

"Ben—"

"What did you expect?" Ben snapped. "That I would have spent the past three years sobbing into my brandy and wishing to have back what was lost?"

"Of course not."

"Then you hoped to be welcomed back into my life as if you didn't betray me?"

"That isn't it, either."

Ben had begun advancing on him throughout their exchange, and Alex soon found himself hauled forward by his waistcoat. Longing heated his belly as he was snatched closer to Ben ... so close Alex could smell the cold night air and light hint of the sweat glistening on his neck. The scents tangled with his signature Bay Rum and the clean whiff of starched linen. Slumbering desires roared to life within Alex in a powerful surge.

"I knew you wouldn't have forgiven me," Alex managed, fighting a losing battle against the urges melting his resolve. "But I had hoped we might talk. You don't even have to listen to me. You can berate me and call me every horrible name you can think of, and I will sit and listen. I just ... when I had settled my affairs in Kent, I found myself wandering around this cold, empty house, and ... I had to come. Even knowing you hate me, even realizing I have no right to intrude on your life."

Ben's fist tightened around his waistcoat as he closed his eyes and issued a harsh sigh. Were it any other person manhandling Alex this way, he would have fought back, perhaps berating the offending party for ruining the starched perfection of such fine silk. However, this wasn't just anyone; this was Ben, and he could do anything to Alex he wanted if only to bestow the touch of his hand—whether harsh or gentle.

"Say it," Ben demanded, yanking Alex closer until they were nearly nose-to-nose. "Tell me why you've come."

Alex gripped Ben's hand, holding it tighter against his chest, desperate for closeness of any sort. His heart lodged itself within his throat as he held Ben's gaze, feeling as if he stood on the edge of a steep precipice. One false move and he would fall to a slow and agonizing death, mourning what never was.

He could bear it no longer. Ben was here before him, whole and warm and real—not just some figment of his imagination, haunting his dreams and waking him in a feverish sweat.

Their lips brushed, and Alex trembled, suspended somewhere between the past and the present, and yearning as he never had. "I came for you," he whispered just before he pressed his lips against Ben's, tentative and questioning.

Alex was sent reeling when Ben slammed both palms against his chest, his lower back meeting the edge of the heavy, oak desk. Bracing his hands on the thick wood, he waited for Ben to make the next move—to either cast him out bodily or ... or, what? Ben had no reason to let Alex kiss him, no reason to trust him after what he'd done. Alex's heart sank with the realization that he had gone too far, as Ben swiped the back of his hand over his mouth. It was too soon for such intimacies, with broken promises and shattered dreams scattered at their feet like shards of glass.

But then, Ben was on him faster than Alex could blink, pushing him tighter against the desk and caging him with powerful arms. His kiss was harsh and punishing, unrelenting and forceful. Alex's skin erupted with sensation, his entire body enlivened by the nearness and taste of Ben. Pure joy swept through him, as the past converged on the present moment. A tortured groan echoed in the cavern of Ben's chest, vibrating through Alex from the outside in. A night's worth of stubble abraded Alex's skin, bringing so many memories flooding through his mind. He used to tease Ben about his facial hair and how hopeless it was for him to shave when a dark blond shadow always made an appearance by the end of the day. His gut clenched at the memory of what that stubble felt like against his neck, his chest, his thigh.

Cupping Ben's jaw, Alex returned the fiery kiss with years' worth of suppressed desire, dipping his tongue between parted lips. The taste of Ben, wild and heady, flooded his senses, familiar and yet somehow new again. Alex felt like a fumbling, desperate boy, wanting everything at once and having no notion where to begin. He drowned in the kiss, which soon became a battle for dominance as Ben's tongue pushed against his. The hands gripping his hair were downright painful, but Alex accepted the pain with the pleasure because it was coming from Ben. Alex would take whatever he could have.

It ended far too soon for his liking, Ben jerking away with a low growl and leaving Alex leaning against the desk, cold and bereft.

"Ben," he pleaded, no longer caring how desperate he might sound. "Would you hear me out? I can explain—"

"Explain what, exactly?" Ben interjected, though where he might have bellowed, he merely whispered. He kept his back turned and braced his hands on a cabinet holding several decanters and clean glasses. "How you made me agree to run away with you so we could be together before changing your mind and deciding to marry a woman instead?"

It was exactly how they had ended, but there was so much more to the story that Ben didn't know, so many reasons marrying Katherine had been the right thing for Alex to do at the time. He hadn't been able to go to Ben and explain afterward, even knowing how it would hurt him.

"It wasn't what it seemed," he replied, taking a step toward Ben, then thinking better of it. "I just want the chance to make things right."

"There is nothing to make right," Ben replied, head bowed and his voice still lowered to that ominous, steely whisper. "You made your choice, and I think we are both better for it. I like my life the way it is and I won't have you intruding on it. Until tonight, I'd quite forgotten all about you. Perhaps you ought to do the same and forget about me."

Alex didn't believe that for a moment, but now was not the time to push Ben. He must suffer the shock and anger he had caused by catching Ben off guard. However, it had been his only recourse. Any letters he sent would have been tossed unopened into the fire, just as Ben had destroyed his father's letters during their college years. Ben needed to know that he was here and would not give up so easily.

Smoothing his palms down his rumpled waistcoat, Alex squared his shoulders. "I'll leave now, but this isn't over. You will see me again."

Ben hadn't so much as turned his head when Alex left the room, didn't come after him once he left the house and set off for his own lodgings. It had been foolish to hope he would, but Alex had hoped all the same.

He blinked as he ascended from the haze of his memories, his vision swimming while the world around him solidified. He'd told himself to give Ben time and space, but seeing him once had heightened Alex's sense of urgency. Having stayed away from Ben and London for nearly four years, the time had come to fight.

Deciding Ben had had more than enough privacy, Alex stood and finished his whiskey with a single swallow. Then, he weaved his way through scattered tables and staggering patrons returning to the bar for more ale, making for the stairs.

Ben was right where the barmaid had said he'd be—the last upper room on the left of the corridor. Alex didn't bother to knock, simply letting himself in and quickly shutting the door. Ben was seated at a small table before the lit hearth, a half-empty bottle of brandy at his elbow and a plate holding the remnants of beefsteak and potatoes before him. Slumped in the chair with his head rested against its back, he made an imposing sight despite his state of undress. He wore a shirt now, but his feet remained bare, and the rest of his clothing had been strewn across the small bed in the corner. His bruises were wrapped in linen, and the scent permeating the room must be some sort of salve, which made Alex's eyes water.

He looked as if he had washed, his damp hair pushed back to curl at his neck and ears. Unfocused, bloodshot eyes met his, and Ben scowled.

"Are you reckless, or just plain stupid?" he muttered.

Alex leaned against the door and reached into his breast pocket for the pouch of peppermint sticks stashed there. Ben watched him push one into the corner of his mouth between his cheek and his teeth, eyes narrowed.

"Neither," Alex replied with a shrug. "Simply curious. Have you grown so bored with normal pugilism? Is that why you engage in underground brawls with drunks and rogues?"

A lopsided smile curved one corner of Ben's lips as he raised the pint of brandy. "I *am* a drunk and a rogue."

Alex couldn't help smiling back, a burst of sugary peppermint flooding his palette. "I see. A gentleman by day, drunken brawler by night. No one can ever accuse you of being boring."

The light humor between them dissipated as Ben sat up straight, brandy bottle raised halfway to his lips. "I thought I made myself clear last night."

"I assumed I had as well."

Ben's nostrils flared, his eyes like penetrating daggers of ice as he stared at Alex over his bottle. "So you intend to become my unwanted shadow. Is that it?"

Alex swirled the peppermint stick, noting the spark of heat in Ben's gaze as he sucked. "Unwanted ... I think not. That kiss last night begs to differ."

Ben swallowed a mouthful of brandy, then snorted. "*You* kissed *me*."

"And you returned that kiss," Alex fired back, raising an eyebrow.

"A thoughtless reaction. I would have done the same with any man throwing himself at me."

"The Ben I knew had higher standards than that."

"Well, you were the one who taught me to lower my expectations."

Alex's teeth clenched around his sweet, severing it in half. He deserved that verbal jab, and they both knew it. Finishing off the peppermint stick, he retrieved a handkerchief and used it to clean his hands.

"You cannot frighten me away," he insisted. "I came to London for you and don't intend to leave until I've earned your forgiveness."

Ben slammed the bottle onto the table, slowly rising to his feet. "On the day London is overrun with flying pigs, you may expect my undying forgiveness. Now sod off."

"Ben—"

"I waited for you," he said suddenly, pausing halfway to the bed and whirling to face Alex. "For hours. I was committed to our plan. I wanted to spend the rest of my life with you, and you left me waiting in the rain with every possession I cared about packed into trunks. I stood in the wet and cold, not caring whether I succumbed to lung fever or some other sickness ... so long as you came, I would survive. As each minute passed, I kept telling myself that you were coming. Something had delayed you, but you would never abandon me. *You* were the brave one, remember? After the second hour, I began to fear you'd been hurt. I paced beside the carriage, imagining you broken and bloodied on the side of the road—waylaid by an accident or a violent highwayman or ..."

Ben clamped his mouth shut and turned back to the bed, snatching up his waistcoat. Alex's heart dropped into his belly, which twisted with an overwhelming mix of guilt and shame. He'd never known any of this, as he and Ben never had the opportunity to talk after that fateful night. He was right that Alex had been stopped from coming to him—but not by an accident or a highwayman. The force keeping them apart had been far more powerful than that.

"Things were happening that you knew nothing about," he protested feebly. "I tried, Ben, I ... I wanted nothing more than to run away with you. I wanted it so badly."

"You never came!" Ben roared, whirling to face him with his waistcoat hanging open, face flushing red. "I waited until sunrise like some idiotic, besotted chit, convinced you would arrive! Then, to see the announcement of your engagement to

Katherine in the papers only days later ..." Ben pressed a thumb and forefinger to the bridge of his nose and sighed, shaking his head. "No, I do not care to hear your explanation now when you never bothered to make one back then. I learned all I needed to know the day I sat in St. George's and watched you bind yourself to someone else. Just because her life conveniently ended doesn't mean I'm eager or desperate enough to have you back."

Alex watched Ben finish dressing in silence, his usual skill for words failing him. During the journey from Kent, he had ruminated over all the things he wanted to say and how he wished to express them. Just now, his mind was a jumbled mess of words unsaid, all of it fighting to slip off his tongue at once.

All he could manage was a pathetic, "I'm so sorry."

Now fully dressed—though his open shirt and lack of cravat made him look as much a rogue as ever—Ben pinned Alex with a baleful glare. "You should be," he spat before taking up his brandy and thundering from the room.

Alex slumped against the wall, each of Ben's heavy footfalls on the steps resounding through him like a nail being hammered into his chest. The wound Alex inflicted had festered over time, and now there might be no healing it. By coming here, was he only tearing into a painful scar? Was it selfish of him to pursue Ben, knowing how hurt he had been by Alex's actions?

Spotting a crumpled, abandoned cravat atop the neatly made bed, Alex went to it. Sinking onto the lumpy mattress, he took up the linen and pressed it to his nose with a deep, slow inhale. Ben still smelled of laundry starch and clean, earthy Bay Rum. No fuss, simple and compelling—like the man himself. He was such a sharp contradiction to Alex, who collected scents, colored cravats, and eclectic waistcoats, and was as fussy about his appearance as a debutante. It was a wonder they'd ever come to love one another at all. The sheer impossibility of it reminded Alex of his determination. Some things were simply meant to exist, and he could never be convinced that he and Ben as a pair weren't among those things. It wasn't selfish to want to make everything up to Ben, to make right what he had broken.

Tucking the cravat into the breast pocket with his peppermints, Alex left the tiny, sparse room—shaken but not broken. As far as he was concerned, he and Ben were far from finished. They had hardly even begun.

CHAPTER 2

ETON COLLEGE, 1799

Benedict clamped his lips shut to muffle a whimper of agony. In his sleep, his mind forgot that movement of any sort was out of the question. The fiery stripes across his shoulders burned at the touch of nightshirt or bedclothes, so he slept in only a pair of old breeches, the sheets draped across his backside. The punishment he'd earned after being caught brawling in the late hours of last evening had been the harshest yet. Dame Culpepper's unexpected appearance in the yard off the back of her house had earned him a caning at the hands of the headmaster. It was bad enough the dame had caught them red-handed; that cowardly bastard Lionel Blackburn had been waiting in the wings to report that the fights had been going on for months—and that Benedict had encouraged the other boys to engage in the vice of gambling by orchestrating bets.

Of course, Benedict hadn't been alone in his actions, but pummeling Blackburn and his friends had painted a target on his back. He had been threatened with expulsion on more than one occasion, and was told after the lashing that this was his final chance. It had taken every bit of his self-control to keep from laughing in the headmaster's face. They both knew all it would take was for his father to make a generous contribution to the college to ensure Benedict's continued education. It didn't matter *that the viscount despised him; no Sterling man had ever been ejected from Eton, and his father wasn't going to allow such a thing to besmirch their illustrious name.*

As he lay there breathing through the pain of half a dozen cane marks, his head rested on a goose-down pillow, and his bedclothes were the finest that could be found in England. The warmth of the coal he'd purchased kept not only him warm, but all the other occupants of the room. He ate like a king every day, having learned that slipping a pint of gin to Dame Culpepper along with the money for ingredients to stock her larder was enough to earn the woman's generosity. While those around him benefited from his improved finances, Benedict couldn't pretend he had done it for any of them. Five of the boys he'd beaten had requested new living quarters, and those who shared his room now were tolerable if not exactly likable. However, a sense of self-preservation and resolve not to suffer another cold winter or half-empty belly drove him.

Benedict had been raised in a world where a good name, blue blood, and a fortune were supposed to make life easier. Yet, he had been denied the ease that guided the lives of his brothers and some of the other lads attending school with him. Despite his youth and lack of experience with the world at large, Benedict had learned one very important lesson: if he wanted anything for himself, he was going to have to fight for it. His father certainly wouldn't smooth his path or give him a hand up, and his brothers were too fond of their places as the favored sons to go against the viscount.

"If you would just try harder to please him, things wouldn't be so difficult for you," his elder brother, Esmond, often said. "You must try."

"You could stop clinging to Mother's apron strings, for a start," Francis, the secondborn, would agree.

Closing his eyes, he shifted his mind away from the wounds on his back and drifted toward slumber.

Benedict snapped open his eyes, his restless thoughts disturbed by the shuffle of footsteps and the thunk of something against the floor. A burst of lamplight made him squint, and he recognize the figure of Alexander Osborne, one of the new transplants from a different boardinghouse. He had replaced Lionel a few weeks before the end of the previous term, and had returned in the spring to resume his place on the other side of the room.

He was a peculiar sort, swathed in his decadent banyans when in their chamber, lounging on his bed to pore over the books he kept organized beneath the mattress. The boy was just as richly dressed outside this room as he was in it—perhaps more so. He stood out like a peacock among the somber, dark colors the other boys wore, seeming not to notice the attention he drew wherever he went.

However, it wasn't Osborne's dandified fashions that made him odd. Often, Benedict would feel a prickle down his spine, registering the sensation of being watched. He was used to being gaped at as the other boys passed rumors about him back and forth. But this was different. It was as if something within Benedict instinctively knew whose eyes rested on him, alerting his senses. Sure enough, whenever he glanced up, it was always to find Osborne observing him with a pensive look in his eye. Even more discomfiting was the fact that he never looked away when Benedict caught him staring. Sometimes Osborne would simply meet Benedict's gaze, almost as if issuing a silent, but not necessarily threatening, challenge—one Benedict didn't understand.

Other times, Osborne would offer a smile. Just the slightest tilt of his mouth in one corner. It disturbed Benedict to find his eyes drawn to those lips every time, an odd sort of fascination making him hot with embarrassment.

The same sensation overcame him now as he noticed Osborne wore another of his banyans—this one yellow, embroidered with green and blue thread. Beneath it was a half-open shirt. He knelt at Benedict's bedside, a lamp resting on the floor beside him and a bowl held in one hand. His thick, dark eyebrows were knit with concern as his gaze swept over Benedict's bared back.

Benedict didn't care for the pity in Osborne's eyes. "What the devil do you want?" he snapped, lifting up on one elbow.

A sharp sting flared in his back, increasing to a burning throb. He fell back onto his belly, issuing a pained groan into his pillow.

Osborne clicked his tongue, giving Benedict a stern look when he raised his head from the cushion. "If you keep that up, you'll wake the others. Does it hurt very badly?"

Benedict scowled. "Does it look like it hurts?"

There was that smile again, coy and teasing, as if he were in on a secret Benedict hadn't yet discovered. "It does, and I am sorry for it. It wasn't well done of Blackburn to set the headmaster on you that way."

"I ought to break his nose again," Benedict said with a dry snort. "Apparently once wasn't enough."

"Ah, yes," Osborne replied with a low chuckle. "I did hear talk of what led you to thrash him. I must say, I wouldn't have done any less. He deserved it."

"I know." Benedict paused, furrowing his brow. "I'm still waiting for you to tell me why you're kneeling beside my bed in the middle of the night."

Osborne raised his bowl. "I heard you tossing and turning, and felt sorry for you. If you'll let me ... my valet has a remedy for such injuries. It might help."

Before Benedict could protest, Osborne had reached into his bowl, lifting a piece of linen dripping with some sort of solution. The scents of peppermint and witch hazel wafted up Benedict's nostrils as Osborne draped the wet linen over one shoulder. A cooling sensation permeated his skin, taking some of the heat from his lash marks. He sighed in relief, the tincture too soothing for him to pretend it didn't feel sublime.

"There, you see?" Osborne crooned, going back into the bowl. "It won't heal you overnight, but it will ease the pain so you can sleep. And if that doesn't work, I have some whiskey stashed in one of my trunks. I only ask that you not tell anyone."

Benedict grunted as another strip of linen was laid over his opposite shoulder. "I think I'd like that drink regardless. And mum's the word."

Osborne laughed again, though he seemed to do his best to keep the sound from traveling across the room. Yet, Benedict felt the laugh more than he heard it, like a deep vibration rippling through him. It made him shift on the bed, a sudden discomfort overtaking him. He wasn't certain he liked the way this boy made him feel.

"What do you care that I'm in pain?" he asked, hoping that by being

prickly, he could maintain some sort of distance between them. The last thing Benedict needed was the blow to his reputation if someone thought he had a friendly bone in his body.

Osborne shrugged, his dark eyes fixed on Benedict's back as he applied more of his strips, covering every inch before starting a second layer to cover the first. "Why shouldn't I care? You are a person with feelings like anyone else. It is difficult for me to see someone in pain and not want to do something to help."

Benedict snorted. "No one is that kind."

"That isn't true," Osborne argued. "I left my bed to mix this tincture for you, and I would hope you might do the same for me."

He might not have before tonight. Benedict suffered enough of his own pain to think of anyone else's. But the thought of Osborne in his place made him feel a prick of guilt. Yes ... yes, he would do the same were it within his power. Osborne had never done him a harsh turn. What did it matter that he stared as if glimpsing a circus attraction? Perhaps he was merely a curious person by nature.

As Osborne continued his task, the tightness in Benedict's muscles began to ease, and lethargy stole over him. Through heavy-lidded eyes he observed Osborne, startled to realize he thought the boy handsome. Osborne was tall and wide in the shoulders, though a bit thin.

A queer feeling erupted in Benedict's belly as his gaze locked on Osborne's chest, and he wondered at the difference between the other lad and himself. He'd grown his first chest hairs at the age of twelve, and they seemed to increase by the dozen each year. He hardly ever noticed Osborne shaving at the washstand, and it seemed he was as smooth beneath his clothes as he was on his face. As he leaned in to reach Benedict's lower back, his shirt gaped wider, revealing even more of that smooth, unblemished skin.

Benedict swallowed and squeezed his eyes shut. He was hot from his scalp to his toes, a sudden restlessness writhing in his belly like a pit of snakes. What the devil was wrong with him? He had seen other boys half-dressed and all but naked over his time at Eton and had never felt the urge to linger. Osborne was made no different than him, lack of body hair notwithstanding. There was nothing fascinating about his chest, his mouth, or the nimble fingers applying the tincture-soaked linen to his back.

Shame flooded Benedict as he forced the unbidden thoughts from his mind. They were backwards and wrong—sinful, just like him. This was the sort of thing that set him apart, and others could see it. His father certainly could, and it was why he'd been trying to crush such oddities out of him.

A warm current of air brushed his ear, and Benedict's eyes flew open just as Osborne whispered, "All better?"

Osborne was close now ... too close. Near enough that Benedict could smell a hint of sandalwood soap and sugar. He ought to put some space between them, his injured back be damned, but Benedict found himself trapped and frozen. Osborne had ridiculously long eyelashes, and with the lamplight just so, they cast shadows on his high cheekbones.

Clearing his throat, Benedict blinked and set his gaze elsewhere. "Yes. Thank you, Osborne."

The bright, full smile crossing Osborne's face drew Benedict's eye right back. He reached out to place a warm hand on Benedict's bare arm.

"Call me Alex."

BENEDICT WAS JOLTED AWAKE BY WHAT SOUNDED LIKE THE screams of a banshee. Jerking his head from a pile of lumpy pillows, he pried open an eye to find the bleary form of his valet at the bedside. He tried to swallow but felt as if his dry tongue had swollen to twice its normal size. Meanwhile, a woodpecker seemed to have taken up residence inside his skull.

"Blast it, Simmons," he rasped. "Must you come in here braying like an ass?"

"I spoke no louder than a whisper, sir," Simmons said drolly, hands folded behind his back.

Benedict blinked, and the outline of his body servant became clear. "Insolence first thing in the morning?"

Humor twinkled in the man's eyes, but his expression was as neutral as his stark attire. "Never, sir."

"What the devil do you want?" he snapped, levering up onto his elbows and shaking his head to clear it. "I asked not to be awakened before noon."

At least, Benedict was certain he had drunkenly slurred that particular order before falling face-down into bed after shedding only his coat.

"It's fifteen minutes after one in the afternoon, sir," Simmons replied with an arch of one ruddy eyebrow. "And I would have left you to rest, but thought you'd wish to know ... a visitor arrived this morning."

"Alex," Benedict ground out as he rolled over to sit up, wincing at the tingle of his blood rushing to his extremities. Of course Alex was here. He had always been annoyingly stubborn and unwilling to accept an answer he did not like. Still, Benedict would have expected at least a day of peace before being forced to face his past again.

"Tell Vautrey I am not at home," Benedict grumbled, yanking off his shoes and tossing them over the side of the bed.

Simmons bent to pick up the shoes without batting an eyelash, but then stood there holding them and watching Benedict shrug out of his sweat-stained waistcoat. "The visitor isn't the earl, sir. I wouldn't have awakened you otherwise, but Ambrose was certain you would wish to know right away."

"Know what, Simmons?" Benedict snapped, impatience worsening his pounding headache. It was his fault for over-imbibing last night, and he'd only made matters worse by going to that ridiculous melee. He would pay for it when he resumed training with his pugilism master.

"Your father," Simmons said with pursed lips. "He arrived this morning."

"Fucking hell," Benedict groaned, pressing the heel of his hand against his eye. It felt as if the blasted thing would pulse right out of the socket. A slight swelling in the lid told him he'd taken more hits last night than he remembered.

"I expected such a reaction, sir. Will you take breakfast and dress before greeting him?"

Benedict met Simmons's gaze, noting the slight curve of his valet's mouth. They seemed to share the same thought, prompting a chuckle from Benedict.

"No, Simmons, I don't think I will. The viscount will want to see me straightaway, and I have kept him waiting long enough."

"Of course."

Benedict was on his feet then, suddenly filled with energy. He didn't particularly desire his father's presence, but wouldn't resist a chance to needle the man. There would be no ejecting him from the premises, as this townhouse belonged to the viscount. Benedict merely chose to reside here to annoy his father, knowing that news of his debauched lifestyle and the bevy of colorful people coming and going from the house would reach him in Norfolk. Perhaps if Benedict acted enough the ass, his father would grow irritated and return to the country.

Neglecting to accept his shoes from Simmons, he trudged to the washstand. The face that greeted him in the mirror was haggard and drawn, the jaw riddled with more than a days' worth of beard. His side-whiskers were untamed, his blond locks tousled and standing on end. The swollen eye was marred with a black and red bruise, the corner of his mouth reddened. Flecks of dried blood stained the linen he used to wash his face. He smelled like a distillery and looked like hell.

Perfect.

Padding down the stairs, he followed the rumbling tones of the viscount's familiar voice to the drawing room. The doors hung open to reveal a pair of footmen working together to remove a portrait from over the mantelpiece, while his father looked on. Hands on hips, he shook his head in disgust at the pockmarks and gouges riddling the portrait of himself. Benedict's stiletto was still embedded in his father's right eye, straight through the pupil.

"Pardon me," Benedict murmured, yanking his stiletto free of the canvas as the footmen passed by. "I believe this is mine."

The servants moved on without a word, though a palpable tension had settled over the household. The entire staff was in Benedict's employ, to prevent the spread of gossip about his proclivities. They were all well aware of the animosity between him and the viscount.

Leaning against the door frame, Benedict pressed the pad of one finger lightly against the tip of his knife. "My lord."

Lord Malcolm Sterling narrowed ice-blue eyes at Benedict, his anvil of a jaw thrusting forward when his lips pursed in disdain. "Benedict."

The crisp diction of the single word did nothing to mask the fact that his voice was nearly identical to Benedict's. Standing before his sire was like looking into a mirror—one that showed Benedict an unwelcome future. It had taken Benedict years to stop hating himself when his face and voice had been inherited directly from someone he despised. For, if he could look so much like his father and someday be forced to take on the title of viscount, Benedict was in danger of becoming just like him. It was the one thing he feared and avoided with every fiber of his being.

"You sent no word of your impending arrival," Benedict challenged, refusing to break his father's stern stare. The man had a way of stripping a person to the bone with his eyes, showing in his expression that he could see all of Benedict's secrets and found him lacking in every respect.

"This house belongs to me," his father retorted. "I am not obligated to announce my arrival to anyone, least of all you."

Benedict entered the room, dropping into the nearest chair and slouching with the stiletto clenched in his fist. The viscount scowled, raking Benedict from head to toe with clear disapproval written all over his face. He could feel his father assessing every aspect of his appearance that didn't align with that of a gentleman.

It had been this way between them since Benedict was a boy
—the youngest of three sons, contrary in every possible way. For
the viscount, Benedict's constant refusal to conform to some
lofty aspiration of nobility was the thing that made him a disap-
pointment. It was the reason his father had spent years stewing
over the fact that the son he hated would inherit everything he
owned.

The deaths of his brothers had ruined the Sterling legacy, and
for reasons beyond Benedict's comprehension, his father chose
to place the blame for that squarely on his shoulders. It didn't
matter that he'd been hundreds of miles away at Cambridge
when a carriage accident had taken both Esmond and Francis in
one fell swoop. Benedict hadn't been driving the carriage which,
traveling in the dark and fog, had overturned on an old and noto-
riously dangerous bridge—sending the footman, four horses, and
his brothers to the bottom of a river. Only the coachman had
survived, and he had nearly drowned trying to save the others.
None of that mattered to the viscount. All he knew was that his
favored sons were gone, and Benedict was all he had left.

"How long do you intend to remain?" Benedict asked, partly
to annoy his father, but mostly for his own peace of mind.

The viscount's appearance in London would draw added
scrutiny to Benedict's already salacious reputation—something
he usually welcomed but didn't need just now.

"Until the matter of your public disgrace has been dealt with
to my satisfaction."

The viscount held up a folded broadsheet in one hand,
making Benedict aware of it for the first time. The fight against
his own curiosity was lost, as it seemed his father didn't intend
to explain without prompting.

"What is that?"

The viscount cleared his throat and looked to the page. "I
have here a copy of *The London Gossip*, released only today. The
author has dedicated an entire section of her paper to you. It
reads, *'rumor has it that the Honourable Mr. S has been seen about Town*

debauching himself with a vigor most unusual—even for him. He has been spotted at several gentleman's clubs, soused beyond coherence. A rather diverting scene was reported to have taken place at Boodles some weeks past, during which Mr. S left destruction in his wake in the form of broken furniture and overturned glasses. One cannot help but wonder where Viscount S is and why he has yet to take his wayward son in hand. Such unseemly behavior does not reflect well upon the family name, which was once highly respected. It would seem Mr. S is determined to rip his father's legacy to tatters. This writer wonders why.'"

The viscount hurled the paper at Benedict with a snarl once he'd finished reading. Benedict bit back a string of curses, not because he wanted to avoid his father's censure, but because he didn't want the man to know how deep his dread went at the revelation that *The London Gossip* had resumed delivering her daily papers. He had gone to great lengths to cut off the popular publication's circulation, but true to form, the wily woman known to the public only as The London Gossip had outwitted him. Again.

He pushed the paper off his lap in a show of childish defiance, taking great pleasure in the way his father's nostrils flared, lips pinching in disapproval. "I hadn't realized you devoured gossip sheets like some nosy society matron. Has country life grown so boring, then?"

The viscount's face reddened as he pointed an accusing finger at Benedict. "When such publications make note of your ridiculous behavior and cast aspersions on my good name, I take an interest. Did you not think word of your exploits wouldn't reach Norfolk?"

"Of course not. I merely thought you had come to understand by now that I will do as I please. Your trip is wasted."

"I think not," his father said, hands folded behind his back as he moved toward a window overlooking the street. "I have given you ample time to weary of your own destructive habits. As you have clearly become a slave to your vices, it falls to me to ensure your future, as well as that of the Sterling name."

Benedict stiffened, his stomach churning as he anticipated what was coming next. This wasn't the first time he and his father had clashed on this subject, and it seemed the viscount was not to be swayed.

"If I wanted your assistance, I would ask for it," Benedict said. "My life is arranged to suit my needs, not to fulfill your expectations. You have made it clear that I will never be good enough to fill your shoes, so why should I exert myself trying?"

"As distasteful as it is for us both, you are my heir. The time has come for you to act as such."

"I am not Esmond, and you cannot make me in his image no matter how much you might wish to."

"You aren't half the man your brother was, on that we agree."

Benedict's jaw ached from the hard clench of his teeth, his gut roiling with intense wrath. It didn't matter how far he distanced himself from caring about his father's opinion; being compared to his eldest brother never stopped putting his teeth on edge. Benedict hadn't stood a chance of gaining the viscount's approval when the heir had been living. Esmond's death had only cemented his place as the favorite, the perfect son, a saint. Francis was just a step beneath him—by no means as perfect as his elder brother but still a Sterling to be respected, worthy.

"I will inherit whether you like it or not," Benedict reminded him. "And I'll do it regardless of how I behave or dress or speak."

The viscount turned to face him, the afternoon light revealing the silver strands interrupting the blond shade of his hair. Those gray strands, as well as the tiny wrinkles at the corners of his eyes, were the only hints to the viscount's age. He was as brawny and robust as ever, and Benedict supposed he could appreciate that he might inherit that same agelessness.

"I have decided to take you in hand," the viscount said. "Your days of a bachelor's idle pursuits are at an end. While I am in London, I intend to compile a list of eligible ladies for you to consider. You will choose the one who suits you and pursue her for marriage. Your reputation will not matter in the face of the family fortunes and estate, as well as your status as my heir. A few months of reformed behavior and public courtship should position you nicely as a groom for your future viscountess. You will marry her and do your utmost to sire an heir within one year."

Benedict's lips quivered, amusement overtaking his annoyance. He searched his father's face for any trace of humor, but found none. Of course he found none—the viscount didn't possess a humorous bone in his entire body.

Shoulders quivering with barely-suppressed laughter, Benedict stared at his father with defiant glee. "No."

The viscount raised an eyebrow. "No?"

"That's right. No to your list of ladies, no to your stipulations of marriage and an heir. No to all of it."

His father rolled his eyes as if dealing with a petulant child. "You intend to be difficult. I expected nothing less, which is why I've taken precautions to ensure my directives are followed to the letter."

Benedict wanted to tell his father to sod off, then quit the room. But, he couldn't afford to ignore the viscount's threats without knowing the totality of his plans. His father had taken him unawares once, nearly breaking Benedict in the process. He couldn't allow that to happen again.

"What precautions?"

Now the viscount was practically overflowing with glee, his eyes glittering with malicious intent. "I paid Dr. Pruett a generous sum to accompany me to London. As of now, he's been put up in a Mayfair hotel to enjoy the lavish accommodations his own funds cannot afford. However, he can be summoned on a moment's notice to take you in hand should I deem it necessary. His methods in treating the insane are very effective ... as you well know."

Benedict's blood ran cold as a dozen memories flooded his mind—being immersed in tubs filled with ice-water, held under until he couldn't breathe through the pain of a thousand icicles pricking his skin. His skin crawled as if assaulted with leeches, his throat burning with acidic bile as he recalled the taste of purgative potions that had nearly caused him to starve.

He didn't fear much, but the threat of a mad-doctor was enough to shatter his bravado. The viscount knew this, his expression like the cat who ate the canary as he watched Benedict process his ultimatum.

"That's right," he said. "If you cannot be coaxed to the altar, then you can be declared insane. After all, only a madman prefers the attentions of his own sex over those of a woman. Such foul acts are an abomination in the eyes of God. I could have you declared incompetent and disinherited. I would rather see my title go to one of your distant cousins than have it sullied by a twisted, corrupted sodomite!"

Benedict shot to his feet, that word jabbing through his spine like the sharpest of daggers. His knuckles ached when he clenched his fists, but the rest of him was on fire, ready for a fight. Benedict would never forgive himself for the carelessness that had led to the viscount learning his secret. He had been paying for it ever since.

"Call me that again—"

"It's what you are," the viscount spat, his disgust clear. "And if it means protecting my legacy, I'll expose you to the world for the disgusting creature you've become."

Benedict bared his teeth in a feral grin "No one will believe it. You see, part of my damaged reputation is due to my connection to a certain woman. Everyone in London has seen me in her company, and knows I spend several nights a week at her lodgings. I've also been seen entertaining whores in public on a frequent basis."

The viscount scoffed. "They will believe the word of a respected peer over that of a notorious scapegrace."

"I'm willing to take that bet."

A tense silence filled the air between them, neither man willing to back down or show weakness. It was the bane of Benedict's life to know the person he loathed most in the world was also the person he had inherited the majority of his traits from. Not only his looks but an uncompromising stubbornness that could rival that of an ass. His quick temper, his athletic reflexes, the ability to read people and exploit both their weaknesses and their best qualities—all inherited from the man who had made his life a constant torment.

The viscount broke first, turning away and striding toward the door. "I realize that my unexpected arrival has caught you off guard. Defiance is typical of you, so I will excuse your impertinence for now. What you need is time to think and to consider all the ways I could make your life a living hell if you refuse to comply."

"You will never control me again," Benedict ground out, staring at his father's back and wishing the heat of his anger was enough to burn away flesh and bone until he was staring at the empty hollow of his father's chest.

The viscount glanced at Benedict over his shoulder with a mocking smirk. "You have one week to make your final decision. For your sake, I hope you will choose the right one."

Benedict remained where he stood once his father had departed, the heavy tread of his footsteps carrying him upstairs. It annoyed him to no end that the viscount would be in residence for the foreseeable future, with Benedict impotent to do anything about it. The house belonged to his father, after all, though he preferred to reside in the country.

He waited until the slam of a door resounded through the house before moving, taking deep, rapid breaths to keep a fit of temper at bay. Just now, he wanted to turn every piece of furniture into kindling, shatter the porcelain and glass across the rug, and pound at the walls until they were riddled with impressions of his knuckles.

But, there was no time for that. His father's arrival had just thrown all his plans off-balance, adding yet another complication to a problem of epic proportions.

Benedict took the stairs two at a time, determination propelling every step. Experience told him that his father's threat wasn't idle, and after years of struggling to bring Benedict to heel, he might finally be ready to play the final card in his deck. That pressing issue was secondary to the real reason Benedict was suddenly in a hurry to leave the house.

He stormed into his room, startling Simmons—whose face appeared from the doorway of the washroom, eyes wide and questioning.

"Sir, I've just finished preparing the shower-bath and water for shaving. Shall I—"

"Yes," Benedict said, already yanking his shirttails free of his breeches as he raced toward the door to the washroom attached to his suite. "I am in a hurry, Simmons. Step lightly."

"Of course, sir."

Benedict felt Simmons's curious gaze as he breezed past, working his fall open. The entire household would speculate over what went on between father and son—and if any of the maids had overheard the conversation downstairs, talk would spread to every servant under this roof by nightfall. Benedict had no need to fear that the gossip would travel outside this house. He had painstakingly selected discreet, loyal servants. As well, Simmons, his butler, three of the footmen, the cook, and one of the scullery maids all had something in common with him. They were too busy keeping the fact that they were attracted to their own sex a secret to go about telling others that Benedict was a molly.

Leaving wasn't an option, either. It annoyed the viscount to no end that Benedict had claimed the family townhouse as his personal residence. It amused Benedict to make a space that belonged to his father into his own domain. If Benedict remained in residence while his father was in London, it might drive the man back to Norfolk. Though, that was a long shot and Benedict knew it. His father would remain until he had his way, which meant Benedict needed to formulate a plan to put a stop to this idea of a forced marriage.

Benedict should have no problem doing this now the matter of Alex had been settled to his satisfaction. He refused to expend another ounce of energy thinking of his former lover. They were finished, and the sooner Alex understood that, the sooner he could return to Kent and leave Benedict in peace.

Settling those matters for the time being and pushing them to the back of his mind, he turned his thoughts back toward The London Gossip. As he bent to pump the fresh, warm water from the bottom of the shower-bath into the top chamber, he fairly trembled with fury at the thought of her. Tipping his head back and closing his eyes, Benedict pulled the cord and allowed the steady shower of water to rinse away the grimy feeling of having slept in his clothes.

For almost a year now, the Gossip had been toying with him, using the details of his life as fodder for the society gossip-mill. In the beginning, it had been easy enough to ignore. She hadn't written anything about him that the rest of the *ton* didn't already whisper behind his back. It wasn't until she'd begun digging into the operations of his secret agency that Benedict felt compelled to put a stop to her malicious ways once and for all.

The idea of putting his friends to work as male courtesans in secret had been born of a desire to help them. Like him, they had all been in dire financial straits with no other means of gaining steady income. Hugh, David, Dominick, and Aubrey had readily gone along with the idea, trusting Benedict to protect their secrets and orchestrate their arrangements. For his part, Benedict received a small percentage of each courtesan's earnings, though he had amassed a tidy sum by his own means. Unlike his friends, who could escort their keepers about London under the guise of respectability, Benedict was forced to conduct his own liaisons in secret. A man couldn't spit in Town without it landing on a man who either knew he was attracted to his own sex, was curious about relations with other men and wished to experiment, or who were in denial about their own natures. Benedict's skill at sniffing them out and making them want him badly enough to pay whatever he asked had reversed his circumstances and helped scratch the physical itch resulting from lack of intimacy with anyone since Alex. The other things Benedict had to go without—closeness, affection, camaraderie—none of them mattered anymore. He had taught himself not to need them, and the men who'd paid to keep him at their disposal over the years seemed content for their arrangements to be about mutual pleasure and nothing else.

As stories about the mysterious Gentleman Courtesans swept through high society like wildfire, The London Gossip had begun using her paper to vilify the courtesans—calling them a foul corruption she intended to ferret out and expose. Benedict's folly had been thinking her harmless, a mistake he would never make again. The woman's vendetta against the courtesans had been one of self-righteous indignation and an inflated sense of so-called morality. Her hostility toward Benedict had felt far too personal, and after a visit to a dear friend with the right connections, he had discovered exactly why.

He scrubbed furiously with a cake of cedar-scented soap, knowing that the cloying scent of lily-of-the-valley was only a figment of his imagination. It had been his first clue to the identity of the anonymous London Gossip, who always obscured her features whenever they crossed paths. The scent had niggled at a long-buried memory, one he had actively worked to forget—along with recollections of the attentions of the mad-doctor. There were parts of his past he had chosen to eliminate from his mind, but some things simply couldn't be outrun.

She had played her hand first, revealing that she knew the identities of most of the men in his employ. He had countered by cutting off circulation of her paper, buying himself time to prevent the exposure of his own secrets, as well as those of his friends. Now, she had revived their little war by finding a way to resume circulation of her paper, and her first issue had skewered him like a fish.

However, he still had the upper hand, for the woman didn't yet know that Benedict had discovered her identity. Now that he had it, they were no longer on uneven ground. He knew his enemy better than she realized and would use what he knew to destroy her.

Resolved, he pumped more water to rinse himself, enjoying the warm deluge over his skin. In one corner of the washroom stood a copper tub he never made use of. Benedict had no idea why he kept the thing, as just looking at it conjured yet another memory best left locked away. Reason told him he was too old, too big to drown in a tub that he had to bend his knees to fit in, but the instincts of one who had endured unspeakable torture could not be rewritten. Bathtubs were off-limits for the anxiety-inducing affect they had on his broken mind.

Tearing his gaze from the empty tub, he strode into the bedchamber with one length of toweling wrapped around his waist while using the other to scrub at his dripping hair. Simmons waited at the washstand with a razor and steaming pitcher of water. Plopping into his chair, Benedict slouched and tipped his head back.

"After you finish my toilette, I need you to take a message to Warin Lyons—he lives over on Half-Moon Street. You remember the address?"

"Of course, sir," Simmons replied while laying a damp, warm towel over the lower half of Benedict's face.

The sound of razor to strop came next, almost soothing in its rhythm, like the ocean lapping at the shore.

"Good. Write nothing down. I need you to deliver this message verbally. Hail a hackney and take pains to ensure you aren't followed."

"Understood. The message, sir?"

"Tell Lyons I need him to meet me at Rowland-Drake Haberdashery in one hour."

"Yes, sir."

Simmons fell silent then, getting to work making Benedict look less like a vagabond and more of a gentleman. He had no care for fashion or the latest trends in men's hair and such hogwash. Simmons was free to dress him as he pleased, as long as he adhered to Benedict's preference for muted, neutral colors and shunned flamboyant embellishments.

Such thoughts inevitably led him back to Alex, who was as much his opposite in this regard as he was in every other aspect. The man was obsessed with fabrics and unusual color combinations, unafraid to be daring and reject the strictures of fashion as dictated by Brummel and his ilk. Most men could never carry off such eclectic style with grace, but Alex was in a league of his own. No one looked as well in cravats died shades of jonquil and burgundy, or waistcoats in contrasting hues of scarlet and tangerine—like the beacon of a robin's breast.

A stirring in Benedict's chest trickled downward as he recalled countless occasions upon which he had stripped Alex out of his finery, delighting in the distress he caused by tearing at buttons and casually throwing articles to the floor. His propensity for leaving his things lying around had irked Alex to no end, but Benedict could make him forget about the clothing strewn over the floor once he got his hands and mouth on bare skin.

Shifting in the chair, he stifled the niggling of arousal in his groin, annoyed with himself for the path of his thoughts. Benedict had left his past where it belonged—behind him—and that included the remnants of what he had shared with Alex. It had all been a lie, a pleasant diversion for Alex until the time came for him to legitimize his standing as a peer with a bride. Raising a hand to his temple, Benedict ran his first finger along the scar that stopped just short of his hairline. Two inches in length, the raised, puckered aberration often burned with phantom pains as imagined as a bathtub drowning that would never happen. But Benedict reveled in the pain. Pain was how he knew he was still alive, how he remembered to stay away from things that could hurt him.

And nothing had ever hurt him the way Alex had, not even his father who excelled at inflicting agony on him. The reminder of where this scar had come from was enough to strengthen his will. Loving Alex had nearly killed him, and Benedict had learned to appreciate his life after fighting to make his own place in it.

Nothing and no one would take that from him. Not even the only person he'd ever truly loved. Clearly, Alex hadn't loved him enough to stay. It was all Benedict needed to know.

CHAPTER 3

Benedict had another call to pay before making his way to Rowland-Drake, the linen-drapery and haberdashery owned by his best friend. Coincidentally, the person he was going to see lived on Half-Moon Street, several houses down from Warin Lyons. However, he couldn't be seen at Lyons's residence, lest the man's connection to the Gentleman Courtesans be uncovered. However, the lady he had come to speak with—Lady Millicent Dane—was the only person in London whose reputation could be called worse than his. The Gossip was also aware of Benedict's connection to Millicent, and that her infamous secret parties had been used to conduct courtesan business. There was nothing left to hide, so Benedict boldly strode to her front door and knocked.

The youngest, most ridiculously attractive butler Benedict had ever seen answered the door, eyes lighting with recognition at the sight of him. The man was like every other servant in this house—beautiful to look at, with the snug fit of his livery flaunting sinewy muscle and brawn. Benedict had to admire the dedication to such an aesthetic.

"Is Lady Dane at home?" he asked.

"She is, Mr. Sterling," the butler replied, widening the door in welcome. "In fact, she has been expecting a call from you. Right this way."

Benedict chose to remain in his greatcoat, the chill of a winter's afternoon clinging to him, though he did remove his hat. He held it in one hand while following the butler to a drawing room. Once the butler announced him, he was ushered into a chamber that, at first glance, looked to be one of elegant taste and style. However, as one took a closer look, the licentious decor made itself apparent. Red wallpaper with gold leaf turned the sunlight streaming through the windows into a pink haze. Erotic paintings hung from them, depicting couples, threesomes, and outright orgies of people engaged in voluptuous acts. Marble and stone statues sat on pedestals about the room, strategically placed to be seen from every angle. They were even more shocking than the paintings in the stark whiteness and multidimensional portrayal of every sexual act imaginable.

In the center of the room, lounging on a sofa and lingering over a scattering of fashion plates, was Lady Millicent Dane. Her blue eyes glittered, and her rouged lips stretched into a genuine smile at the sight of him. Her lush proportions were encased in a simple dressing-gown of black damask, which made the milky hue of her skin and white-gold of her hair appear ethereal. Her feet, covered in dainty slippers, peeked out from beneath the hem.

Millicent didn't bat an eyelash at the notion of him seeing her thus undressed, but that had nothing to do with her knowledge of his predilections. The woman was unashamed of her sexual nature, and shunned the strictures of a society that would tell her she could not receive a friend dressed in something that covered more skin than most of her ball gowns.

"Ben, darling! I'd been hoping you would pay me a visit."

"So I was told," he said while sinking onto the loveseat facing her sofa, with a low table between them. "New butler?"

Her grin grew wicked as her gaze darted toward the door, which hung ajar to reveal the figure of the butler striding by. "Isn't he delectable? The entire household is enamored with him already, though I cannot decide whether the women want him more, or the men."

Benedict chuckled. "And what does Peter think of him?"

Millicent's smile grew wistful at the mention of her body servant and longtime lover. Peter had begun his service in her house as a footman, but he had soon earned her favor, then eventually her heart. Benedict didn't quite understand their arrangement—knowing only that Millicent's dominant nature meant the man was willing to do anything she asked, no matter how debasing. The two had no boundaries to their tastes and were known to share lovers of both sexes whenever the mood struck. However, despite there being no benefit of marriage, he'd never seen a pair more dedicated to one another than Millicent and Peter. The servant loved his mistress, and Benedict liked to believe she loved him back.

"Peter is the most enamored of all. They've been trading lingering looks all week. I do believe he'd be amenable to ... an additional duty along with all his others."

Benedict couldn't help but envy men like Peter and this butler, who were capable of feeling desire for both men and women. For his part, while he could admire a woman's beauty or form, his appreciation of the fair sex ended there. He had long ago accepted who he was, but couldn't pretend life wouldn't be easier for him if he could conjure the slightest interest in a woman. It would protect him from ruin, solidify his viscountcy when the time came to inherit, keep him from having to hide who he was, living a lie every day. Apparently, Alex shared this trait with Peter, for he'd had no problem joining with a woman in marriage. Thinking of Alex consummating the union, enjoying the attentions of a wife in the dark, and taking pleasure from it made Benedict's chest ache. The thought of Alex being intimate and tender with a doting wife hurt more than Benedict wanted to acknowledge. It baffled him to realize that Alex still held such power over him. Even after turning him away twice, Benedict still felt an acute agony at the thought of what could never be.

Seeming to sense that his thoughts had taken a disagreeable turn, Millicent sat up straight, feet touching the floor as she pushed her fashion plates aside. "Something is wrong."

"No ... yes. My father arrived this morning."

Millicent pulled a face, knowing full well the sins the viscount had committed against Benedict. "My condolences. Would you like to take a room here until he leaves? I don't care who he is; he would not be allowed over the threshold. I have an army of footmen who could toss him out on his ear on a moment's notice."

"Thank you, but no. I refuse to be intimidated into leaving my own home."

"Good show."

"I do have another request to make of you."

Her eyes widened in realization. "You are ready to act on the information I gave you."

"I am. There is a ball this evening in the home of the Duke and Duchess of Avonleah."

"Yes, darling, the duke and his wife are dear friends of mine."

"So, you've been invited."

"Of course. Weren't you invited?"

"No. But, Avonleah doesn't strike me as one to shun a man with a bad reputation."

Millicent snorted. "Hardly. He was once the biggest rake in London. The duchess is a special woman, indeed, to have tamed him."

"Do you suppose I could garner an invitation, if you were to request it? I take it *she* will be there."

They both knew the 'she' he referred to, and Millicent's jaw hardened in disdain. "Naturally. She sits quite far down the ladder of high society, but has made some influential friends. I wouldn't be surprised to know she has blackmailed her way into higher circles. How else could she find herself invited to a ball in the home of a duke?"

It was something Benedict had never considered, but it made perfect sense. The woman he remembered from his youth was the daughter of a gentleman with only a tenuous hold on respectability. She and her father had been willing to do anything to better their status. When using Benedict to do so hadn't worked, she must have devised this London Gossip scheme as a way in. With the information she had on him, it stood to reason she knew many other secrets—the kinds of secrets she could use to bribe her way to the status she desired.

"How, indeed," he murmured, lost in thought.

"Consider it done, darling. It is no trouble at all, and Avonleah would give me anything I wanted for an invitation to one of my parties. I'm hosting another Tuesday next, you know. I hope you will come. Perhaps it will prove a pleasant respite."

"Perhaps. I can make no promises right now."

"I understand. What else can I do to help?"

Rising to his feet, Benedict shook his head. "Nothing for now. You have already helped me so much. I could never repay you."

Millicent stood, rounding the table and pulling him into an embrace. He had to crouch to meet her, bracing a hand at her back as she wrapped both arms around his shoulders and squeezed.

"You are one of the few people in this godforsaken city who accept me as I am," she said. "That alone is enough to make me willing to do anything you ask. I am the one who owes you a debt of gratitude."

"Nonsense," Benedict insisted as they pulled apart. "You aren't the only one grateful for accepting friends."

She walked him to the drawing room door. "I will have your invitation delivered right away. If you need me at the ball, you have only to seek me out."

Benedict took his leave with a half-hearted promise to do what Millicent had asked. However, he couldn't explain why he would not take her up on such an offer. Only he could confront this unpleasant part of his past and lay it to rest once and for all.

THE BELL ABOVE THE DOOR TO ROWLAND-DRAKE LINEN-Drapery and Haberdashery tinkled as Alex pushed it open, entering an establishment that had grown and flourished during his absence from London. What had once been a small, one-room shop was now transformed. The removal of a wall had opened the ground floor of this building into one next door. The first main room overflowed with fabrics in an array of vibrant hues, and counter displays offered the necessary trimmings for various garments. Fashionable hats, gloves, shawls, and other accessories were artfully arranged in the newly attached room.

Searching the area, Alex caught the eye of the young man behind a large oak counter. He was tall and wiry, with smooth, light-brown skin, dark hair cropped close, and a pair of startlingly vibrant green eyes. The combined parentage of a black parent and a white one dueled for dominance on his face.

"Welcome to Rowland-Drake, my lord. Might I help you find something? A gift for a lady perhaps ... or fabric for a new waistcoat? I can see you're a man of extraordinary taste."

He dipped his head to indicate Alex's waistcoat—a pale lavender silk printed with tiny silver fleur de lis. Alex smiled at the young man, obviously an assistant to the owner who was an old school friend of Alex's. Apparently, Aubrey Drake had trained his protégé well.

"Perhaps in a moment," Alex replied, eying a jade green fabric spilling from the massive rolls mounted to the wall. "But first, I wondered if Mr. Drake might be in this afternoon?"

"He is, my lord, but he's very busy today preparing for a new shipment. I can inquire if he will see you."

"He will. Simply tell him the Earl of Vautrey requires his attention."

Instead of bustling off to deliver the message, the young man goggled at Alex in clear shock. "Lord Osborne, is that you? I mean ... you said 'earl' so you must be Lord Vautrey now. My God, I thought you looked familiar."

Alex furrowed his brow and took a close look at the assistant. No one called him Lord Osborne anymore, as his viscountcy had simply been a courtesy title until he'd inherited the earldom. His eyes widened as he realized what a dolt he'd been. The man's features were too distinct to be forgotten, though the last time Alex had seen him, he'd been skinnier than he was tall and still carrying the softness of youth in his face. But the eyes didn't lie. Before he was the shop assistant, Christopher Sanders had been a young apprentice in this very shop.

"Kit?" Alex blurted. "By Jove, look at you! The last time I saw you, you appeared as if a strong wind could carry you away!"

Kit rounded the counter and offered Alex a hand with an exuberant smile and a deep chuckle. Alex marveled at the depth of the voice he heard, unable to believe his eyes or his ears.

"Well, there have been quite a few changes around here," Kit said while giving his hand a hearty shake.

"So I see," he replied, glancing about the renovated shop. "Aubrey has done well for himself."

"Not better than you, I see," boomed a third voice from across the room.

Alex turned to find the man he'd come to see, coming from within a small back office. Aubrey Drake's wide, white smile contrasted starkly against his dark-as-night skin. He hadn't aged a day, though a few strands of gray salted the wool of his short, close-cropped hair. Standing as tall as Alex and as broad as Ben, Aubrey Drake was a sight for sore eyes. Alex hadn't seen Aubrey since the day of his wedding, and had missed the company of one of his closest friends.

"Aubrey," he murmured, emotion straining his voice as a handshake was transformed into a tight embrace. "I am so happy to see you."

Aubrey pounded his back, then leaned back to stare Alex in the face. "The feeling is entirely mutual. I didn't know you were in Town."

Kit moved back to his place behind the counter, but looked on with a curious gaze as Aubrey drew Alex out of earshot.

"I only arrived two nights ago," Alex said. "I didn't want to impose on you while you are working, but I hoped you might have time for a word. I will not take up too much of your time."

"Nonsense," Aubrey insisted, already guiding him toward the open door of the office. "I have all the time in the world for you, my friend. Come, we'll have a drink and—"

"Aubrey! Haven't you heard me calling? I had hoped you could tell me what you think."

The interrupting voice had been feminine, and Alex looked up in time to find a woman appearing from behind a curtain, the skirts of an unfinished gown swishing around her heels. She halted at the sight of Alex, cheeks flushing pink as her cerulean eyes darted from him to Aubrey.

"Oh, I'm sorry," she murmured, dipping into an elegant curtsy—one that could not be ruined by the pins and hanging bits of lace marking her gown as a work in progress. "I didn't realize you had left your office, my love. Forgive me."

Aubrey offered a soft smile, and Alex noted the clear affection in his eyes as he looked upon the woman. "There is nothing to apologize for, darling. Actually, I was going to send for you. I want you to meet one of my oldest friends. We attended Cambridge together. Lord Vautrey, my wife, Mrs. Lucinda Drake. Lucy, this is Lord Alexander Osborne, the Earl of Vautrey."

"It is an honor to meet you, my lord," Lucinda replied with a smile. "Though I would make a better impression in a gown that isn't pieced together by pins."

Alex took her hand and bowed over it. "Please, you must call me Alex ... and you would make a grand impression dressed in rags."

She smiled up at her husband. "Oh, I like him."

Aubrey chuckled. "Always the charmer."

"You shall call me Lucinda," she said, turning back to Alex. "Aubrey has told me so many stories of his time at university, and many featured you. You, Dominick Burke, and ... Benedict Sterling."

Alex suppressed a flinch at the knowing look in her eyes. Aubrey and Ben had always been close, with Aubrey conscious of his and Ben's preference for men. Of course Lucinda would know the truth about Ben. Aubrey would never have married a woman who wouldn't be willing to know and accept his best friend.

"Yes, the three of us were inseparable," Alex answered.

"What a shame that you have been away so long. Perhaps a reunion is in order now that you've returned to London."

"All right, you busybody," Aubrey quipped, gently taking Lucinda's arm and steering her back toward the curtain. "Off you go. You look beautiful, and the gown is coming along nicely."

Resisting Aubrey's prodding, she glanced at Alex over her shoulder. "It was so lovely to have met you, Alex. Will you join us for dinner one evening?"

"I would be delighted," he replied just before she disappeared in a billow of silk.

Following Aubrey into the office, Alex shook his head in disbelief. "Aubrey Drake ... married. I never thought I would see the day."

Aubrey rounded the desk to a small cabinet pushed into the corner, where a single decanter and four clean glasses rested. "I was once engaged," he reminded Alex while trickling what smelled like brandy into two of the tumblers. "Surely you haven't forgotten that."

Alex accepted his drink and took one of the chairs facing the desk. He gave Aubrey a pointed look. "You and Philippa were ill-suited. While I was sorry to hear she cried off, I did have my reservations."

Aubrey chuckled. "That's what Ben said."

Their mutual friend's name fell between them like a ten-ton boulder, sending a wave of tense silence through the room. Alex stared into his glass, skin tingling with the phantom memory of being near Ben again—kissing him, touching him, breathing in the scent he knew so well and had longed for.

He took a drink and then cleared his throat, crossing one leg over the other and doing his best to appear unruffled. "Yes, well ... Lucy seems lovely. You look happier than I think I've ever seen you."

Aubrey smiled, proving Alex's point. The lines of strain that had once perpetually marred his brow had disappeared, and even with gray hairs at his temples, he looked younger and more content than ever. A prick of envy and longing reminded Alex that this might have been him had he chosen his path differently. However, he was here because he believed it wasn't too late to have the future he'd always wanted.

"I am happy," Aubrey said. "I suppose you've heard about Nick?"

Alex laughed. "I was even more surprised to hear of his

nuptials than yours. I thought for sure he would die a bachelor—still chasing skirts until the bitter end."

"You'll understand when you meet Calliope. She's a lovely woman and perfect for Nick. He's a new man."

"I am glad to hear it. I look forward to seeing him and meeting her."

They grew silent again, Aubrey's expression growing pensive as they sipped their brandy. After a while, he set his half-empty tumbler on the desk. "I was deeply sorry to hear about your countess. I had not realized she was ill."

"She wasn't," Alex hedged, unwilling to divulge more than he was ready to. There were things he wanted Ben to know before he began speaking of Katherine to anyone else. "Her death was sudden and ... and devastating."

Aubrey's sympathetic look also carried understanding. He had not known Katherine well, but knew how close she and Alex had been. While Alex hadn't loved her as a husband should love a wife, their deep friendship had made their pretense of a marriage bearable. Having her to rely on had lessened the pain of losing Ben as much as was possible.

"Alex," Aubrey began with a deep sigh. "I know why you're here."

Alex tensed, hearing the warning note in Aubrey's voice. "You disapprove."

"Not precisely. I think, were I in your shoes, I would have made the same decision. You love Ben and always have. You want him back."

"More than anything," he admitted, having no reason to hold back with Aubrey.

"Have you seen him?"

"Twice since my return. He doesn't want to see or speak to me, and I cannot say I can blame him."

"Neither can I," Aubrey stated, though there was no malice behind it. "I do not blame you for your choice. Ben does, but he doesn't know what I know. You were placed in an impossible situation."

"You never told him?"

"You trusted me to keep your confidence."

Alex wasn't certain whether to be relieved to hear this, or disappointed. On the one hand, if Ben had known the reason Alex had been forced to marry Katherine, he might have understood. He might have gone on with his life knowing that Alex hadn't left him for lack of love or devotion, but to protect him. But then, Ben was known for his obstinacy and willpower. He would have tried putting a stop to the wedding, insisting that anything could be overcome as long as they were together. And Alex, weak, romantic fool that he was, would have been powerless to resist. Ben would be far worse off than he was now as a result.

"What happened after I left London?" Alex asked. "Ben is angry with me, but there's more to it than that, I can feel it. He's changed."

"He has," Aubrey agreed. "As far as what went on once you were gone ... I'm sorry, Alex, but I cannot divulge that. Ben's story isn't mine to tell. I want the two of you to make amends, and am willing to help in whatever way I can. If you want me to try to talk to him and smooth the way for you, I am perfectly willing to do that, but ... don't ask me to reveal things he would prefer to keep to himself. I promised to keep your confidence, but I also promised Ben the same. I owe him that much after all he has done for me."

"I understand," Alex said, though he couldn't help but feel disappointed. He had been hoping for any insight into Ben's state of mind, any information that could help get through to him.

As if having plucked his thoughts out of thin air, Aubrey leaned in, gaze intently locked with Alex's. "I can tell you that he wouldn't be so angry if he didn't still feel something for you. If you can withstand his anger in the beginning without faltering, you can get through to him. That is one thing that has remained the same."

It wasn't much, but Alex would accept that. It had never occurred to him that when it came to Ben, heated fury was better than cold apathy. If Ben could be made to feel rage, he could also feel affection and desire. Those emotions were still there somewhere, however deeply they had been buried.

"Thank you," he murmured before finishing off what was left of his brandy. "I don't intend to give up, and will remain in London as long as it takes."

"Good," Aubrey replied. "Then I can expect to see you fairly often? Perhaps for dinner as Lucy proposed."

Alex chuckled. "Most certainly." Catching sight of the array of newspapers resting at the corner of the desk, Alex gestured toward them. "May I?"

Neatly stacking a mess of documents at his elbow, Aubrey nodded. "Of course."

Flipping through crisp copies of the usual papers, Alex frowned when he noticed one that was unfamiliar to him. "*The London Gossip*? Aubrey, I never took you for being interested in *ton* scandals and such."

Aubrey's mouth drew tight, his expression changing from open and inviting to shuttered in a matter of seconds. "I'm not ... not really. But the woman who writes that paper has been known to print unflattering things about me in her columns—Lucy as well. It's simply good sense to keep up with what she's printing and consider how it can affect business."

Alex scowled while skimming reports of debutantes who had ruined their marriage prospects with scandalous behaviors, gentlemen who had blown fortunes at the gaming tables, and a running list of impending marriages and births. There was even a betting guide for those who might wish to wager on any of the happenings of high society: whether a duchess might bear her husband a son or daughter, if a betrothal would be called off before the wedding, if the mistress of a viscount would be set aside after he was married.

"By Jove, she sounds like a right harpy," he muttered. "In one section she complains that the vice of gambling is ruining the society gentleman, but in the next she prints a betting guide."

"She is both a harpy and a hypocrite," Aubrey replied, the words laced with disgust. "But you know how high society thrives on gossip. That's the most popular scandal sheet in town."

A certain column caught Alex's eye, and he quickly read a report concerning Ben's recent activities. "It says here that Ben has a mistress. Some dowager countess."

Aubrey made a low sound of amusement from his throat. "A pretense, and a rather effective one. Matchmaking mamas steer their daughters clear of him, thinking him a rake. The courtesans keep their distance as Celeste is said to have quite the hold over him. She's a friend, and has her reasons for going along with the charade."

It made sense, though it struck Alex as something Ben would never have done in the past. His irreverence meant he didn't give a fig what anyone thought of him, and didn't need pretense of any kind to explain why he wasn't married or never seen in the company of women. Perhaps more had changed in Alex's absence than he'd thought.

"I see. This Gossip woman certainly seems to dislike Ben. She is almost detached when writing about others, but seems to have reserved a great deal of animosity for Ben. Have you any idea what that's about?"

"Not in the slightest." Aubrey sounded bored as he stood and stretched. "Who can pretend to know the mind of a woman like her? Enough about that. Come, I want to show you the expansion on the shop and our new renovations. Then, I have some fabrics I think you will like in the storeroom. No one else has purchased them yet, so you will make quite a splash should you choose to wear one."

The abrupt change of subject puzzled Alex, but then Aubrey must be used to this gossip columnist's peculiarities. Alex was only so curious because his distance from London had kept him in the dark about such matters. Not one to pay much attention to idle gossip, he was willing to let the matter drop.

He followed Aubrey out into the shop, noticing that Kit was busy charming a female patron over a tray of fastenings and other baubles. Two young apprentices were busy tidying the shop, while a pair of gentlemen browsed a display of gloves.

The expansion of Aubrey's shop became more impressive now that Alex allowed himself to really take it in. Rowland-Drake had gone from a small establishment in Cheapside, to a luxurious, sprawling place in the West End.

Alex could hardly fathom it, when he'd known the shop to be heavily in debt and on the brink of failure just three years ago. Curiosity niggled, but he ignored it. Despite their closeness and long friendship, Alex drew the line at probing questions about another man's finances.

An hour later, he had purchased five different waistcoat fabrics and the buttons to embellish them, a pair of gloves, two mufflers, a hat, embroidered stockings, and burgundy broadcloth for a new coat. His valet would swoon over the new pieces once they were commissioned, and Alex couldn't deny a little thrill at adding to his already expansive wardrobe. There were so many things about himself he had to keep hidden, but his clothing could always serve as an expression of who he was. His unconventional style often drew stares and murmurs, but no one was ever bold enough to call him out for going against the austere color palette and constricting modes of men's fashion as dictated by those whose opinions meant nothing to him. It always amused him to see younger men emulating his fashions, sporting yellow-dyed cravats and brightly-colored waistcoats, and patterened stockings—a sure reminder that being an earl came with all manner of influence.

Deep down, he wrestled with the appropriateness of his

attire as well as his purchases. Katherine had been gone for just over six months now, and as a man he was freer to shed deep mourning than a widow would be. When guilt plagued Alex, he reminded himself that Katherine would have wanted him to dress like himself again. She had loved helping him select his garments, and seeing him miserable and unable to explore his passion for clothing would have saddened her. Besides, continuing to wear mourning would have only reminded Ben that he'd had a wife—by far the sorest point of contention between them.

Aubrey followed him to his carriage, his apprentices following behind with the wrapped parcels. They had just been handed off to the footman, when another carriage pulled up behind his, followed by a hackney coach.

Every hair on Alex's body stood on end as he recognized the Sterling family crest emblazoned on the door. He could only stand there holding his breath in anticipation as the footman opened the vehicle to reveal Ben, who fit a hat over his bright blond locks while stepping out, a stark black greatcoat swirling around his ankles. Alex felt as if he'd been punched in the gut when those electric blue eyes landed on him, flaring with recognition first, then heat. An answering need sparked within him, making it damned hard to keep from crossing the distance between them and planting his lips on Ben's.

Ben's expression hardened in an instant, eyes going blank as if a pair of shutters had been slammed closed over them. He looked to Aubrey. "Are you busy at the moment? Lyons and I need a word."

Alex noticed the man who had emerged from the hackney for the first time. He wasn't nearly Alex's height, but taller than average and slender, with dark hair pulled back in an unfashionable but flattering queue. His eyes were a light, honeyed shade of brown and his features were pleasing but sharp and cold, his lips drawn tight.

Who was this Lyons fellow, and what was his relationship to Ben and Aubrey? It was ridiculous to be jealous, and he had no right to be annoyed at the thought of Ben having a lover. There was no sense of secrecy or intimacy between them, but Alex had a feeling Lyon wouldn't let it show if there were. The man had a stoic face, unlike anything Alex had ever seen.

"Not at all," Aubrey replied, though there was a questioning note in his voice. He was looking from Alex to Ben with unease in his eyes. "The lads and I were just carrying out these packages. Lord Vautrey, this is an associate of myself and Ben, Mr. Lyons. Lyons, this is an old schoolmate of ours, Lord Vautrey."

Lyons offered him a stiff bow. "My lord."

"A pleasure," Alex replied, studying the man closely, then looking to Ben. As looks went, he was certainly Ben's type—dark-haired, tall and broad without being too bulky. He even seemed to share Ben's surly disposition.

Alex told himself he was being ridiculous. If Ben had a sweetheart, Aubrey would have told him. Besides, even if he did, Alex could not be put off. Anyone standing between him and Ben would be pushed aside.

"We will wait in your office," Ben declared before sweeping past Alex and disappearing inside without a look back.

Mr. Lyons followed, leaving him alone with Aubrey. Alex's questioning look wasn't answered verbally, and just as he had in the office, he had the sense that Aubrey was holding something back. There was nothing unusual about three men meeting in a place of business during the day, but Alex's instincts couldn't be ignored. Something was going on, and curiosity over it was eating him alive.

"Perhaps we could have dinner this evening?" Aubrey said suddenly, as if what had just occurred was of no consequence.

"I am otherwise engaged tonight—a ball at the Duke and Duchess of Avonleah's house. There will be gossip if I'm not there."

"Tomorrow, then? I have a friend I would like you to meet, and he's currently in town."

"Tomorrow it is. Thank you, Aubrey."

They clasped hands, and Aubrey tightened his grip before Alex could pull away. "I hope things work out in your favor, Alex. For what it's worth, I believe it would be good for Ben as well as for you."

Alex took those final words and locked them away, bolstering his will. Tonight, he would attend the infernal ball and endure sympathetic glances and condolences from people he barely knew. Tomorrow, he would resume his mission.

CHAPTER 4

"The Duke and Duchess of A are hosting a ball this evening in their lavish Grosvenor Square home. This author will be in attendance, so those who intend to be present would should remain on their best behavior, lest you find yourselves the subject of tomorrow's column."
-*The London Gossip*, 26 January 1820

"I take it you've called this meeting because *The London Gossip* is back in circulation," Aubrey said, once he, Benedict, and Warin were shuttered away inside the office. Beyond the door, Lucinda had taken over helping Kit and the apprentices service an afternoon rush of customers.

Benedict hated to interrupt his friend's work, but Aubrey would have no livelihood if their involvement with the Gentleman Courtesans was publicly revealed. As far as he was concerned, nothing was more important than stopping that consequence at all costs.

"My scheme to stop her distribution was never going to be permanent," Benedict replied I only did it to buy some time."

"Time for what?" Warin asked, his voice low and somber. The man had the austere presence of an undertaker, but made a fine apprentice. Once business had become more than he could handle on his own, Benedict had taken Warin under his wing and taught him the ins and outs of his operation. Warin had become Benedict's right hand, an extension of him that could be trusted to act in the best interest of the men in their employ.

"To discover her identity," Benedict murmured. "I knew once I had that information, it could be used to silence her. With the things she's written about the members of the *ton*, she's made enemies out of many influential people—present company included."

"And have you?" Aubrey prodded, leaning in over the desk in anticipation. "Discovered her identity?"

"I have."

Silence descended among the three men, the muffled voices from the shop penetrating the office door. Aubrey looked shocked, while Warin's face remained a blank slate.

"Her name is Cynthia Milbank. Aubrey, the name will be familiar to you."

Aubrey's goggled at Benedict as if he'd been struck by lightning. "Miss Milbank? Are you certain?"

"I wasn't at first, but there was something too familiar about her. Millicent confirmed it. It's her."

Warin darted a puzzled look at Benedict. "Would either of you care to enlighten me as to just who this woman is and why she's doing this?"

"She was Benedict's fiancée for a short time," Aubrey offered.

For the first time, Warin's expression faltered, clear surprise registering on his face. He knew of Benedict's preference and had never judged him for it.

"It was an arrangement made by our fathers," Benedict said with a shrug. "No one involved wanted it, but my father found it necessary. He assumed marriage would reform me."

"He also assumed you would go through with it," Aubrey said with a derisive snort. "It's almost as if he doesn't know you at all."

"Oh, he knows me," Benedict spat. "He simply doesn't care.

He is determined to have his way, regardless of what anyone else wants."

"What happened?" Warin asked. "Since you are still unwed, I'm assuming she cried off."

"She didn't," Benedict replied. "I did."

Warin's stoic expression had been completely obliterated by now. While not born of the *beau monde,* Warin's connections to people such as Benedict had taught him the various faux pas that could bring a man to ruin. He knew as well as Benedict and Aubrey that it was the height of incivility for a man to end an engagement—one that could lead to him being shunned from polite society.

"Dear God," Warin said with a shake of his head. "It's no wonder your reputation is such shite."

"Indeed," Benedict said. "I refused to go through with the marriage, and no one could make me—not my father, not Mr. Milbank, not Cynthia."

"I think it's safe to say we now know why her writings about you are so venomous," Aubrey remarked. "During your engagement, did she happen to discover the truth of your ... inclinations?"

"That, I do not know. It is my belief that she's angry that I jilted her and out for revenge. She started out with a vendetta against the Gentleman Courtesans, which comes as no surprise to me. The Milbanks are merchant class social-climbers looking for status and prestige, which they thought to gain through marriage. Cynthia was always such a haughty little chit, looking down on those she thought were beneath her due to their immorality."

"How did she come to learn that you were the proprietor of the agency?" Warin asked.

"I cannot say," Benedict replied. "However she learned the truth, she has intensified her efforts against all of us ... because of me."

"This isn't your fault," Aubrey insisted.

"It sort of is his fault," Warin said under his breath.

Benedict snorted a laugh. "I take full responsibility for bringing her wrath upon us. Which is why it falls to me to end this."

"What are you going to do?" Aubrey asked.

"Millicent is obtaining my invitation to a ball hosted by the Duke and Duchess of Avonleah. I have it on good authority that Cynthia will be there. I intend to confront her ... discreetly, of course."

Warin frowned. "I don't know if that's a good idea. She's sure to be furious with you for temporarily halting circulation of her paper."

"I don't doubt it," Benedict said. "But I cannot do this any longer. The last time I encountered Cynthia, she told me she wanted something. I intend to find out what that is."

"Do you intend to give it to her?"

"Not a chance. But if I know what she wants, I have all the control. I can deal with her more effectively. Besides, I need her to know I'm on to her."

"What can I do?" Warin asked.

"I need you to visit every man in our employ in person and tell them to lay low for the time being."

"Consider it done. What about those who don't have keepers at present?"

"Those between arrangements will need to wait until it's safe for us to resume business," Benedict replied. "The ones with keepers must exercise caution. We don't know who she has gained her information from, and cannot risk her learning new details she might use to oust us."

"Understood," Warin said. "What else?"

"Before you do any of that, I need you to visit the Dowager Countess of Langford and inform her to prepare to attend a ball with me this evening. I will need her at my side for the sake of appearances."

"Right away," Warin said, coming to his feet and replacing his hat upon his head. "Send for me if you have further need."

Once he departed, Benedict turned to Aubrey. "I need you to make contact with our friends. Marriage hasn't made Hugh, David, Dominick, or you any safer. Who's presently in London?"

"Hugh and Evelyn intend to retire to the country in the coming weeks ... it is nearly Evelyn's time. The arrival of their babe should keep them out of the public eye for a good while."

"Good," Benedict said. "Perhaps you can convince him that it would be best to make their journey sooner than planned. I don't suppose you and Lucy can be convinced to vacate London as well."

"Not a chance," Aubrey said. "I won't leave you alone to deal with the consequences of this."

"You should."

"I won't."

"You have a wife to think of now," Benedict pointed out. "There is also Elizabeth to consider."

Aubrey's young niece had recently reached an age to begin considering marriage, with the hope that she would snare someone of means and good social standing. Benedict had watched Elizabeth grow from a sweet girl to a lovely young woman; she was like family to him. The last thing he wanted was to ruin her chances.

"Both Lucy and Elizabeth would want me to support you. Besides, I have as much stake in stopping Cynthia's machinations as you do. There's my business to consider, and my reputation is tied to my livelihood. I've worked very hard to make a good name for myself, and while some will never consider me anything more than the son of a former slave, I like to think I've gained what respectability I can."

Benedict looked upon his friend, whom he admired more than anyone. It wasn't only Aubrey's steadfastness or constant state of calm confidence that made Benedict feel safe and understood. Aubrey had always been the model of what Benedict thought all men should aspire to be. He hadn't been born with great wealth or status, and had earned everything that was his by the sweat of his brow. Benedict's status had been given to him at birth, and his current position as the viscount's heir was a matter of privileged circumstance. Understanding that drove him to forge a life independent of his father and the strictures of a title he didn't want.

"I intend to ensure you retain everything you have earned," Benedict said. "Elizabeth will have her good marriage, and your success will never be marred by my folly."

Aubrey sighed, and ran a hand over his face. He suddenly appeared weary and worn down. "We must all take responsibility for our parts. You didn't force any of us into this, nor did you ever make a single courtesan do something he didn't wish to. In truth, I have you to thank for my improved circumstances, as well as the blessing of Lucy. I would never have met her had she not hired me as her courtesan. I daresay Hugh, David, and Dominick share the same sentiment."

Benedict supposed the happiness of his closest friends proved the silver lining of this entire business. While he couldn't fight off the gnawing pangs of envy, seeing them settled in lives that didn't include him, Benedict knew they were all better off. He was the only one who would be left alone when all was said and done, nursing his bitterness and regret.

"I should go," he said, coming to his feet. "There is much to do before the ball."

Aubrey wasn't inclined to let him off so easily. "Ben," he said, piercing Benedict with a sharp stare."

Benedict paused halfway to the door, sensing the direction this conversation would take and dreading it.

"Aubrey, don't—"

"What will you do when this is all over?" Aubrey interjected. "The courtesan enterprise is still a lucrative one, but we began this as a temporary solution to our financial problems. Between the agency and your pugilism winnings, I imagine you have quite the nest egg saved."

Benedict did his best to remain composed. Aubrey was far too good at seeing through his pretenses, rightfully interpreting his apathy and rigidity as an armor he wore for the sake of self-preservation. He had seen Benedict at his lowest point and understood how he'd come to be this way.

"That is irrelevant. The other courtesans depend on me for their livelihood. They need me."

Aubrey raised one dark eyebrow. "Do they? It seems Lyons has learned all he needs to from you. He would make a fine proprietor for the agency."

A low growl of frustration tore from Benedict's chest. "Do you intend to arrive at the point of this lecture sometime today?"

As always, Aubrey remained unruffled by his outburst. He had always been the one person Benedict couldn't intimidate into silence. Well ... there was also Alex, but Benedict refused to allow both men to occupy the same space in his mind. One was like a brother to him and had been there when Benedict needed him most. The other had abandoned him, tearing his heart out in the process.

"It is no coincidence that your father and Alex have turned up in London at the exact same time," Aubrey said. "Call it fate if you like, but I only know that the past has a way of forcing a reckoning, and yours is overdue."

Benedict clenched his fingers around the brim of his hat. "My father wants to arrange a marriage for me under threat of commitment to an asylum. Should I capitulate to such a *reckoning?*"

Aubrey's expression melted into one of empathy and sadness. "Of course not. I only meant that you will have to settle matters with him eventually. Running away or rebelling will only make him more determined. As for Alex—"

"He has been made to understand that nothing more will happen between us. I'm finished with him."

Aubrey slowly shook his head, eyes lowered as he rifled through a ledger sitting open on his desk. "I don't think you are. I cannot tell you what you ought to do, but if our friendship means anything to you, you will listen. There is more to what happened between you and Alex than you understand. I realize he hurt you, and you have every right to be angry with him. But, the two of you were inseparable for years. He loved you, Benedict, you know he did. Has it never occurred to you to find out his reasons for calling off your plans and marrying Katherine?"

"He did it because he's a coward," Benedict growled. There was a wall behind him in danger of having a fist-sized hole smashed into it. "And apparently, he didn't love me as much as we thought, because he never bothered to explain himself. Why should I hear him out now?"

Aubrey didn't meet Benedict's heated gaze, casually flipping through his ledger book and making notes here and there with a pen. "Why, indeed?"

As Aubrey seemed inclined to remain silent, Benedict didn't bother offering a farewell. He stormed from the office, ignoring the questioning stares of Lucy and Kit. His carriage waited where he had left it, allowing for a swift escape.

He didn't have the time or the strength to expend on these matters of Alex and his father—not when Cynthia Milbank had the ammunition to destroy his life and the lives of those he held most dear. He was in control, always, and he would not be made to feel guilty for shunning Alex's ridiculous notions of reconciliation.

The future spread before him, a path that was his to forge and shape as he saw fit.

Nothing and no one would dictate that path to him.

. . .

LADY CELESTE BROWNING, DOWAGER COUNTESS OF Langford, had been Benedict's saving grace the past several years, and continued to be so this evening as she walked into the ballroom of the Duke and Duchess of Avonleah on his arm. As a pair, they attracted quite a bit of notice, almost every eye in the room following their progress into the throng of guests. Benedict had timed their arrival with precision, wanting to be seen by as many people as possible—including Cynthia Milbank.

Petite and ethereally lovely, with inky black hair and startling blue eyes, Celeste was used to being the center of attention. Of course, the rumors that she had murdered her husband to gain his fortune only made her a more polarizing figure amongst the *ton*—her association with Benedict adding fuel to the fire. She handled it all with grace and aplomb, head held high as she clung to his arm and smiled at those who gaped at her like an exotic bird in a menagerie.

She had been posing as his mistress to mask the truth of his predilections, with no care for what it would do to her reputation. Her state of widowhood had freed her to act as she pleased, and being one of the few friends who knew the truth about him made Celeste the perfect ally. When he visited her townhouse three nights a week, it wasn't to go to her bed, but to use one of her spare bedrooms for his own purposes. The various men who had paid to keep him came there for their pleasure, ensuring both their secrets were kept safe.

Thankfully, he had been without a client for the past two months and was in no mood to take another. The commission he earned from the arrangements of the other courtesans kept him comfortable, and Aubrey had been right about his savings. After losing everything to speculation once, he had become smarter about managing his funds. He had enough to live on for years to come if he was careful.

"My God," Celeste murmured as Benedict halted a passing footman and procured a flute of champagne for her. "One would think they'd never seen a courtesan and her cull before."

Benedict's cheek twitched with a smile that never came. "If only they knew the truth."

Celeste sipped her champagne, scanning the room with eyes that missed nothing. "If it didn't mean the ruin of us all, I would dearly wish for them to know the truth. Can you imagine the delicious scandal it would cause?"

"I do and I have … every day for the past three years or so."

Releasing his arm, she gave him an apologetic look. "I'm sorry. That was insensitive of me. Of course I don't want you and your friends to be exposed."

He waved her off. "Think nothing of it. Now go … mingle and dance and make every woman in this room green with envy. I will find you later."

Flicking open a painted fan, she wafted it before her face while sauntering through the crowd, exchanging pleasantries with those shamelessly slavering over her.

Benedict moved in the opposite direction, scanning the crowd for his unwitting prey. She had only ever presented herself to him wearing veiled hats to conceal her identity, but could do no such thing tonight. Try as he might, he'd never forgotten her face—mottled red and soaked with tears as it had been the last time he saw her. Her false innocence and wiles hadn't been enough to trick him then, and they wouldn't sway him now. Benedict knew Cynthia Milbank for the viper she was, and intended to make that clear at the first opportunity.

As he weaved through the occupants of the room, pausing to greet acquaintances, a sudden foreboding trickled down his spine. He was being watched, quite intently. He took his time seeking the source of the prickle on the back of his neck, expecting to be confronted by Cynthia. Instead, it was Alex who locked eyes with him from a short distance away.

He stood near a potted plant on the periphery of the crowded ballroom, lifting a half-empty champagne flute to his lips while staring unflinchingly at Benedict. Despite wanting to present Alex his middle finger and storm off, Benedict was held in the other man's thrall, powerless to resist the siren's call of those striking brown eyes.

Gritting his teeth, Benedict reminded himself all the reasons his attraction to Alex didn't have to mean anything. He'd fucked at least six of the men in this room—though he hadn't made his way through enough of the guests to be certain there weren't more. He liked his men tall and broad in the shoulders, firm but not too bulky, dark-haired. He had a weakness for full, plush lips, much like the ones Alex pressed against the rim of his glass.

This was a matter of primal instinct, nothing more. That Benedict could admire the cut of a dark blue coat that hugged Alex's shoulders and arms to perfection, or the way his silk breeches clung lovingly to powerful thighs only meant he'd gone too long without a man in his bed. His mind had been occupied with other matters, but he could rectify that whenever he wanted. Aside from a long list of past clients who would leap at the chance to spend a night with him, there were places a man of his tastes could go in London to have his needs met.

Alex approached him now, not bothering to mask the determined set to his face. Short of turning tail to flee, Benedict had no other recourse. Everyone in the room knew he and Alex to be old school friends. To give him the cut in front of the majority of the *ton* was to invite speculation and gossip—something he didn't need at the moment.

So, as Alex came to stand beside him, Benedict turned his attention to the couples on the dance floor. Celeste was among them, engaging in a minuet with a man busy ogling the low cut of her bodice.

Alex's sugary scent wrapped around him. He stood so close their shoulders brushed, his hand briefly coming against the back of Benedict's. Alex had been eating sweets again—a pastry coated in sugar and cinnamon if Benedict's nose hadn't missed its guess. He would forever wonder how Alex managed to keep such a trim figure while shoving sweets down his gullet.

"I see you still dress like a man in mourning," Alex murmured.

When Benedict jerked his head in Alex's direction, he found him watching the dancers, lips quivering with amusement. Unlike Benedict, he was turned out like a fashion plate. The deep blue of his tailcoat was brightened by a waistcoat in shades of cerulean, plum, and gold, the gilded threads gleaming in the candlelight. His cravat had been dyed a deep yellow that appeared gold when juxtaposed to his waistcoat. His clocked stockings featured a blue stripe up the back of his calf. There wasn't a hair out of place, and the scent of a fresh shave mixed with that of the peppermint and cinnamon on his breath to create an intoxicating aroma.

Benedict's fingernails bit into his palms as he tore his gaze away from Alex. It annoyed him to realize that others had taken up where he'd left off, admiring the display of Alex's wardrobe. Beside him, Benedict's traditional black and white evening kit was somber and stark.

"I miss dressing you," Alex went on. "How well you look in shades of purple. It brings out the color of your eyes magnificently. You grumbled and complained over the clothes I selected for you, but you wore them. Because you loved me, or because you secretly knew you looked splendid? Perhaps a bit of both."

"What the devil do you want, Alex?" Benedict ground out, his palms beginning to ache from the tight clench of his fists.

Alex's little finger lightly caressing Benedict's. A crackle of electricity raced over his skin, reminding him of things best forgotten.

"I told you what I want, Ben. You."

"I wouldn't recommend holding your breath. You might die and then I really would be in mourning."

To his surprise, the white flash of Alex's broad smile lit up the periphery of his vision. "Why, Ben, I'm flattered. I never would have thought you'd care enough to mourn me. I'm touched."

Benedict ground his teeth rather than reply. Alex was his polar opposite—cool and relaxed, sipping from his champagne flute.

"Will you dance tonight?" Alex asked. "You were always a magnificent dancer. You taught me to waltz, remember? I was abominable at it, and am now barely passable. I suppose your natural grace is what makes you such a skilled pugilist."

When Benedict offered no response, Alex issued a soft sigh.

"You're going to have to face me eventually," he murmured. "I won't go away just because you growl and gnash your teeth. I am used to it, as you well know."

"You are wasting your breath and your time," Benedict snapped.

"I don't think I am. But, even if I were, I wouldn't stop. You are that important to me."

Irritation shot through Benedict. A distraction of this sort was the last thing he wanted. Alex needed to understand that Benedict wouldn't allow himself to be maneuvered into yet another pointless conversation—one destined to end as their previous ones.

He opened his mouth to say just that, when his attention was snared by the person he'd come to confront. The annoyance of Alex's presence faded as he narrowed his eyes at Cynthia Milbank. His anger turned from the man at his side to the woman who had taken part in ruining his life.

"I have other matters more pressing than entertaining this foolishness," Benedict said. "Bugger off."

"Was that an invitation?"

The quip registered in Benedict's mind only after he had walked away, and Alex's laughter followed him across the ball-room. Shrugging it off, he kept his gaze fixed on Cynthia as he tracked her slow progress through the room. She greeted friends and acquaintances with a tight, fixed smile, her movements stiff and controlled. Despite knowing that she was the London

Gossip, Benedict couldn't help but feel slightly shocked at the sight of her. After he'd ended their engagement, the Milbank family vacated London. Because Benedict had been so absorbed in his own problems, he never bothered to notice when they returned. By his calculation, Cynthia had resided in London for at least the past two years, if not more—which perfectly positioned her to launch her scandal sheet and skewer him with her pen.

While Benedict had been busy rebuilding his life and making the Gentleman Courtesans into a lucrative business, Cynthia had infiltrated the spaces of high society. Her seminary school education gave her access to the daughters of men high up on the social ladder. Over time her connections had flourished, and now she was a force to be reckoned with. Benedict's mistake had been in underestimating her. He wouldn't be so arrogant again.

He approached Cynthia's back as she chatted with a group of ladies, the scent of lily-of-the-valley wafting up his nostrils to make him nauseous. Swallowing past the sensation, Benedict pressed on. He couldn't allow the trauma of past events to affect his actions now. There was too much at stake.

Her grating voice wrapped around him as he hovered, lying in wait and trying to keep hold of everything he'd eaten throughout the day. Laughter floated up from the cluster of ladies, Cynthia's practiced and false. She was the perfect representation of a woman groomed to claw her way into the beau monde. Her family's desperation for status, and the viscount's need to marry Benedict off to anyone who would have him had made their engagement a perfect one—save for the fact that Benedict, even if he were attracted to women in any way, would never desire someone like Cynthia for a bride.

A lull in the conversation provided Benedict an opening. Four heads swiveled toward him, and Benedict offered a polite bow. He kept his gaze on Cynthia, who stared back at him with cold calculation hardening her dark eyes.

She had changed very little, and looked as if she'd stepped right out of Benedict's memories. How could he have stood in any room with Cynthia and not know she was there? Being face to face with her now made him go cold, as if a sheet of ice coated the surface of his skin.

"I beg your pardon, ladies," he said in his most cordial tones. "You all look lovely this evening."

Giggles and flickers of fans were followed by choruses of 'thank you, Mr. Sterling,' and 'you're too kind.' Cynthia remained silent, lips compressed.

Benedict grinned, her discomfiture emboldening him. "Miss Milbank, I haven't seen you in an age. I pray you have been well."

"Quite well, Mr. Sterling," she replied. "Thank you."

"I will admit to crossing the room in the hopes that you had not promised the next dance to anyone else. Please say you haven't ... I'll be wounded if you are."

Sly glances and flirtatious smiles came from Cynthia's companions, and Benedict indulged them with an upward tick of one eyebrow. Cynthia's chin jutted defiantly, but he could see that she realized she'd been trapped. If she cut him, rumors would swirl as to why. Their short-lived engagement wasn't a widespread fact, but the connection between their families was.

Forcing another one of her humorless smiles, Cynthia accepted his proffered hand. "You are in luck, Mr. Sterling."

"Splendid."

Benedict placed her gloved hand on his arm, stiffening in revulsion at the nearness and scent of her. His stomach roiled as his mind sprung forth with things he'd rather forget. This woman and her father had conspired with the viscount to trap him into an unwanted marriage, and added further trauma to what had already been an impossibly difficult time in his life. He would not forgive them for it.

"Ah, a waltz," he murmured as they entered the dance floor.

"You are permitted to dance it, are you not? While still unmarried, you are certainly *old* enough to be allowed a waltz."

Cynthia's fingers dug into his forearm. "It is impolite to remark upon a lady's age, though I should not expect decorum from an impertinent wastrel such as yourself."

Benedict kept his gaze over her shoulder as they positioned themselves for the dance, every part of him rebelling against her nearness. He closed his eyes and took a deep breath, conjuring up a more desirable situation. His mind inundated him with memories of guiding Alex through the steps. Instead of being annoyed at the thought of Alex, Benedict was relieved. There was something comforting about the memory of leading Alex through the steps, chuckling when a mistimed step resulted in sore toes.

Will you dance tonight? ... You were always a magnificent dancer.

The first refrain of the music jarred Benedict back to the present, and he led Cynthia into the dance. She executed the dance with a stiff awkwardness that forced him to compensate.

"I am surprised you approached me this evening," Cynthia remarked, her tone suddenly light and nonchalant. "A few years ago, you could not be away from me quickly enough."

"I didn't ask you to dance so we could rehash the past. I was never going to marry you, and you were foolish to believe our fathers could bring me to heel."

"And you were naive to think calling off our engagement wouldn't result in consequences. I warned you not to do it, but you didn't listen."

"You are right," Benedict conceded. "I underestimated how vindictive you could be."

"You destroyed any chance I had of making a good match."

"Your father did that, with help from mine. Or have you forgotten that after I refused to go through with the engagement, the three of you conspired to drug me beyond comprehension so you could slip uninvited into my bed?"

Cynthia swiveled her head toward him, causing a near

misstep, which Benedict corrected with a sharp turn. "You certainly *rose* to the occasion readily enough," she spat.

"I was out of my mind with opium, and never consented to your advances," he hissed, his face flushing hot. He was fairly trembling now, feeling as if some monstrous beast had awakened within him and fought to burst free of his skin. "Did you honestly think forcing yourself on me would gain my compliance? I wouldn't have you if my life depended on it."

Her laughter pierced his eardrum like a dagger, and he nearly hurled her away from him then and there. "Suppose I told you that your life did depend on it ... as well as the lives and social standing of your friends."

"This old threat?" he scoffed. "It has grown tiresome. You do not know enough to publicly accuse us, and the fact that I know you are the London Gossip means that if I go down, I will take you with me. If you can be sure of nothing else, you be certain of that."

A viper's smile appeared, and Benedict half expected a forked tongue to flick from between Cynthia's lips. "You *could* take me down with you, that I know. But, you might wish to withhold judgment on how much I know and what I'm willing to do with that information. You may have temporarily outsmarted me by changing the logistics of the operation, but I was determined to uncover the truth. I kept digging. Do you want to know what I discovered?"

"The suspense is killing me."

"Along with the account given to me by Lady Carlotta Thrush—who conducted an affair with Mr. Dominick Burke and is willing to risk her own reputation to publicly tell her story—there was the rather diverting story I was told by a Madame Hershaw. You know, the old windbag is quite fond of you, as well as the obscene piles of money you paid her to provide a shelter for your secret enterprise."

Benedict's heart stuttered, his pulse quickening in his throat. Madame Hershaw had provided an office for him in the back of her shop, and a discreet way for clients to meet with him and negotiate their contracts. The woman was a modiste caring for a crippled, widowed son and three young grandchildren. Benedict's payments had gone a long way toward helping her provide for her family. She would never set out to expose him without provocation and Benedict had given her none. After vacating his office, he had bestowed enough money on Madame Hershaw to keep the family afloat for a year or more. As well, his presence in her shop had increased her business tenfold.

No, she couldn't have turned on him, and that left only one other possibility.

"What did you do to her?" he demanded.

"Oh, nothing as nefarious as you might think. I simply made her aware of my intention to expose the names of all the men involved in the Gentleman Courtesans in my paper, and that if she doesn't aid me in that endeavor I will name her as your co-conspirator. Once she was made to see that her business would be ruined unless I painted her as an innocent victim blackmailed into helping you, Madame Hershaw was more than willing to see things my way."

"You bitch," Benedict growled. "You sneaking, cowardly little bitch."

"Now, now," she crooned. "I'm not finished yet. Perhaps you should reserve your epithets until after I've given you the other piece of information I uncovered. You see, there is a certain gentleman who one of my guards witnessed in the act of buggery some weeks past. When threatened with exposure, this gentleman offered anything for my man to keep his secret. As I trade in information, my servant was able to extract the most titillating bit of gossip. Imagine my surprise to know that there are *men* who have frequented your business for the use of male courtesans. It was easy enough to deduce which of you was depraved enough to take on such clients. Of those closest to you, all have gone on marry, and one has even begun breeding. I find it interesting that you, Mr. Sterling, have never been publicly connected to any woman ... or that the little love nest you keep with Lady Celeste Browning has seen a number of other male visitors over the years. Were you in residence when they called, I wonder?"

Benedict showed no outward reaction to Cynthia's revelation, though he was a turbulent swell of panic and fury inside. This woman was far more dangerous than he'd ever supposed, and proved that by reminding him she was willing to hurt anyone standing in her way. Madame Hershaw, this mysterious gentleman who had likely been one of his past clients, his friends.

Taking a deep, slow breath, he forced himself to remain outwardly calm. He hadn't lost yet.

"I fail to see why you would tell me all of this rather than expose it to the world. When last we met, I asked you what you wanted, and you weren't ready to tell me then. But, I don't think I need you to. You want to repay me for tossing you over."

They came to a stop as the music's final notes dispersed through the room and stood facing one another, shoulders squared.

Cynthia never looked away from him, her mouth twisted into a grotesque sneer. "There is something I want more than your public downfall, and if you want me to keep my mouth closed about what I know, you will give it to me."

For the sake of the eyes watching, Benedict offered his arm. She took it, and a current of heated malice flowed between them as they made their way off the dance floor.

"I'm waiting," he grumbled, knowing she currently had him over a barrel and hating her even more for it.

"Your refusal to marry me after ruining me—"

"After you ruined yourself by taking advantage of my drugged state," he interjected with a sharp glare from the corner of his eye.

"Semantics are unimportant. The fact is, my ineligibility for marriage has left me dependent upon my father—a circumstance

I am sure you understand. Your invention of the Gentleman Courtesans freed you from the viscount, and I want the same."

"And you think I can offer you that?"

"I know you can. With the money you've earned with your indecent activities, you are more than capable of ensuring I can live the rest of my life as I please."

Realization dawned on Benedict, leaving a bitter taste in his mouth. "Name your price."

"Fifty-thousand pounds. It is far less than I could have asked for, but I'm not entirely unreasonable. Consider it restitution for what you did to me."

Benedict could hardly believe her gall. She had aided his father in violating him, yet could stand here and so smugly make demands of him? Jerking his arm out of her hold, he turned to face her. They now stood on the edge of the bulk of the crowd, going unnoticed by those reveling around them.

"And if I refuse?"

"You can expect an issue of *The London Gossip* dedicated solely to exposing the truth about you and the Gentleman Courtesans—including the involvement of Madame Hershaw, Lady Browning, and Lady Dane. Fifty thousand pounds is nothing in the face of ruination for everyone you hold dear. The mention of your *male* clients is sure to be included as well."

Benedict was rapidly losing the battle with his body, his nape prickling with sweat. His stomach threatened to embarrass him at any moment.

"I am a patient woman," she added. "I'm willing to give you three weeks to produce the funds before I print my story. I understand you need time to fully grapple with the implications of all this. You see? I can be generous."

Benedict glowered at her, not trusting himself to speak. He swayed on his feet, suddenly mortified to realize he might swoon. His mind clouded with too many thoughts to sift through, and he was drowning.

A lifeline appeared in the form of Celeste, who materialized at his side like an angel. She took Benedict's arm, but kept her fiery gaze on Cynthia.

"Begone, you foul creature," Celeste commanded. "Or I will scratch your eyes out in the middle of this ballroom and damn the ensuing gossip."

Cynthia offered her chilling smile, snapping her fan open and wafting it before her face. "Mr. Sterling, you know where to find me."

Benedict choked down bile, craning his neck to search for an avenue of escape.

Sensing his crisis, Celeste gently steered him toward one of the ballroom's side doors.

"Come with me," she said. "The duchess is a thoughtful woman who always makes drawing rooms available for a reprieve from the crush. Steady now ... we're almost there."

Benedict breathed easier once they were free of the bright lighting and cloying heat of the ballroom, and he numbly allowed Celeste to guide him through an open door. Once safely inside, he paced away from her, jerking at his cravat—which seemed to have formed a noose about his neck. Fumbling with the nearest window, he jerked it open and sucked in deep pulls of fresh, cold air.

"Ben?" Celeste called from the doorway. "What can I do? What did that witch say to you?"

Benedict bowed his head and slowed his greedy breaths to a steadier rhythm. "I cannot speak of it just now, Celeste. I need time ... I need ..."

What did he need? His entire life was disintegrating, after years of building a fortress of wealth and independence around himself. He had thought himself so clever, outfoxing Cynthia in their little game. Benedict had never expected her to uncover his closely held and most dangerous secret.

"Ben?" Celeste prodded.

"Go," he murmured, slumping into the nearest armchair and squeezing his eyes shut. "I will be all right. I just need a moment.

Return to the ball, and I will send for you when I'm ready to leave."

Benedict felt her concerned gaze on him, but was unable to open his eyes. Within the dark void there was comfort, a temporary respite from an impending storm.

The door clicked shut, and Benedict slumped in the chair, feeling as if he had been pummeled from head to toe. The urge to march back into the ballroom and tell Cynthia that he'd die before giving her a single ha'penny was potent. However, he couldn't discount what she knew or how she'd come to know it. He and his friends might be able to combat their exposure as Gentleman Courtesans, but Benedict wouldn't recover from being outed as a sodomite. He might have brushed it off as a libelous rumor, if not for his father's determination to bring him to heel.

With Cynthia's claims as ammunition, it would be appallingly easy for the viscount to have Benedict committed and disinherited. While he didn't care a whit about the title, he did value his freedom and would slit his own throat rather than allow mad doctors to have their way with him. While being hanged for sodomy was also a possibility, it wasn't nearly as frightening as what the viscount had in store.

Benedict was jarred out of his reverie when the door swung open. A gentleman rushed through the door, then leaned against it. Benedict scowled as Mr. Martin Lewes stared at him with wide, frantic eyes. Benedict hadn't spoken to the man in weeks, and saw no reason Lewes would accost him publicly. He had been engaged to the wife of his friend, Dominick Burke, and made it as far as the nuptial altar before she'd jilted him. The runaway bride had eloped with Dominick immediately, snatching her enormous fortune right out from under Lewes—who was desperate for funds to supplement the crumbling estate he would soon inherit.

"Lewes," he snapped. "What the devil do you want?"

Lewes cleared his throat and took a timid step away from the door, wringing his hands. "I ... I had hoped we could talk ... negotiate."

Benedict snorted and rolled his eyes. "We've been over this, Martin. You are destitute, and I am no longer willing to go on siphoning what little funds you do have. It bothers me to see you pawning your things to pay my fee. We're done, and I will not change my mind."

Lewes's wide, sky-blue eyes pleaded with Benedict as he came farther into the room. He was a pretty man, not to Benedict's taste, but that never mattered where money was concerned. Not long after Lewes's ruined wedding, Benedict had discovered him prowling Bowling Green in Marylebone in the dead of night—a well-known and convenient place for a man to find himself a renter for the night. The discovery that Lewes hid secret sexual urges didn't surprise Benedict, as he had suspected the man from the start. A short conversation revealed that Lewes had never carried through with his plan to pay for a companion for the night. It had been far too easy to gain him as a client, though the man's limited funds had made it a brief one. Now that Lewes's appetites had been awakened, he'd become a chore to deal with. This was his third time approaching Benedict about resuming their arrangement.

"I can pay you," Lewes pleaded, going down to his knees and resting his hands on Benedict's thighs. His soft, manicured hands stroked upward, his gaze fixed on the fall of Benedict's breeches. "Perhaps not as much upfront, but I'll make it up, I promise. Please ..."

Benedict pushed the invading hands away from his buttons and rose to his feet. "Get up. You're making a fool of yourself."

"Only because you so skillfully introduced me to pleasures I could never have imagined, only to take them away. I'll give you whatever you want if you only consider it."

Benedict stepped around Lewes. "For Christ's sake man, have some pride! You're kneeling on the rug like a besotted fool. I will not tolerate you accosting me."

"I can be discreet ... you know I can!"

Benedict paused halfway to the door, a sudden thought occurring to him. "Are you acquainted with Miss Cynthia Milbank?"

Lewes staggered to his feet. "Miss Milbank? I wouldn't say I'm particularly familiar with her, but we have encountered one another on occasion."

Benedict advanced on Lewes, making the other man yelp with fright as he took hold of his lapel and jerked him closer. Lewes stood several inches shorter than Benedict, and had to crane his neck to gape up at him. Benedict stared into fearful eyes and searched for any glimmer of dishonesty or malice. The man had been upset at being cast aside. Had he then retaliated by ousting him to Cynthia?

"Did you happen to encounter one of her servants at a molly house?" he demanded.

Lewes's mouth gaped open, unintelligible sounds of protest emitting from within. "I say! What an accusation for you to make! I've never stepped foot inside such an establishment!"

Benedict stared Lewes down, but aside from the terror of a man poised on the other end of his fist, there was nothing. He released Lewes, reminding himself that paranoia would only lead to irrational action. What he needed was to clear his head and think rationally.

"The London Gossip is on to me and the other courtesans, so you would do well to keep your distance," he said.

Lewes pressed a hand over his mouth, chin trembling while he gazed about the room as if searching for an escape route. "Dear God. How?"

"You don't need to worry about that. I intend to put a stop to her machinations. Do as I've said and stay away from me if you value your reputation."

Lewes's cheeks flushed pink as he moved toward the door with disjointed, clumsy movements. "Yes, of course ... I ... I'm sorry, I ... I'll go."

Benedict sank back into his chair once Lewes was gone, bracing his head in his hands. He felt as if a sword hung over his head, but he couldn't move from beneath it because more deadly blades surrounded him on all sides—threatening both his security and his sanity. There must be a way out; he simply needed to find it.

CHAPTER 5

Alex paced from one side of the drawing room to the other, hands clasped behind his back. He trembled with anxiousness and anticipation, waiting for the moment Ben would appear. What he had overheard while eavesdropping outside a drawing room during the ball had shaken him to his core. He wasn't ashamed to have spied on Ben, desperate for any hint of what his bizarre exchange with Cynthia Milbank had been all about. Before marrying Katherine and leaving London, Alex had known of Mr. Milbank's plans to ingratiate himself into the ton, and that they included his only child—a daughter. Rumors had begun to swirl that he'd become fast friends with Viscount Sterling. It was easy enough to deduce that the two fathers had marriage on the mind, but Alex had never thought Ben might acquiesce to such a scheme. Ben was stronger than him and didn't have a cowardly bone in his body. Yet, seeing him dance with her and watching what appeared to be an intense conversation, Alex had found himself questioning his beliefs.

After the waltz, Ben had retreated in the company of his presumed mistress, and Alex couldn't allow such an opportunity to pass him by. He had followed them, watching from the shadows of the corridor as they entered one of the drawing rooms. Alex thought it odd for Lady Browning to leave alone, and his curiosity had been piqued when another gentleman appeared from the other end of the corridor, melting away from the darkness to be illuminated by firelight once he'd opened the door.

He was a slight man but handsome—ridiculously so. Jealousy and annoyance had prompted Alex to listen at the keyhole, and what he'd heard had changed his entire strategy. Alex would never have pegged Ben as one who might resort to selling himself, but the more Alex thought of it, the more it made sense. Since Eton, Ben had been determined not to rely on his father, which was why he'd supplemented his meager monthly allowance using his fists all the way through his completion of university. Not long after amassing an impressive pile of winnings from his brawls, Ben had returned the most recent payment of his allowance to his father, along with a letter in which he told the viscount to go to the devil. From then on, he had won everything that was his by fighting and with smart investments, which had afforded him the comforts he had lacked during his first years at school.

Ben had managed to support himself without going to the viscount for a single pence for years. But, Alex assumed something had changed Ben's circumstances in the past few years. With no other recourse, Alex could imagine him crafting the idea of going to business as a paramour to men who secretly desired other men. But there was more to it than that, for he had overheard Ben claiming that the London Gossip was on to him and 'the other courtesans.' There were several others, which made him the likely orchestrator of the entire thing. It was so like Ben to not only scheme to earn the income he needed, but to take others under his wing in the process. Ben had many flaws, but no one could accuse him of not caring about those in his inner circle. At times he cared too much, and that presented its own set of problems.

With this new knowledge tucked away in his mind, Alex had decided on a new course of action. He'd known from the start that to reveal everything to Ben would be difficult, and his last few attempts proved that. Using this new information, Alex could take control of the situation and limit Ben's options to flee —creating the opportunity to resolve their issues. In the process, perhaps he could learn more about what was going on between Ben and Cynthia Milbank, and lend a hand in helping put a stop to this London Gossip business. In the end, if he couldn't win Ben's heart again, perhaps Alex could solve this problem for him.

Alex went still, glancing up as the butler appeared on the threshold.

"Mr. Sterling will receive you in his study. Right this way, my lord."

The door to the study hung ajar, allowing Alex a view of Ben sitting behind his desk. He didn't look up from the paper he scribbled on when the butler closed the door, furrowing his brow as he studied a row of figures jotted on a scrap of paper. A ledger sat open before him, riddled with Ben's haphazard, nearly illegible handwriting.

Alex sank into a chair, crossing one leg over the other as he watched Ben work, content to drink in the sight of him. His lack of cravat and coat exposed the thick column of his throat and offered the barest glimpse at tufts of chest hair. He hadn't been shaved this morning, and dark blond whiskers had already overtaken the topography of his jaw. Alex's face tingled at the memory of that facial hair tickling him during a kiss, and his fingers longed to trail through the wiry strands of his side-whiskers.

For lack of something to do with his hands—short of hauling Ben out of that chair and kissing him soundly—Alex reached into his coat pocket and retrieved the small pouch of sugarplums he had stashed there this morning. The flow of sugar through his veins mingled with the heady rush of being near Ben again, making him feel slightly giddy. He was chewing his fifth sweet when Ben spoke, though he kept his head lowered over his work.

"This is an interesting change," he muttered.

"How so?" Alex asked.

"You've decided you prefer to sit and observe me as if I'm under a microscope, rather than resuming the campaign to convince me to forgive you."

"Ah. Well, that's because I haven't come to beg for forgiveness."

Ben's paused, pen hovering over his paper, and Alex briefly made out random figures being added together.

Ben's gaze flicked to him briefly before he resumed his task. "Then why are you here? I have no intention of allowing you to dress me, if that's it."

Alex smirked. "Pity. I just purchased a stunning damask from Aubrey that I think would make the perfect waistcoat for you. Oh, and this burgundy broadcloth I just adore ... it'd make a stunning pair of coats for us both."

Ben snorted and shook his head. "It's as if you *want* to advertise to the entire city that we're a pair of backgammon players."

Alex chuckled. "Nonsense. They'll all simply assume you were inspired by my exquisite taste, as the rest of the men of London are. I spied four men on my way here wearing yellow-dyed cravats."

"People without sense are easily influenced. Don't allow it to make you think too highly of yourself."

"It is too late," Alex argued. "I consider myself quite the thing."

With an exasperated sigh, Ben laid his pen aside and met

Alex's gaze. "I don't have time to play games, Alex. If you could get to the point of your visit—"

"I've come to make a deal with you."

Ben frowned. "What kind of deal?"

Alex replaced the sugarplums in his pocket and rose to his feet, planting his hands on the surface of the desk and leaning in. Ben slouched, meeting the challenge in Alex's gaze without wavering.

"I know the truth, Ben," Alex began. "I know you're one of the Gentleman Courtesans. I also suspect you're the ringleader of the entire operation. I must assume Aubrey was a courtesan as well. I couldn't puzzle it out at first—how he could afford such extensive renovation and expansion of his shop. And he's a fine catch for any woman, but a former countess as a wife? Something didn't add up until I realized both of you are wealthier now than you've ever been."

He wouldn't reveal that he'd eavesdropped on Ben's conversation with that Martin fellow. There was no time to argue over semantics.

Ben showed no outward reaction to Alex's accusation. Folding his hands over his abdomen, he pursed his lips. "I'm still waiting for you to tell me about this deal you wish to make."

"Name your price. I want you for one month, exclusively, and am willing to pay whatever you demand."

For several seconds, Ben didn't speak. However, Alex watched him too closely to miss the flick of his gaze toward the figures he'd been adding. From here, Alex could only see numbers, the amount of commas and zeroes leading him to believe Ben was adding sums of money. It looked like an astronomical figure, and apparently, he wasn't finished tallying. Based off the open ledger, Alex assumed he was searching his assets for a certain amount of money. But, for what reason? If it was something important and Ben needed funds, then Alex had the upper hand. His inheritance had left him with more money than he could spend in four lifetimes, and a number of his own assets to draw on if need be.

"I need to ensure I understand what you're saying," Ben replied, slow and succinct. "You have abandoned your quest to resume our previous relationship and now wish to purchase me to warm your bed? And just what brought on this sudden change of heart?"

It was excruciating to remain placid and feign nonchalance, when what Alex wanted was to insist that nothing had changed and he still loved Ben beyond all reason. But appealing to Ben's emotions wasn't working. A more mercenary approach was necessary until Ben had softened toward him. Once that happened, Alex would do everything in his power to prove his love, and just how unwilling he was to live without Ben.

Alex shrugged as he stood upright, slowly making his way around the side of the desk. He rested his hip on its edge, now close enough to notice the dark smudges beneath Ben's eyes— proof that he hadn't slept last night. A quick peek at the numbers on the paper, and Alex's theory was confirmed.

"I have decided to forgo the impossible in favor of what I *can* have. As you may know, it has been some time since ... well, there hasn't been another man since you. I miss that. I haven't forgotten how good we were together, and I know you haven't either. If money is what you need, I have plenty. I feel no shame in paying for what *I* need."

"You mean to say there were no other men because you had a *wife*," Ben retorted. "I hardly believe you have lived as a monk all this time."

Alex offered a rueful smile, though his stomach twisted at the reminder that there was still so much to tell Ben, so many secrets to reveal. Some of them would make matters worse between them, but only if Alex wasn't careful with his timing. First, he needed Ben near and unable to ignore him. Proximity would eventually force a reckoning between them, and all would be laid bare.

"You would be surprised to know the truth," Alex hedged. "Katherine and I did not share a relationship that included physical passions. We were friends."

"I couldn't care less about what you had with Katherine. I am far more interested in your reasons for trying to manipulate me into letting you back into my life. Whatever your game is, I'm not interested in playing."

Alex pushed off from the desk and moved closer, grasping the arms of Ben's chair and wrenching it to face him. Ben's shoes scraped the floor, his eyes widening at the reminder that Alex was no weakling. Ben was heavier than before, but Alex's country lifestyle had given him idle hours to fill with physical activity. He was in the best shape of his life.

Hands still braced on the chair, Alex dipped his head and allowed his lips to skim along Ben's hairline, making his way toward his ear.

"Your body in my bed, naked and willing ... that's all I require. It is all there has to be between us. Can you honestly look me in the eye and say you no longer want me? I'm certain you could have your pick of men—have had many while I was away—but I wonder if any of them know what you really like. Do they know how sensitive you are, just here?"

Ben shuddered when Alex found the hollow behind his ear and stroked it with his tongue. The reaction emboldened Alex to push him further.

He skimmed his lips down Ben's neck, nuzzling into the opening of his shirt. Wiry hairs tickled his lips and nose, and the sharp scent of Bay Rum and linen starch permeated his senses.

"Do your past paramours know what makes your eyes roll back into your head?"

Alex placed a hand on Ben's chest, allowing his fingertips to trace down the simple cloth-covered buttons of his waistcoat one by one. He made his slow way downward, toying with one of the silver fastenings of his breeches before skimming the prominent bulge showing against his fall.

"Do they know all the ways you like to be touched and kissed … fucked?"

Ben's breathing grew harsher by the second, his legs parting as Alex teased along the length of his swollen cock. He was rock-hard and pulsing eagerly against Alex's fingers, tension thrumming through him in a palpable current.

"My keepers don't fuck me," Ben murmured, pulsing his hips to urge his cock against Alex's palm. "If they want to fuck someone, they can go home to their wives. They pay *me* to fuck *them*."

Alex groaned, satisfaction flooding him at the revelation that Ben hadn't given others what had been entrusted to him. It had to mean something, even if Ben would insist it didn't.

"I'd pay you to fuck me," Alex whispered, rubbing his palm against Ben's prick, enthralled by the heat and solidity of him. "Whatever you want … you can have it. All you have to do is say yes."

Ben's resistance was gone, the lust that surged between them overtaking any argument he might have offered. Alex kissed his way along Ben's neck and jaw, a rough hand falling over his to apply greater pressure against the turgid organ begging to be pleasured. Alex's own cock wept with need, and he wrapped his free hand around it, stroking and pulling as Ben guided his other hand. Fingers intertwined, they worked Ben's cock through his breeches, the sound of their harsh breaths mingling together in the eerie silence of the room.

Alex angled his lips toward Ben's, craving more, needing to experience him in every way possible. It had been too long, and he was desperate to recapture some of what he'd thrown away.

Ben jerked his head away before their mouths could meet, his heavy hand clasping the back of Alex's neck. His eyes burned like the blue flickers inside a raging fire, and his chest heaved with every breath. A cruel yet alluring smirk lifted one corner of his mouth as he tightened his grip, urging Alex to his knees.

"If I say yes, there are rules that must be followed. First and foremost, you might be paying me, but it will be with the understanding that I'm the one in charge. I set the terms, and any deviation from them will result in the termination of our contract."

Alex braced his hands on the arms of the chair, his rapt gaze snared by the slow motions of Ben's fingers over the buttons of his fall. They slipped through their holes one by one, with teasing precision.

"Agreed," he rasped, lips parting at the first glimpse of Ben's cock through the white linen of his shirt. A circle of wetness caused by preliminary surges of his seed left the fabric like a veil over the broad head.

"You might want to ask me how much such an arrangement is going to cost before you agree."

Ben pulled at his shirttails, allowing his cock to bob free. It stood high and proud, curving toward his navel. Alex sucked in a sharp breath at the sight of such magnificence. He was impossibly thick, his base surrounded by a thatch of curling golden hairs, his bollocks drawn up tight. A bead of moisture glistened at his slit, and Alex licked his lips as the urge to lap it away came over him. He leaned in to do just that, but Ben stayed him with nothing more than a stern look. Alex shivered at the promise in that look, remembering very well what it was like to concede to Ben's dominance. It was no surprise that he liked to be in control; that fact guided his very existence. Alex was more than happy to oblige him.

"How much?"

Ben gripped his cock with a grin and gave it a slow stroke, using his thumb to smear his head in his own seed. "Twenty-five thousand pounds. I want ten upfront."

Alex's fingers tightened around the arms of the chair, desperation clawing in his gut. "Yes. I'll pay it. I would have paid more."

"Twenty-five will do," Ben replied, slowly and steadily pumping his cock, his expression smug in the face of Alex's hungry gaze.

"Before I agree, I have conditions of my own."

A flash of wariness lit in Ben's eyes before he masked the reaction. "You are in no position to make demands."

"Not demands," Alex chided. "Requests I'd like you to consider. Firstly, we will leave London and spend at least a fortnight in Kent."

Ben nodded. "I need a reprieve from London anyway. What else?"

"You must accompany me on one outing before we leave, to the establishment of my choosing."

"Fine. Anything else?"

"No."

"Good. Hands behind your back. Let's see how well you obey."

Alex almost protested, wanting his hands on Ben so badly it hurt. But, he had already pushed their negotiations far enough. Now he needed to play Ben's game.

Clasping his hands behind his back, Alex stared expectantly at Ben, who was still lazily stroking himself. He seemed relaxed now, his position of control proving to be comfortable territory.

"Open your mouth," he said, his voice heavy with command.

Alex couldn't obey fast enough, eagerly leaning in to accept the offering of Ben's cock. The tumescent head nudged against his lower lip, the salty taste of skin and semen teasing his palate. Alex flicked his tongue against it, noting how the muscles in Ben's lower belly hardened and contracted in reaction. With a slow, controlled exhalation, Ben thrust his hips, slowly easing his way into Alex's mouth. Alex closed his lips around Ben, his mouth stretched and filled. With his tongue, he caressed a bulging vein along the underside, detecting Ben's throbbing pulse.

Ben's fingers tangled in the hairs at the nape of his neck, pulling him closer and pushing his way deeper. A rough groan fell from his lips when his cock found the back of Alex's throat. He withdrew, and Alex sucked, absorbing the taste of Ben and the scent of his musk. He clenched his hands together so hard his fingers ached, but couldn't let go for fear he'd give in to the need to explore with his fingers. Alex wanted to wrap his hand around Ben's cock and stroke, fondle his bollocks, ease a finger past them and toward the hidden pucker of his arse. Ben knew him too well not to know what he desired, and would surely enjoy denying him that.

Alex kept his eyes open and fixed on Ben, taking in every nuanced expression as the hardened veneer of indifference melted away. His lips softened and parted, his eyes hooded by the pale fringe of his lashes as he eased his cock in and out of Alex's mouth. The room seemed charged with tangible energy, tension coiling between them like a spring. It increased as Ben tightened his grip on Alex's hair, guiding his head downward with each surge of his hips, his strokes coming harder and faster. Alex gasped around Ben's cock, accepting the deep invasion rather than fighting it, wanting to take as much of Ben as could fit. It seemed a near impossible feat, but that didn't stop him from sucking and bobbing his head, opening himself to everything Ben had to give.

The telltale taste of Ben's impending climax coated his tongue, and Alex intensified his efforts, sucking harder and faster, his face and neck flushing from the effort, his own cock pushing against his fall and begging for reciprocal stimulation. Even his own hand would do, bringing him off within seconds, but he kept both firmly behind his back. He would do nothing to prematurely end what surely must be the most transcendent moment of the past few years of his life. Nothing was certain, and the future could be affected by any number of variables, but none of that mattered right now. Being connected to Ben again, even amid so much turmoil, was the manifestation of countless sleepless nights and waking daydreams. It felt right and real and true.

Ben's head fell against the back of his chair, hissing moans trapped behind clenched teeth as he gripped Alex's head in both hands and thrust like a madman, chasing his finish. A string of profanities was the only warning Alex had before Ben's cock shot streams of hot, salty seed into his mouth. Alex closed his eyes and took every drop, his scalp stinging from the tightness of Ben's hold. Ben jerked and convulsed in the chair, thrusting through every second of his climax. Once fully spent, he released Alex and slumped, legs spread and shoulders relaxed.

Alex went back on his haunches, drinking in deep breaths and trying to will his stubborn erection away. The vindictive gleam in Ben's eyes just before he had commanded Alex to his knees meant he wouldn't be allowed his own pleasure just yet. That was fine by him for now; his mission had been accomplished. Ben would be solely his, and in the privacy of his estate, they could begin to mend what had been broken.

"I'd forgotten how good you are at that," Ben said while putting his clothes to rights and then coming to his feet. "Twenty-five thousand pounds and the efforts of your skilled mouth ... I do think I am receiving the better end of this bargain, Alex."

Alex stood, wincing at the ache in his knees. "That's the idea."

Ben readjusted his chair, gripping its back as he observed Alex from the corner of his eye. "At least until you grow bored of the novelty of having me as your courtesan."

I could never grow bored of you, Alex thought, still able to taste the remnants of Ben's spend on his tongue.

"You mentioned something about a contract?" he asked aloud, keeping the thought to himself.

Ben lifted a decanter from one corner of his desk and poured himself a measure of brandy. "We usually have our clients agree to the terms on paper, but considering the danger of being caught, we will simply have to shake on it."

Alex promptly extended his hand. "Very well. You can trust me to adhere to your terms."

As he accepted the extended hand, Ben's expression clearly

said he didn't trust Alex farther than he could throw him. However, they shook with a firm, decisive grasp—as if Alex hadn't just swallowed the length of Ben's cock.

Ben turned away and stalked to a nearby window, gazing out over the back courtyard as he sipped his brandy. Just to the right of the window, an aberration made itself apparent in the mahogany paneling of the wall. Alex frowned, drawing closer to study what turned out to be a circular hole. A smooth, shiny object appeared just beyond the scar ruining the precious wood, though for the life of him he couldn't determine what it was.

"What happened here?" he asked.

Ben turned just as Alex pointed at the spot, his expression darkening like a thundercloud had passed over him. Turning back to the window, he tightened his jaw. "Nothing that need concern you. When do we leave for Kent?"

Alex blinked, stunned by what he had just witnessed. It was an odd reaction for a man to have concerning a hole in his wall, but he dared not press further. There were so many mysteries of Ben's changed personality to untangle and absorb, and now Alex had plenty of time to do just that.

"Three days, if it suits you."

"It does. Our outing?"

"Tomorrow night."

"Very well. Until then."

He didn't even gaze away from the window, making it clear that Alex had just been summarily dismissed. It took a great deal of his will to turn and walk away, reminding himself that this was only the beginning. If he had his way, what he and Ben shared would never end.

ALEX STARED AT BEN'S SHADOWED SILHOUETTE, ANTICIPATION making him restless. The sway of his carriage intensified his anxiety, and his left leg bounced in a manifestation of it. He had arrived at Ben's residence to collect him half an hour ago, and they'd nearly reached their destination. Alex could feel Ben's annoyance from across the carriage but brushed it off without a second thought. Alex would have to deal with his companion's surliness through the first days of their arrangement. It wasn't enough to deter him. Besides, his hope was that this outing would help ease some of the friction between them, reminding Ben of times long past but hopefully not forgotten.

"Where are you taking me?" Ben asked.

It was the first time either of them had spoken during the ride, and Alex was grateful he hadn't been forced to break the silence.

"It's a surprise," he teased.

"I hate surprises," Ben grunted.

"I think you will like this one. Besides, when was the last time you did something fun? I imagine you spend quite a bit of time training for your boxing matches and ... and tending to your ... business."

Ben's teeth flashed in the dark in a mocking grin. "Fucking. My business is fucking."

A shiver raced through Alex as the crude words fell from Ben's lips. His pleasure-starved body had been vexing him since yesterday; fevered dreams of kneeling before Ben and swallowing his cock having tormented his sleep. Knowing Ben as well as he did, Alex had a feeling he'd be made to wait until they reached Kent for their *business* to truly begin. He felt as if he might die between now and then.

He groped about for something to say lest his wandering thoughts cause him to do something stupid. "Doesn't it concern you? The potential for being caught, I mean. There is greater risk for you than the other men involved."

Ben shrugged. "No more risk than sneaking around in parks with renters or meeting lovers in public house rooms. At least, by attaching a price to my services, the risk is outweighed by the potential for wealth."

"You make an interesting point. I hadn't thought of it that way."

"I daresay you never thought of men as courtesans at all before now, let alone male courtesans who service other men."

"No," Alex agreed. "Though I have to admit the idea is ingenious. It certainly seems to have improved your fortunes, as well as Aubrey's." He had a certain thought and sat up straighter, eyes widening. "Dear God ... Nick was involved, too, wasn't he? You're thick as thieves, and I cannot believe you'd start such a venture without him."

Ben didn't even bother to deny it. "Nick was one of the best before he met Calliope and settled down. Earned himself a king's ransom and gambled most of it away within a few years. His inheritance has set things right again, and he's become better at managing his funds."

Alex wasn't surprised to hear that their old school friend had allowed his vice to lead him to destitution. Dominick Burke had joined their small circle of friends once they'd reached university. Benedict resumed his secret bare-knuckle brawls in this new setting—though he took greater care to avoid being caught. Alex had been curious enough to sneak away to watch the spectacle, both horrified and entranced by the beauty and brutality of Ben —bare-chested and sweating, pummeling this man or that one with his hammer-like fists.

It was at one of these matches that they'd met Dominick, who approached them while counting his winnings and praising Ben for his skills. His obsession with gambling led him to wager on just about everything—from footraces and fights, to the changing of the weather and the probabilities of certain boys being sent home in disgrace after some lark or another. That he was now reformed came as a greater surprise than the realization that his gambling had continued to plague him up until recently.

"Good for him," Alex murmured. "Where is he living these days? Now that he's no longer at Albany, I don't know where to find him."

"He hasn't been to London in months, but I cannot say where he might be at present. There's an estate in Cornwall and another in Leicester. His father-in-law also owns property in Surrey, and he and his wife visit regularly."

That was disappointing, only because Alex hadn't laid eyes on Nick in years ... since his wedding day, in fact. Their close friendship wasn't enough to let Dominick in on Alex's secret, and he wondered if Ben had ever come clean. As far as Alex knew, Aubrey and Lady Dane were the only mutual friends who knew about their history and preferences.

What would Nick think if he knew? He would likely discover the truth eventually. Once Alex had achieved the desired outcome, he didn't intend to be without Ben ever again. From the outside looking in, others would see a close and enduring friendship between two men. Being as close as he was to both of them, Nick was sure to notice that something deeper was at play. It was one of many challenges they would have to navigate together—presenting themselves to society as bachelors who had been the best of friends since university, and hiding the true nature of what they shared. For many, it might seem like a bleak future, but Alex saw the silver lining of it. When they were alone, they would be free to carry on as they pleased —free from prying eyes and scrutiny. Free to love one another and be loved.

He wanted to express such thoughts to Ben, but now was not the time. As the carriage slowed to a stop, Alex reminded himself that he was playing the long game. He would have to earn Ben's heart back piece by piece, and thus far he didn't even have the barest sliver.

Patience, he reminded himself. *It will take time.*

The door swung open, and the footman laid the steps. Alex emerged first, turning to watch Ben peer cautiously at the building illuminated by gas lamps. The light showed the scowl that marred his face as he looked at Alex.

"No," he snapped. "Absolutely not."

Alex pursed his lips. "You promised. We shook on it. One outing to the place of my choosing."

"I wouldn't have agreed had I known *this* was where you intended to take me ... which, I suppose, is why you decided not to divulge our actual destination."

"Indeed. But we are here now, and a bargain is a bargain."

Here turned out to be Mother Morton's Coffee-House and Tavern in Soho Square. From the outside, it appeared like any other respectable tavern. However, one must procure membership and pay a yearly fee to be allowed entrance to the evening suppers. Despite having been away from London for years, Alex had kept up his membership, looking forward to the day he might be able to return. Katherine had been well aware of his nature, and was both understanding and accommodating. They had never returned to London after their marriage, but if they had, she wouldn't have begrudged him a trip to Mother Morton's. It wouldn't have been his aim to find another man for an assignation, as the hurt over being forced to let go of Ben was still too fresh. But there was something to be said for having a place to go where a man could simply be himself without fear— especially when who he was could earn him time in the pillory, the loss of his title and lands, or a dance on the end of a noose

Now that he could experience it again, Alex very much wanted Ben to share it with him.

"Fine," Ben huffed, hauling himself out of the carriage.

He blew past Alex toward the entrance while avoiding his gaze. They paused for Alex to present the card he carried as proof of his membership, vouching for his companion before being allowed entrance. His shoulders slumped in dizzying relief as the door swung shut behind them. They were ushered past a velvet curtain into the wide, open room of the tavern, which was filled with the haze of cigar and cheroot smoke, as well as a clamor of voices and laughter. Atmospheric lighting from the chandelier and candelabras revealed a long bar along one side of the room, around which were crowded a colorful array of patrons. The middle of the room had been cleared of all furniture for dancing, and upon a stage draped in green and gold curtains, a group of musicians filled the air with lively music.

The right side of the room was reserved for those who wished to dine—the tables ranging in size from intimate settings for two, and sprawling accommodations for larger groups.

"Shall we have dinner first?" Alex suggested, his stomach rumbling. He hadn't eaten since this morning, too nervous to think of taking a single bite.

"Whatever you want," Ben grumbled, allowing Alex to take his arm and guide him toward an empty table.

Alex leaned in to whisper in his ear. "I will hold you to that."

Ben glared at him but didn't bother to put any distance between them. Here, two men leaning into each other and linking arms was the mildest of affections on display. All around them, men clasped hands, embraced, and traded kisses without second thought, safe in the knowledge that it was safe to do so.

Mother Morton's hadn't changed much during Alex's absence. As he and Ben settled into a small table for two in a shadowy corner, he felt a warming sensation like coming home after a long time away.

He and Ben had frequented this tavern many a night, and everywhere Alex looked, he saw something that reminded him of those days. Phantom memories materialized before him like wisps of smoke.

Feeling Ben's eyes on him, Alex glanced up and offered a shy smile.

"Why here?" Ben demanded. The sparse words were strained and heavy with the weight of the past.

"You know why," Alex countered.

Ben neglected to respond as a flamboyantly dressed waiter approached them. He wore the signature scarlet and gold colors of all the staff at Mother Morton's, though his attire was anything but conventional. From neck to waist, he was respectable in white shirtsleeves and a bright red waistcoat with gleaming gold buttons. It was the billowing tufts of a matching skirt that drew the eye, the darts and gatherings reminiscent of an older style in women's fashion. A pair of heeled shoes with gleaming silver buckles peeked out from beneath his hem. His head was covered by a red and gold turban adorned with a brooch made of paste jewels, a jaunty red feather arching along his jaw. His face was painted with rouge and kohl, a few hours' worth of stubble showing through white face powder. A heart-shaped beauty patch stood out beneath one eye.

"Good evening, gentlemen," he said in a deep voice belying his feminine attire. "Can I interest you in a late supper? The mutton is exceptionally good tonight, and there are a scrumptious array of selections for dessert."

Ben barely spared the waiter a glance as he ordered beefsteak and ale, while Alex requested the mutton, a bottle of Burgundy, and a selection of every available dessert.

Their waiter was off with a swish of his skirts, disappearing through a crowd of other men dressed in sedate evening attire mingling with those whose cuffs and collars dripped with lace, their faces painted, their heads adorned with towering, powdered wigs. Here and there, Alex spotted men in corsets and skirts and gowns ranging from homely to decadent. Painted fans fluttered, and jeweled hands waved through the air amid animated conversation.

Ben took in the scene with a clenched jaw, his entire body radiating tension. Alex knew this reaction to be his fault, not the fault of those congregating around them. Being reminded of a place they'd once gone together to be alone and free made Alex happy, as it clearly had the opposite effect on Ben. It was Alex's hope that by the end of the night, that would change.

After all ... Mother Morton's was where they'd shared their first kiss. As they awaited their dinner, Alex leaned back in his chair and remembered it with fondness and longing tightening his chest.

CHAPTER 6

"That noxious creature, the so-called 'Ravishing Widow D', is hosting
another of her exclusive parties this coming Tuesday. This writer has
heard rumors of the arrangements being made ... the likes of which are
too scandalous for the eyes of my esteemed readers. Suffice it to say that
Lady D has proven yet again that you may take the woman out of the
gutter, but you cannot remove the stains she left it with."
-The London Gossip, 27 January 1820

Benedict hung close to Alex as they stood at the bar waiting for
their drinks, afforded a bird's-eye view of the entire front room
of what he now knew to be a molly house. He had accepted
Alex's invitation to accompany him to London for Christmas, not
wishing to spend the break with his family before heading off to
Cambridge. His mother's death the year before had been a stunning blow,
one he couldn't have endured if not for the friendship of Alex—who
seemed determined to brighten his days when he required it, or simply sit
in silent grief with him when it was what he preferred. To return to a
home devoid of her sparkling presence would make tolerating his father
and brothers even more unbearable.

He had not known what to expect as a guest in the Vautrey family townhouse, but he'd never fathomed being welcomed by the earl and countess and treated like a son. Benedict and Alex spent their days roaming London, attending plays at the theater, dining in coffee-houses, and exploring museums. They played cards before the fire in the drawing room some evenings, a thick, heated tension swelling between them.

It had been this way for the entirety of their friendship, with Benedict hovering on the cusp of a monumental decision. As they came to know one another, Benedict had mustered the courage to ask Alex why he always stared at him with those secretive eyes of his.

Alex had stunned him by replying, "It's only that find you beautiful. I cannot help myself."

That had been the first real insight into Alex's nature. Benedict's first instinct had been to place distance between them, for surely such feelings were sinful. They were young men, and the natural thing to do was join forces to gain the attention of the ladies they would one day court for marriage. Only, every time that thought crept into his mind, he was besieged with the memory of standing before a naked Jemima. His disinterest in her wasn't a singular event. No woman had ever provoked him to the sort of lust the other lads were afflicted with.

Alex, however, filled him with queer feelings he would rather not examine too closely. Only, as time went on, Benedict was forced to admit that what he felt for the other man was something beyond friendship.

"You do it, too, you know," Alex had said after Benedict confronted him for staring. "You look at me when you think I'm not paying attention. Care to explain?"

Despite Alex's teasing tone, Benedict had been overcome with sickening dread. Alex was right; he did spend an unhealthy amount of time observing Alex from the corner of his eye. He couldn't seem to help himself either, and eventually decided to stop fighting whatever was happening to him. Benedict could hardly help that the sight of Alex's bare throat or exposed forearms made his face heat, or that the sight of him in dishabille in the privacy of their bedchamber made a knot form in his throat.

There was nothing to be done about such inclinations but to fight them. But it didn't stop him from wondering about kissing those plush lips, or slipping his hands into the opening of Alex's shirt to experience the feel of that smooth, firm chest.

One evening, they had sat awake later than the other boys, huddled close to the hearth in which they'd just lit a fire. Alex had stared at him in silence for a long while, with Benedict helpless to do anything other than gaze back at him, paralyzed by fear and curiosity. Finally, Alex had moved, one hand creeping across the rug toward Benedict's. Benedict didn't resist when their fingertips brushed, or when Alex turned his palm over and rested his own atop it. Fingers intertwined as if by instinct, and Benedict was stunned by how right it felt, how pure and perfect. While he gaped in astonishment, Alex had merely smiled knowingly at him—as if nursing a secret Benedict wasn't yet aware of.

Benedict had wrestled with the slow but significant changes developing between them, until they'd come to a head on a spring evening. Alex had coaxed him to take a walk into town for dinner, after which they'd ambled down darkened streets, companionable silence stretching between them. Suddenly, Alex took Benedict's hand and pulled him into a narrow alley between a tavern and a haberdasher's that had closed for the day. Taking Benedict's face in both hands, Alex had leaned in until their lips brushed.

Stunned, Benedict had reared away from Alex, heart thundering in his chest. "What the devil are you doing? Are you mad?"

Leaning against the wall of the tavern, Alex had sighed. "Yes, and it would seem you are the cause. Haven't you ever wondered why there always seems to be this ... connection between us? And I don't mean the friendly sort. You feel it when I hold your hand, or when I look at you. I know you do, because it's how I feel."

Benedict shook his head, though recognition niggled the back of his mind. His body had lit up like a struck match at the slight touch of Alex's lips, and tendrils of heat now snaked through him.

"No, I don't wonder," he protested. "It isn't right for us to wonder, Alex. This can't happen. We can't ..."

Alex had lowered his eyes, shoulders slumped. "Of course. Forgive me, I ... I thought perhaps you ... well, it doesn't matter. I've known the truth about myself for a long time. Perhaps you are yet to discover your own truth."

Benedict clenched his teeth around a vehement denial, knowing it would be a lie. He reached up to wipe the remnants of the brief kiss from his mouth but found his fingertips lingering along the edge of his lower lip instead. He didn't want to obliterate those small traces of Alex, despite his protestations.

"Can we forget this ever happened?" Alex pleaded. "I couldn't bear to lose you as my friend."

Benedict had agreed and they hadn't spoken of it again. Yet, Alex's overture had changed everything. Benedict's curiosity over his burgeoning appetites had been stoked and he found it difficult to turn his mind toward the more acceptable pursuit of the female sex. He didn't want any woman; he wanted Alex.

Alex seemed to sense this, even as he pretended not to. Now that Benedict had put a stop to what Alex began with his fleeting kiss, it was up to him to make the next overture ... if ever there was to be one.

While ruminating over the possibilities and pitfalls, Benedict had made another surprising discovery. While searching for a book to borrow among Alex's trunks, he uncovered literature and tomes filled with drawings of a scandalous nature. His mouth had fallen open as he thumbed through depictions of men with other men—kissing and lying together undressed, holding one another's cocks, and even taking each other's pricks into their mouths. His throat tightened at a particularly frightening image of one man on his hands and knees while another knelt behind him, his cock buried in the other man's arsehole.

Slamming the book of drawings shut, he was then startled by footsteps. His anxiety eased as he realized it was only Alex. They were thankfully alone in the room, though the threat of discovery had been very real. His recklessness had nearly gotten them both in serious trouble.

Gaze roaming to the cover of the book Benedict held against his chest like a hidden treasure, Alex's lips quivered with amusement.

"Keep it for as long as you like," he said. "Perhaps you'll find it as diverting as I do."

Benedict had stashed that book beneath his bed, along with an erotic novel telling the story of a young man learning of forbidden pleasures with his school's headmaster. While poring over them both, Benedict had been unable to fight his bodily reactions, the arousal that such lurid descriptions inspired. It had shamed him to frig himself to the imaginings of a mind that was now enlightened, his body awakened into a fury of need now that he knew what he truly wanted.

Now, as they took their final break before beginning their time at Cambridge, Benedict faced the possibility of knowing what it was like to give in to his needs. He could hardly believe it had come to this, but what he felt seemed as natural as drawing breath. This was who he was, and Benedict wasn't certain he could fight it much longer.

Apparently, Alex harbored similar hopes for their time away from school, as he had brought Benedict to Mother Morton's—a coffee-house and tavern that became an exclusive club in the evening, a place for men who desired other men to congregate.

Benedict goggled at the scene before him, stunned at the uninhibited display of men dressed as they otherwise wouldn't have in society. Most were dressed like him, in waistcoats and breeches, though a few were as dandified as Alex in bright colors and heavy adornments. Others dressed as women, or in some odd combination of male and female attire, walking about as if they didn't care what anyone thought of them. And perhaps they needn't care, as it seemed Benedict was the only one staring at these men in disbelief.

Alex's lips brushed his ear, and Benedict nearly leaped out of his skin.

"Calm down," he whispered, his breath tickling the side of Benedict's neck. "Being a man who prefers other men doesn't mean you have to start wearing corsets and gowns."

Benedict reared back to find Alex grinning, shoulders shaking with suppressed laughter. "I never said—"

"I'm only joking," Alex crooned, giving his shoulder a light squeeze. "Being who you are is as simple as what you see in this room. We are different in many ways, but in others, we are the same. You can be whoever you want to be, but still love who you love. And, in a place like this, you needn't be afraid to show it."

To illustrate his point, Alex slid his hand down Benedict's arm, then took hold of his hand. Benedict stiffened as their fingers locked together, but a quick glance around the room revealed that no one had noticed. In fact, other men could be found behaving in the same way—holding hands, kissing, leaning close to one another. Benedict had never seen anything like it. However, it came as second nature to stand there holding Alex's hand as they waited for their ale, knowing they wouldn't have to pull apart unless they wanted to.

As the night went on, Benedict found it easier to enjoy himself, the ale going a long way in that regard. They drank and had dinner at a table filled with friends of Alex—other young men who frequented Mother Morton's when time permitted. They were like any other males Benedict knew, except for their natures, which were clear based on their presence in a molly-house. They came and went from the table to dance with one another, prompting Alex to turn to him with an outstretched hand.

"Well?" he urged when Benedict merely gaped at him. "I am a horrible dancer, but am willing to embarrass myself for you."

Accepting Alex's hand, Benedict allowed himself to be led to the edge of the dance floor, which overflowed with men twirling and spinning and clutching at one another while laughing. The song was a waltz, played at a dizzying rhythm that made Benedict's head spin as Alex guided him through the steps.

He grunted when a heavy foot came down on his, jerked off balance by Alex's graceless steps.

"Christ, I thought you were joking," he yelled to be heard above the music. "You really are terrible."

Alex shrugged. "Alas, I am good at many things, but dancing isn't one of them."

Benedict winced when Alex crushed his toes again, adjusting their positions so he was the dominant partner. "For the love of ... Let me lead before you break every bone in my foot."

Alex threw his head back and laughed, but seemed to follow the steps better with Benedict holding him tight, guiding him through every turn. They were closer now than they'd ever been, mashed together from chest to thighs and breathing the same air. Alex grew suddenly serious, his fingers tightening around Benedict's. Benedict had become a bundle of exposed nerves, new sensations overwhelming him all at once.

Alex smelled like the peppermint stick he'd eaten after dinner, and honeyed ale. He was solid and warm in Benedict's hold, his chest firm and broad, his thighs taut and sinewy. His face flushed at the feel of Alex growing hard against him, the pulse of blood in his cock in tandem with Benedict's own. With each step and turn, they brushed against one another, further inflaming the unmistakable surge of desire growing between them.

They came to a stop almost at once, though the music continued. Alex had grown two inches in the past year and now looked down at Benedict with heavy-lidded eyes, his lips parted on panting breaths. Benedict was having trouble breathing as well, the feelings he'd tried to repress bursting from him in a sudden rush. Before he could talk himself out of it, he lunged, seeking Alex's mouth with his own. This kiss was clumsy and unskilled, Benedict's hunger driving him to mash his mouth against Alex's, clutching at his shoulders for dear life.

Alex pulled away, framing Benedict's face in his hands. He was smiling, his lips reddened and his eyes bright. Benedict shook with the force of his fear that Alex would reject him. It would serve him right after that night in the alley, but hope made him lean in, yearning and waiting, desperate where before he had been reticent.

Long, dark lashes lowered over Alex's eyes as he met Benedict in the middle, his lips soft and seeking. Benedict sighed against his mouth, leaning in to accept the kiss. Alex was methodical and controlled, slowly accustoming Benedict to the invasion of the kiss. He nibbled at Benedict's lower lip, stroked his tongue into the seam of Benedict's mouth. Threading his fingers through Benedict's hair, Alex tilted his head and delved deeper with his tongue. Benedict's palate was overwhelmed by the sugary sweet taste of Alex, drunk on the need for more, and then more. An entire world of possibility had just been opened to him, and he hardly knew where to begin now that he'd decided to stop fighting it.

One thing was clear, as he and Alex stood drinking from each other's mouths as if starved—he didn't have to figure it out alone. He had Alex and hoped to God that wouldn't change any time soon.

. . .

"Ben!"

With a blink, Benedict ascended from a drugging haze of memory, his head swimming and his limbs heavy yet somehow weightless. His beefsteak sat before him untouched, and he'd been so lost in recollections of the past that the waiter returning to deliver it had escaped him. His stomach had tied itself in knots, so the sight of the food only made him feel sick.

Alex seemed to have suffered no such debilitation. His plate was clean, his wineglass emptied. It was his voice raised over the music that had snatched Benedict out of his musings—his mind chasing the wisps of memory that filled this place like a heavy fog.

What had he been thinking, agreeing to step foot inside Mother Morton's? After Alex's departure from London, Benedict had avoided what had once been one of his favorite haunts like the plague. Alex, the crafty bastard, had to know how difficult it was for Benedict to maintain his apathy within these walls. Sitting across from him at a table he was certain they had shared before, Benedict found it far too easy to forget where they stood now. Against the backdrop of Mother Morton's, they were young men again—free from the burdens they now carried, and discovering what it meant to be in love.

Alex was watching him with a pensive expression, fingers toying with the stem of his glass. Benedict returned his gaze as if meeting an unspoken challenge. Alex could bring him here and make Benedict feel things he didn't wish to feel ... but in the end, it would change nothing. Trying to find the words to express those thoughts, Benedict ground his teeth, annoyed that they wouldn't leap off his tongue as easily as before. It was this tavern, the place where he and Alex had experienced so many firsts together. It was Alex himself—too perfect to be real, too close to be ignored.

The music changed from a dizzying tempo to a slow, swelling

one that made Benedict's chest constrict around his lungs. With a soft smile, Alex inclined his head toward the dance floor, crowded with men drawing close to one another for a waltz.

"Dance?"

No. No, he didn't care to dance with Alex. A waltz was too intimate. He hadn't danced with another man since Alex left him, hadn't wanted to spoil his coveted memories with a different partner. It didn't make sense, considering the hatred Benedict had fostered for his former lover over the years, but there you had it. There were some things he was simply unwilling to taint by drawing one of his temporary lovers into them, regardless of how he'd come to feel about Alex.

Despite himself, Benedict spit out the first answer that came to mind. "Are you still terrible at it?"

Shrugging one shoulder, Alex's grin widened. "No better than the last time we danced, but certainly no worse."

With a labored sigh, Benedict came to his feet. "Then, I'm leading."

Alex rushed to follow Benedict into the crowd of dancers like an eager puppy, his smile both charming and infuriating. This wasn't some romantic gesture or olive branch; it was a test. Benedict needed to remind himself that being near Alex again wasn't enough to change him, or heal his festering internal wounds. It would be a way to prove that he could survive this arrangement without losing himself in the process. He was in this for the promised money, nothing more.

They drew into each other with an ease born from years of practice, Alex submitting to Benedict's dominant hold with satisfying pliancy. Hands clasped and arms around one another, they fell into the dip and sway of the waltz, Benedict's controlled movements guiding Alex's. There was much raucous laughter and jostling on the dance floor, but the drunken revelry seemed far removed from them. Benedict refused to break Alex's stare, taking the other man's probing gaze as a challenge.

I am in control here, he said without speaking, resolve driving his every thought, his every move. *I'm here because I choose to be, because I intend to exact every penny of the money I need to save my skin before leaving you as you left me.*

Alex was far too stubborn to be cowed, staring back at Benedict with unspoken challenges of his own. If he could read Alex's thoughts, Benedict was certain they would echo the things already said. He was determined to win, to break through the walls Benedict had constructed around himself and reclaim a heart that had long shriveled up and died. There was the rub. He was almost tempted to warn Alex off, to tell him that there was no heart left for him to win. But it was far crueler and more satisfying to allow Alex to discover that for himself. It seemed a just reward for his unpardonable offense.

"You're still as graceful as ever," Alex said, his expression growing wistful. "The only partner who could manage to make me look good on the dance floor."

"It's simply a matter of residual skill," Benedict replied. "I'm good enough for no one to notice how terrible you are."

Alex chuckled. "Indeed. It's one of the reasons I'll be glad to quit London so I can shun all the invitations piling up in my study. If I'm not here to attend their balls, no one can coerce me into dancing with their daughters. The poor ladies' toes will be trampled into dust by the time I'm finished with them."

"I'm certain dear Lady Vautrey didn't mind, as your massive fortune must have been a comfort to her, crushed toes notwithstanding."

Alex stiffened, coming to an abrupt halt and nearly causing Benedict to stumble over his next step. The amusement faded from his face, replaced by stony ire. Without a word, he pushed Benedict aside and weaved his way through the other dancers without bothering to offer an apology.

Annoyed at having been summarily dismissed, Benedict gave chase, his warning glare enough to make the other men skitter out of his way. He stalked Alex toward a door to the left of the stage, which he knew led to a corridor giving access to a row of private rooms, as well as an exit to the outside privy. The door slammed against the wall when Alex threw it open, his anger apparent in his brusque stride and the stiff set to his shoulders.

"What the devil is your problem?" Benedict hurled at his back. "Does speaking of your dearly departed wife trouble you so much?"

Whirling on his heel, Alex strode back toward him with clenched fists, nostrils flaring. "It does if you're going to be an ass! We were having a perfectly nice time, and you ruined it."

Leaning against one of the rough doors to a private room, Benedict pursed his lips. "I was just making conversation."

"No," Alex insisted. "You were trying to get under my skin by speaking on matters you know nothing about, because you won't let me explain why I had to do what I did."

"Because it doesn't matter. What's done is done."

"It damn well does matter, and you know it!"

Pushing away from the door, Benedict closed the distance between them. He took hold of Alex's shoulder and shoved him against the opposite wall, crowding him against it and offering no escape. Alex sucked in a sharp breath when Benedict's other hand fell against the front of his breeches, his cock twitching and beginning to swell. Tightening his hold on the stiffened shaft, Benedict stroked, watching as Alex's anger faded in the face of pleasure.

"*This* is the only thing that matters between us now," he growled. "The sooner you realize that, the easier this will be for us both."

Alex flexed his hips, grinding his erection against Benedict's palm with a shudder. "The sooner you realize that *this* means more between us than you're willing to admit, the easier this will be for *you*."

Benedict kissed Alex, primarily to shut him up—but also to smother the feelings such sentiments provoked. If Alex was kissing him back, he wasn't trying to use words against Ben, or reminding him of how good it felt to know someone cared for him so deeply. They didn't need to talk to fulfill the obligations of their contract. Alex's assertion that the physical nature of their arrangement had meaning was a load of hogwash. Benedict had spent three years proving that he didn't have to care about someone to fuck them; hell, he didn't even have to like them. Skin on skin, lips on lips, tongues pushing and writhing. It was all mechanics leading to a pleasurable end, and fattening Benedict's purse. The difference between ruination and freedom ... that was all this meant to him.

However, it became far too difficult to hold on to such notions with Alex clinging to his lapels and kissing him with desperate fervor. Benedict's mind went empty of all conflicting thought, and he gave himself over to sensation only—Alex's mouth on his, the thud of his own heart and the pulse of blood racing to his cock.

He was moving against his own will, propelled across the corridor with each of Alex's forward steps. Benedict's back came against the door, and Alex bit at his lower lip while fumbling for the knob, panting as if starved of breath. The door fell open and they stumbled into the empty room, devoid of all light save for a waning fire burned down to simmering coals. They had inhabited every room in this corridor at some time or another, Mother Morton's proving one of the only places they could safely be alone during their university years. The memories followed him here, but Benedict ruthlessly shoved them aside as he turned Alex to hurl him against the door.

Alex tried to move away from the door when allowed the barest few inches of space, but Benedict disabused him of any such intentions. Taking hold of Alex's coat, he yanked it down his arms and left it at his elbows, the tight fit acting as the perfect restraint. Alex grunted and tried to pull free, but was left to slump helplessly against the door as Benedict tore at the buttons of his fall with one hand while yanking his shirttails free with the other. The heavy length of Alex's cock strained toward him from a light thatch of dark curls, shorter than his own but impressive in its girth.

"Do you still want to talk?" he taunted, lightly flicking the swollen head and producing a pained groan from Alex. "Or do you want me to make you come?"

Alex closed his eyes and let his head fall back in silent surrender. Benedict's own cock pushed against the front of his breeches, begging for freedom and release. There was no time for slow and steady finesse, or even to make their way to the bed. Benedict had a point to make, and his impatient cock-stand demanded he make it right here, right now, against this door.

Bracing a hand at Alex's throat, Benedict opened his own fall, his movements bumbling and clumsy. A button skittered across the floor due to his carelessness, but Benedict ignored it. Gripping his pulsing shaft, he stroked himself, allowing the tip of his cock to brush against Alex's. Alex gasped, arching his back and trying to get closer, a desperate sound resounding in his throat. Benedict tightened his grip just enough to feel the rapid flutter of Alex's pulse, commanding him to stillness. Alex opened his eyes, his dark gaze wide and pleading, his chest heaving with panting breaths.

"Please," he begged in a hoarse whisper. "Please, Ben."

Benedict edged closer, slowly pumping his own cock, his knuckles brushing along the turgid length of Alex's. He fed off the desperate plea in Alex's voice, the need radiating from his eyes. It was nearly enough to finish him then and there, but he wasn't nearly done with Alex. All the years of wanting and being denied, needing and being starved, drove Benedict to tease and torment, to exact his own form of revenge.

Alex tried to take hold of his cock, but Benedict slapped his hand aside and took it in hand, working them both in a slow, aching rhythm. Alex groaned, pumping his hips to match Benedict's pace, his fingernails scraping against the door. He grew wet after a few strokes, the drip of his semen slicking Benedict's hand. Benedict's cock answered in kind, his head smeared with the evidence of his matching desires.

Benedict rubbed over his slit to collect a drop, then braced a hand at Alex's jaw before pushing the glistening thumb against his mouth. Alex parted his lips, allowing Benedict's thumb to caress his tongue. Then, he closed his mouth and sucked, his cock leaping in Benedict's hold as if in reaction to the taste of him. Benedict delved his thumb deeper, his balls drawing up tight to his body as Alex sucked, cheeks pulling inward.

"Fuck," he muttered, nearly unmanned at the rasp of Alex's tongue against him. He edged even closer, pulling his thumb free of the sucking mouth to replace it with his tongue.

Alex responded eagerly, lunging to capture Benedict's lips, suckling at his tongue as if it were one of his beloved peppermint sticks. The taste of wine and his own seed mingled on Benedict's palate as he opened his grip to take Alex's cock against his. They moaned in unison as the tight grip of Benedict's fist pressed their shafts together. Benedict worked them both in tandem, his other hand tight against Alex's jaw as he plundered his pliant mouth. Alex trembled and bucked against him, adding more friction to the pulls of Benedict's hand.

Gritting his teeth and fighting for time, Benedict kept each pump of his hand slow and steady, reveling in the feel of Alex's thighs against his own, the hairs soft and wispy, the muscles firm. Alex was unraveling fast, arching away from the door and thrusting into his grip, his hands still trapped by his coat and searching for purchase on the door.

Benedict moved his hand to the back of Alex's neck and held fast, quickening his strokes as he sensed the inevitable end. Alex let his head fall against Benedict's shoulder, moaning and shaking and nuzzling into Benedict's neck. His lips and tongue found the sensitive patch of skin beneath his ear, and Benedict pressed against Alex's neck, urging him on. It was as if they'd never been separated, Alex knowing exactly what he wanted. As Alex stiffened and groaned his release, he sank his teeth into Benedict's neck, just hard enough to produce a sharp sting. Benedict growled his approval, stroking even faster as Alex's cock spurted hot streams of semen, slicking Benedict's pulsing cock. He followed within seconds, his release coming on the heels of Alex's. He fell into Alex, still holding the other man's face against his neck and wringing them both dry amid a chorus of deep, visceral groans. Neither of them moved right away, leaning into each other and simply breathing. Benedict closed his eyes, helpless in the face of the warmth coming over him in the aftermath. He didn't *want* to cling to Alex, his chest swelling and his throat burning with suppressed emotion. Despite his insistence that only the physical mattered between them, Benedict was struck with the realization that Alex had been right. Somehow, what they'd done felt like so much more, though he was loath to acknowledge that.

Alex slumped against the door as Benedict slowly peeled himself away, his hand and groin sticky with a mixture of their seed. His heart pounded like a drum. His body was sated, slowly climbing down to steady calm—yet his mind was still awash in turmoil. He could hardly hold onto one thought before another one descended on him. With a whispered curse, he stumbled to the rough bedside table, which was thoughtfully stocked with a basin of water and linens. Benedict offered Alex a wet linen without meeting his gaze, before turning away to clean himself. Ignoring the sounds of Alex shuffling about, Benedict took his time. All the while he told himself that they had only done what their agreement stipulated. He was a courtesan and Alex a paying client like any other. What did it matter that he knew how Benedict liked to be touched and kissed or that they'd come together as if they'd never parted?

Alex was nothing but flesh and a bank draft to him—a means to an end so that he could see his plan through to the end. Cynthia Milbank needed to be dealt with, and then his father. Alex was instrumental only within the framework of those plans. Benedict couldn't let himself forget that.

"You have to admit," Alex remarked. "We're still good together. Always have been."

Benedict turned to find Alex composed, his clothes straightened and his expression placid—though his color was high and his eyes bright.

Benedict raised an eyebrow. "I'm good with all my lovers. It's my job, after all."

He had meant the remark as another barb, a defense against the truths Alex was forcing him to confront. But Alex had the most curious reaction. Instead of growing cross, he simply approached Benedict with a sly grin, reaching out to adjust his rumpled cravat.

"I'm glad your lovers have enjoyed your skilled attentions," he purred, leaning so close that his lips brushed Benedict's. "It is good to know you've put all the things *I* taught you to good use."

With that, he pressed an abrupt, punctuated kiss to Benedict's lips before turning to exit the room without a look back—leaving Benedict with a hot face and a jaw dropped in stunned disbelief.

CHAPTER 7

*"It would seem the Earl of V's visit to London is coming to an abrupt
end. Apparently, the excitement of London does not compare to the
serenity of the Kent countryside. Will he return for the start of the
Season? With no countess or heir, the earl must soon set his mind to
fulfilling his duty as a peer of the realm. Time will tell, I suppose."*
-The London Gossip, 28 January 1820

Benedict woke the next morning with a splitting
headache and a foul disposition. He and Alex had
returned hours after midnight, and Benedict spent what
was left of the night tossing and turning, his mind refusing to
allow him rest. When he wasn't turning over the events of the
evening with Alex in his thoughts, he ruminated over the prepa-
rations he'd made for the impending journey to Kent.

On the afternoon that he and Alex had agreed on the terms
of their arrangement, Benedict paid a visit to Madame Hershaw's
dress shop in Cavendish Square. Taking care to use a hat and
muffler to conceal his identity, he entered through a door off the
back alley, coming upon the modiste as she exited her office. The
woman burst into tears at the sight of Benedict, blubbering
apologies between hiccups and sobs.

"It's all right," he crooned, pulling her into his arms and patting her quivering back. "You had no choice. I don't blame you."

"That venomous shrew of a woman!" Madame Hershaw wailed, pounding a tiny fist against his chest. "She threatened me and my girls. This shop is our livelihood, Mr. Sterling. We'd all starve without it."

"I know. Don't worry about it a moment longer. The Gossip and I have been in touch and are coming to an agreement. We'll all be safe soon enough. I simply need you and your girls to continue as if nothing has happened. Can you do that?"

Madame Hershaw nodded, accepting his handkerchief and using it to mop at her reddened cheeks. "I'm so sorry. All I ever wanted was to help you."

"And you did," Benedict assured her. "I'm the one who brought that woman's wrath down upon us all. So, I must be the one to fix it."

Once the modiste had been comforted and calmed, he left the shop, then paid final visits to Aubrey, Celeste, and Millicent. His friends had assured him they had matters in London under control. Millicent and her contacts would keep a close eye on Cynthia Milbank and write to him at Alex's estate if she seemed up to anything more unscrupulous than usual. Aubrey would work with Lyons to ensure their friends and the other courtesans were kept calm and discreet, while combing their daily copies of *The London Gossip* for any hint that Cynthia was making a move against them.

His final order of business had been to visit the Milbank residence. Cynthia's father had left town on business, leaving her in the company of a spinster aunt. The old woman suffered from unreliable hearing and rheumatic eyes, so she heard none of their conversation as Cynthia guided him to the corner of a drawing room.

"Well?" she prodded. "Have you already come to a decision regarding my offer?"

"I have," Benedict replied. "I will pay you, but I'll need one month to produce the money. Do you think you could exercise patience long enough for me to do that?"

He hated to bow to her demands, but that she had uncovered his most damning secret changed everything. Each of them held the power to destroy the other—but Benedict knew as well as Cynthia did that both secrets would prove more detrimental to him than her. Even if everyone believed that Cynthia had assaulted his person, no one would think of him as a hapless victim. Benedict would be painted as an effeminate weakling, and once Cynthia ensured the entire beau monde knew of his proclivities, he'd be known as a sodomite as well. As well, he had his friends to think of. The money would silence talk of them and their families, not just Benedict himself. He would never forgive himself if he gambled with their lives and lost. For now, bowing to blackmail seemed his only option.

If there was a way out of this conundrum, Benedict hadn't found it yet. Asking Cynthia for time to procure the money gave him room to think and plan. If there was a way, Benedict would find it.

Cynthia's cat-like smile made his blood run cold, her signature scent agitating his nostrils. Nausea roiled in his gut and his head spun, but he maintained his outward composure.

"I've waited this long to see you receive your comeuppance," she murmured. "I am certainly patient enough to wait for this."

"Good. In the meantime, my names and those of any man previously or currently in my employ are to be kept out of your paper. I am leaving London for a short time, but will be kept apprised of your writings. Should I find a single sly mention of anyone associated with me, the deal is off. That includes Lady Browning and Lady Dane, as well as Madame Hershaw and her girls."

Cynthia puckered her lips in distaste. "*The London Gossip* is my livelihood. It cannot survive without the lifeblood of rumor that maintains it."

"This city is filled with any number of scandalous people you can use as fodder for your columns. I daresay you will never be short on titillating material."

"Fine," she huffed. "But if I haven't received the funds within one month, I reserve the right to print whatever I choose."

"Agreed. And one more thing. I want your word that once you've taken the money, you will not breathe or write another word about the Gentleman Courtesans. If you do, I will ensure everyone is made aware of the identity of the London Gossip, as well as the events of that night you climbed into my bed. I won't do myself any favors revealing that last secret, but I'll gladly suffer the blow to take you down with me. You'll never be able to show your face in polite society again."

Cynthia's face drew tight, her eyes blazing with malice and disgust. "Very well. I will keep your secrets as long as you pay and keep mine."

She offered him a hand to shake, but Benedict turned and walked away, refusing to ever let that woman touch him again. His skin crawled with the hazy memories he had of the night she'd taken advantage of him. For a time, he had forgotten the details entirely, remembering only waking next to her and finding specks of blood and semen staining the sheets. His father had pretended to 'discover' them, feigning umbrage at the evidence of Cynthia's ruination and demanding Benedict do what was right.

Now, small snatches of the encounter were coming to light, muddled as they were by his drugged state. Just thinking of it made Benedict want to strangle Cynthia where she stood. Had she touched him, he might have given in to the urge.

Thankfully, he escaped with his sanity intact, and was now positioned to get on with his and Alex's agreement.

Simmons silently readied him for the trip, sensing Benedict's mood. Throughout his toilette, Benedict reminded himself that he was still in control. Alex seemed willing to do anything to have the smallest pieces of Benedict, which gave him the advantage.

With that thought fixed firmly in his mind, he descended the stairs behind the footmen carrying his things to Alex's waiting carriage. Simmons was on his heels, urging the servants to take care with his master's luggage. As they reached the ground floor, the viscount appeared from within the dining room—devoid of his coat, with a napkin dangling from his fingers. Peering through the open front door, Benedict spied Alex approaching from his waiting carriage. Behind him, the coachman assisted the footmen with his baggage.

Recognizing Alex, his father frowned and then turned back to Benedict. "What the devil is this? When did you begin associating with Osborne again?"

Benedict grinned at his father's expression of consternation. The viscount might have discovered the truth about Benedict years ago, but when it came to Alex, he was left to wonder. His father knew them to be old school friends but had never caught wind of their secret connection. He stared back at Benedict now with suspicion, seeming to silently ask if this was what he assumed it to be.

"Ah, careful," Benedict murmured under his breath. "He's Vautrey now. Besides, a man can resume a prior acquaintance with an old friend."

Alex was upon them now, having declined the butler's offer to take his coat and hat. "Good morning."

Benedict offered a bow, as was proper, lips twitching with amusement as his father was forced to do the same. "Vautrey, you remember my father ... Viscount Sterling. Father, my good friend, the Earl of Vautrey. He has graciously invited me to enjoy the countryside with him in Kent for a few weeks. You will be glad to have the house to yourself, I'm sure."

The viscount narrowed his eyes at Benedict, a muscle spasming in his jaw. "I see. How ... gracious of him."

Benedict furrowed his brow as Alex cleared his throat and

studied a painting on a nearby wall. Benedict shook his head, certain he only imagined the strain between them. His father was merely being an ass and making Alex uncomfortable. The two had only met a handful of times, when he and Alex had been home from Cambridge. Alex had been as much a fixture in his life back then as Aubrey and Dominick.

"I do believe your baggage is secure," Alex said to Benedict, still pointedly ignoring the viscount. "Are you ready?"

"Almost," Benedict said, moving closer to the door and peering out at the street. "I'm waiting for ... ah, here he is. Fisher, you're right on time. Come and meet the earl."

Benedict couldn't help another smile as Alex cast a curious glance at the man standing on the front step, a worn and dusty valise held under one arm. John Fisher's clothes were years out of fashion, his heavy paunch of a belly threatening his waistcoat buttons. But then, the man had been a Corinthian work of art in his days of glory as one of London's fiercest heavyweight pugilists. He now plied his trade as a boxing master for men like Benedict, who were willing to pay to keep the man at their beck and call.

"I hope you don't mind," Benedict said, casting Alex a smug look. "I have a match next month to train for and can't allow myself to grow lazy and soft while we're in Kent."

"My Lord," Fisher drawled with a graceless bow.

Alex's nostrils flared as he eyed Fisher. Benedict's jaw ached from a smile that wouldn't abate as he watched Alex struggle with his tongue. He had no choice but to let Benedict have his way, and they both knew it.

"Of course," Alex relented. "Mr. Fisher, you can share the second carriage with my valet and Mr. Sterling's man."

"I'm that grateful, my lord," Fisher said before glowering at Benedict. "You've been brawling behind my back."

Benedict shrugged as Fisher took in the faded bruises along his jaw and under his eye. "Fish must swim, Fisher."

"Hmph," Fisher muttered. "You'll pay for it, mark my words."

"Looking forward to it," Benedict called at the man's retreating back. Then, Benedict waved a hand toward the open door. "Shall we, Vautrey?"

Without another word, Alex preceded him to the door.

The viscount took hold of Benedict's arm before he could follow, his lips twisted into a hard sneer. "Have you forgotten my ultimatum?"

Benedict feigned surprise. "Of course I haven't forgotten. I thought we had settled the matter to both our satisfaction. You ordered me to find a wife, and I told you to go fuck yourself."

His father's grip tightened, his face flushing a furious shade of red. "You insolent little—"

"Yes, yes," Benedict said, snatching his arm free. "We both know you despise me and hate that I will be your heir. I'm a twisted, broken sodomite, and you will expose me as such if I don't comply. Except ... I don't think you will. You see, I think you've run out of tricks to use in bringing me to heel and are bluffing. Exposing me destroys your precious legacy, and we both know you love that more than you've ever loved me or anyone else in your life."

In all actuality, Benedict knew very well that the viscount wasn't bluffing. However, Cynthia currently posed the greatest danger to not only him, but those closest to him. By placing a few hundred miles between himself and his father, Benedict could buy himself more time to distinguish the second most pressing threat.

The viscount looked as if he might grind his teeth into dust or suffer an apoplexy. For a long moment, he and Benedict merely stared at one another, neither willing to back down and both taking the measure of the other.

"This isn't over," the viscount whispered, a steely edge to his words. "I will still be here when you return, and Dr. Pruett remains at my beck and call. I warn you not to challenge me in this. You cannot win."

Benedict offered a derisive smirk to hide the trickle of dread threading through him. He *could* win, but only if he managed to outwit his father.

"I suppose we'll see," he replied before donning his hat and going after Alex.

The viscount remained where Benedict left him, glaring daggers at his back. Once free of the house, Benedict pushed his father from his mind. The viscount couldn't touch him in Kent, which meant he would be safe enough for now. Everything was still under his carefully planned control.

Alex awaited in the first carriage, so Benedict hauled himself in and took the squabs opposite him. Within seconds they were on their way, the curtains parted to allow in the glow of the afternoon sun. Benedict laid his hat beside him and watched the scenery of London pass them by.

It took ten minutes for Alex to speak, almost as if he wanted to be as far from the Sterling townhouse as possible before saying a word.

"He knows," he said, voice low and strained. "Your father ... he knows about us."

Benedict frowned at Alex. He had taken great pains to ensure his father never discovered the truth of his association with Alex. Benedict had never wanted his lover to stand on the other end of the viscount's machinations. "Of course he doesn't. Whatever gave you that idea?"

"Didn't you notice the way he looked at us?"

Benedict snorted a dry laugh. "He *always* looks at me like that. He hates me ... you know that."

Alex shook his head, staring down at his hands. "Ben—"

"Calm down," Benedict interjected. "He is suspicious, but it would be no different if you were some other man. He knows I have no interest in women, but seems to have learned that I'm capable of being friends with other men without wanting to debauch them all. It has everything to do with me and nothing to do with you. Don't tell me you've become paranoid."

That seemed to help a bit, and Alex slumped against his seat with a sigh. "When did he find out about ... you?"

Benedict propped his feet up beside Alex. "Years ago ... after university. He found your letters hidden in my bedchamber. We were smart not to use our names. He knew they were from another man, but I refused to name you when he confronted me. The bastard gave me such a thrashing."

He had made that last remark without second thought, only realizing the weight of it when Alex reacted—drawing in a sharp breath and going preternaturally still.

"He beat you because of me?"

Benedict waved a dismissive hand. "He has beaten me in the past for far less. You should know it was the last time he ever raised a hand to me. I'd grown too old and too big to be anyone's whipping boy."

Those words had done nothing to comfort Alex, who was still watching Benedict with mournful eyes. "You should have told me."

"It's water under the bridge now," Benedict said.

Alex looked as if he wanted to protest but snapped his mouth closed. They sat in the rocking carriage in silence for a while before he spoke again, his voice low and hoarse.

"My father knew. Not just about me, but about us ... together."

Benedict hadn't known that, but was hardly surprised. He would never spend much time at home between terms if he could help it. The company of men like Alex, Aubrey, and Dominick had offered him a haven away from the tyrannical rule of his father. His constant presence at the earl's London residence had to have made the man suspicious.

"He was a good man," Benedict murmured. "Far kinder to me than my father ever was."

"Yes," Alex agreed.

"But he and my father did have one thing in common. Both

are and were determined to do whatever it took to preserve their names and their legacies."

"Yes," Alex said again, his gaze unfocused and detached. "Do you remember how we always vowed to never become like them?"

Benedict stared at Alex's profile, sharp and smooth along the jaw, strong and stubborn through the chin. His dark brows shadowed eyes that betrayed nothing, though Benedict could feel the disquiet emanating from him. The concern that rose in Benedict was uncontrolled and unwelcome. Shoving it aside, he tore his gaze away, arms folded over his chest.

"Yes, well, one of us held true to that promise," he said, ignoring how words meant to hurt Alex also made his chest ache. Was he really so different from Alex? He might not have made the same choices as the man he'd once loved, but Benedict never passed a day unencumbered by bitter rage. He looked and sounded more like the viscount every day, as the people he relied on to keep him out of the darkness faded away one by one.

But then, he couldn't be angry at his friends for taking wives and being happy. Such was expected for men who craved the companionship of women and the pride of a growing family.

It was Alex who had truly abandoned him, leaving Benedict to carry on alone and misunderstood. Yet, as he leveled an accusing look at Alex, needing some outlet for the turmoil welling within him, his heart sank.

Alex stared morosely out of the window, a forgotten peppermint stick hanging from his limp hand. His brow was pulled down, his lips pressed together, and he looked as if someone had just punched him in the gut.

For reasons Benedict didn't want to examine, pity and curiosity afflicted him as he wondered what Alex might be thinking. The mention of their fathers and the unresolved questions of the past floated on the air between them, heavy and oppressive.

But, Benedict couldn't allow himself to deal with them, so he went on pretending they didn't exist. Alex wouldn't be part of Benedict's life long enough for the resolution of their past to matter, so it was better to leave things as they were.

With all he had lived through already, Benedict knew he wouldn't survive another loss. If he never allowed Alex to get too close again, he wouldn't feel anything when it came time to walk away. He was different now, fundamentally changed. There could be no going back.

ALEX BREATHED A SIGH OF RELIEF AS HIS CARRIAGE ENTERED the gates leading into his estate. The slow, two-day journey from London had worn him thin, with tense silence between Alex and Ben punctuating the long hours. Alex's attempts at small talk had been met with half-hearted responses, in a clear attempt at discouraging him from making conversation. When Ben wasn't reading or sleeping, he was staring out the window, outright refusing to meet Alex's gaze. No attempts at seduction were forthcoming, and it felt as if their night at Mother Morton's had become nothing more than a distant memory—one as cloudy and far away as their past encounters.

But he was home now. Despite the longing, perpetual ache he'd suffered, his years at Vautrey Park with Katherine had also offered solace. His childhood home, the place that had always kept him safe from the world, opened its arms and accepted Alex into its warm embrace. That Ben seemed determined to hang over their time like a dark storm cloud didn't ruin Alex's happiness at being here. With distance between them and other distractions, there was nothing to do but face one another. Ben would resist, but Alex was more determined now than ever.

Ben had perked up the moment they'd reached Vautrey lands, gaze sharp as he took in the scenery. The weather was pleasant, fluffy clouds and a beaming sun illuminating the splendor of the ancestral seat. The weight of being responsible for so much land and the people depending on it for their livelihood never eased.

Alex had been made aware of what his inheritance meant from the time he was old enough to understand. Once he'd come to recognize his preference for men over women, Alex had shunned the expectation of marriage and children. He'd never wished to subject a lady to life with a man who couldn't truly love or appreciate her as she deserved.

Alex had been content to be as good an earl as he could, managing his holdings so that his uncle or cousin would come into a prosperous inheritance. Having a legacy to pass down to a son hadn't been important to him. Even taking his place as the rightful earl had paled in comparison to his true aspirations.

Glancing to the other side of the carriage, Alex was startled to find Ben looking at him for what felt like the first time this entire trip.

"It's beautiful," Ben said. "And enormous. I can see why it was so important to you."

Alex winced at the unspoken taunt threaded through Ben's words. *It was important enough for you to give me up.* Alex glimpsed the house as the carriage rounded the circular drive—perfect and secure, his haven in a world that forced him to make impossible choices.

"It wasn't important to me," he whispered, pangs of regret making his chest echo with a pulsing ache. "The house, the title, the money ... I was prepared to give it all up for you."

"But you didn't," Ben reminded him tersely.

The door swung open to reveal the waiting footman, and Alex's butler hovering in the opening of the front door.

"No," Alex murmured just before stepping down. "I didn't."

He wanted to add that he regretted it but stopped short, knowing it to be a lie. Alex still believed he had made the best decision he could have at the time. Reminding himself of what had been at stake, he took solace in knowing that his decision hadn't been selfish or even self-preserving. Soon, Ben would be made to understand that.

They were greeted by Hodge the butler, who offered a crisp

bow as Alex and Ben ascended the white front steps. "Welcome home, my lord. All is prepared for you and your guest, as requested in the note you sent ahead."

"Very good, Hodge. This is Mr. Sterling, and he will be in residence for several weeks. I did not realize we'd have an additional guest, but please ensure that accommodations are made for Mr. Fisher."

Hodge followed Alex's gaze to the pudgy man heaving himself out of the second carriage. He emitted a sharp whistle while slapping a dusty hat onto his head, gazing around in wonderment. Hodge's face didn't shift a bit, but Alex was familiar with his moods. The slight tick of his left cheek always gave him away, and he clearly found this new guest to be beneath his distinguished master.

Ever the consummate professional, Hodge gave an acquiescing nod. "Of course, my lord."

"I'll need a place to train," Ben put in. "A large room with a lot of open space. Preferably without a collection of precious knickknacks that run the risk of being broken. Fisher has trunks of equipment to store as well."

"Of course," Alex replied before turning back to Hodge. "Ensure that the designated trunks are taken to the gallery. The maids will clean it early and leave the space available for Mr. Sterling's particular use."

"I train at sunrise," Ben argued. "Have your maids clean at their usual time."

Hodge's nostrils flared at the high-handed command, but Alex gave the butler a covert nod of approval.

"As you wish," Hodge said to Ben before addressing Alex. "A light luncheon has been prepared, and hot baths can be drawn at a moment's notice."

"Lunch first, I think," Alex replied as he and Ben entered the house to be greeted by footmen who divested them of hats and greatcoats. "It's been a long day ... I'm famished."

Hodge bustled off to execute Alex's instructions, leaving him in the entrance hall with Ben, who was inspecting his surroundings with a guarded eye. While Ben had visited his family's townhouse in Mayfair, he had never stepped foot inside this house. Alex had imagined him here so many times—treading the corridors with heavy footsteps, riding horses across the grounds, lounging in the library ... sleeping in his bed. His throat grew tight as he absorbed a fantasy come to fruition, but under the worst of circumstances. It was his hope to convince Ben never to leave; a task that currently seemed as impossible as taking the blazing sun into his hands.

"The dining room is this way," Alex said, guiding Ben toward the corridor on the left. "Your things are being delivered to my chambers and accommodations are already prepared for your valet."

Ben's footsteps faltered just shy of the dining room doors. "Your chambers?"

Alex grinned. "Well, of course. This entire arrangement is about you being in my bed, isn't it?"

"To fuck you," Ben said, arms crossed over his chest. "Not to sleep."

"It's been years, Ben. I'm not going to be satisfied with you slinking across the corridor when you're finished with me."

"I have to assume your staff is discreet, otherwise you would never have brought me here."

"Of course. Discreet and loyal."

Ben stared at him with silent accusation in his eyes, as if Alex had somehow swindled him into something he hadn't agreed to. Truthfully, he'd expected Ben to balk at the suggested sleeping arrangements but had decided it was worth a try.

One that paid off, handily.

"Fine," Ben huffed. "But I want the left side of the bed."

"Naturally. I've always preferred the right, anyway."

Ben glowered at Alex as if suspicious of his claim, but gave a grudging nod before sweeping a hand to indicate Alex should precede him. Alex couldn't help a sly smile as he led the way. It was a small victory, but after Ben surprised him by bringing his boxing master along, Alex was due.

Inside the dining room, footmen were busy arranging dishes on the table between place settings—one of which was hastily being added for Mr. Fisher.

"Does he know?" Alex asked before the man could impose on them with his presence.

"No," Ben replied, without needing to ask what Alex referred to. "And I'd like to keep it that way."

"Of course."

Fisher entered the room just as they seated themselves—Alex at the head of the table and Ben to his right. Fisher took the place to his left.

"I'm grateful to you for allowing an old man to impose on your hospitality, my lord," Fisher said while eying the various dishes laid out for them.

"Think nothing of it, Mr. Fisher," Alex replied. "I want your time here to be enjoyable, so if you need anything, alert any member of my staff, and you will be accommodated."

"While we're on the subject," Fisher said while piling several finger sandwiches onto his plate. "Mr. Sterling will be on a strict diet during his time in the country. No fancy French foods or heavy sauces. No desserts. No wine, beer, ale, or spirits."

Alex's lips quivered at the low, pained sound Ben made in the back of his throat, but kept his attention on Fisher. "I see. Anything else?"

"Beefsteak and eggs for breakfast," Fisher replied, adding a cluster of grapes and a handful of lemon tartlets to his plate. "Or ham and eggs. Coffee is to be taken black, no cream or sugar."

"For the love of Christ," Ben grumbled.

Ignoring him, Fisher pointed his fork at Alex. "And ... a mixture of water, salt, and oats three times a day. Pugilists gruel ... good for the muscles and the bowels."

"Fisher, I hardly think the earl wishes to discuss my bowels over his meal," Ben griped while serving himself from a dish of cold meats and cheeses.

"Oh, let the man speak freely, Ben," Alex said. "It's all very interesting. So, this mixture of oats ... does he eat them with a spoon or suck them down like a glass of milk?"

"I'm going to kill you," Ben whispered, stabbing viciously at a grape with his fork. "Slowly. Painfully."

Alex laughed him off and continued peppering Mr. Fisher with questions about Ben's training regimen—which he truly did find interesting. Ben had always been a fighter, and Alex had witnessed several informal brawls like the one at The White Cock. What he really wanted to witness was a legitimate pugilist match—Ben testing his strength and skill against someone trained, just like him, to wreak havoc with his fists. Perhaps he could attend this upcoming fight Ben had mentioned.

After an hour of listening to Fisher's plans for Ben over the next four weeks, while Ben sulked over his food, they parted ways to wash the dust of travel away. Fisher informed Ben that he would have the rest of the day for a respite, but was expected to report to the gallery for training at dawn and no later. With that, Fisher ambled off in the company of a footman to his guest chamber. Alex led Ben upstairs to his own rooms, pleased to find that the promised bath had been drawn in the washroom. Ben's toilette items had been neatly arranged beside his on the washstand, and a small trunk rested on the bench at the foot of Alex's bed.

Ben stood in the midst of the room, taking in the chamber's colorful decor—the furnishings and bedding coordinated to match the magenta, gold, and royal blue pattern of the Chinese wallpaper.

"Why am I not surprised?" Ben muttered, toying with one of the gold cords tying back the bed curtains. "Decorated yourself, did you?"

Alex hesitated only a moment before replying, for he couldn't continue to dance around the subject of his marriage. He had brought Ben here to reveal the truth, and could start by edging closer to the massive elephant in the room. "I didn't do it alone. Katherine had a keen eye for colors and fabrics—it was one of the things we had in common. She chose the furnishings, and sent for the fabrics to upholster the chairs so they matched the curtains."

Registering Ben's disdainful expression, Alex rushed on before he could make some degrading remark about Katherine.

"I understand that the subject of my marriage is a sore one between us," he said. "But I'll not tolerate any disrespect toward her under this roof. There is so much for me to tell you, but I'll begin with this ... Katherine was a dear friend, and my memories of her are important to me. I cannot put that aside just because I've brought you here."

Ben didn't offer a verbal reply, but a quick nod of acquiescence proved to be enough.

Alex decided to let matters lie for now. They'd had a long, trying few days , and he had another resident of the house to visit before he could make himself more comfortable. "Help yourself to the bath. I have something to see to, but I'll return shortly. There's a library three doors down from the dining room —on the left. But there are books in the attached drawing room, through that door. Or you could explore the house. The third floor is in a bit of a shambles ... renovations that won't be completed until spring. I wouldn't suggest going up there. But the rest of the house is yours. I want you to be comfortable here."

Ben leaned against a bedpost and gave him a knowing look. "As comfortable as one can be in the home his former lover shared with his wife."

Alex issued a weary sigh, in no mood to verbally spar with Ben right now. "You never seem to have trouble making space for yourself anywhere. I'm sure you'll do so here, as well. I'll return soon."

Without waiting for a response, Alex fled the room, his

steps hurried as he made for the stairs. His heart was in his throat as he made his way to the third floor, a bitter taste flooding his mouth at the lie he'd just told Ben. However, if his memories of Katherine were precious, then this final secret was even more so. Ben didn't trust him enough to forgive him yet, and Alex could well understand that. As much as he loved Ben, Alex wasn't certain he could trust him to accept what he was keeping hidden on this floor of the house—albeit temporarily.

He breathed a bit easier as he trotted down a corridor with windows on one side overlooking the back lawn. Alex didn't relish having to divide his time between the two loves of his life, but it was a necessary precaution for the time being.

He knocked before entering, not wanting to intrude on the nurse if she was busy with a feeding. A soft voice bade him enter, and Alex stepped into the nursery. Cheery tones of canary yellow and soft pink enveloped him, and the gurgles and coos of the babe seated in the nurse's lap brought a smile to his face.

"Welcome home, my lord," said Rosalind, the nurse who had been caring for the babe since the day of her birth. "This one must have sensed you were near. She's in a wonderful mood, just cooing and singing her little heart out."

Alex accepted the muslin and lace bundle of his daughter from the nurse, who stood back and looked on with tender fondness. "Thank you, Rosalind. I'd like some time alone with her. I'll put her down for her nap."

"Of course, my lord. Ring if you need me."

The nurse was gone after a hasty cursy, leaving Alex to take up her abandoned place in the chair. Settling the six-month-old girl on his knee, Alex took stock of what he and Katherine had created—not out of love, but out of a need to at least attempt to fulfill their duties as an earl and a countess.

Alex had pushed aside all desires for fatherhood ages ago. A man needed to bed a woman to create a child, and Alex had never experienced the desire to do so. Even his forced marriage to Katherine hadn't changed his mind right off. It was Katherine who had convinced him to try.

"You need an heir," she had said to him over dinner one evening. "And I want ... Oh, Alex, I want to be a mother like I've never wanted anything in my life. I know you are not ... fond of me in that way, but ... could we try? Just until I conceive?"

Alex had been helpless to refuse her. Katherine had sacrificed just as much as Alex in their union. She would never know the true love of a husband, never experience real and deep passion. Her husband was incapable of giving her any of it. But, he wasn't incapable of siring a child.

So, after two years of celibacy, he had gone to Katherine's bed and done his best to impregnate her, if not please her. It had been difficult for them both, with Katherine feeling guilty for coercing Alex into such an agreement, and Alex hating himself for being unable to throw himself wholeheartedly into the endeavor. Their only hope for putting an end to it and entering the next phase of their lives was to conceive. After a few months of trying and doing their best not to speak of what went on in her bedchamber each night, their efforts had paid off.

Nine months later, Lady Isabella Harriette Osborne was born —bright-eyed and rosy-cheeked, with a fine fuzz of blonde down matching her mother's locks. Katherine had worried that Alex would be disappointed in her for birthing a girl, but Alex had never fallen so rapidly in love. One look at his daughter, and he decided that all the nights of trying to conceive had been worth it.

"She's perfect," he told Katherine while holding Isabella for the first time. "I don't need an heir. I just want her."

Katherine smiled up at him from her bed, dressed in a clean nightgown but still glistening with sweat. She had then promptly fallen asleep. She awakened only twice after that, so weak from childbirth that she couldn't even hold the babe to her breast without assistance.

She had lost too much blood, the doctor informed Alex as he

stood over the body of his dead wife, stunned beyond reason. Something had gone wrong ... there was nothing anyone could have done ... her soul was in the care of God now.

None of it offered him solace. He had wanted to give Katherine her heart's desire, because there was so much he could never offer. In the process, he'd sent her to her grave.

Isabella sputtered and murmured unintelligibly while pulling at one of his waistcoat buttons, her tiny chin slick with drool. Alex smiled at her, finding it impossible to remain morose with his daughter being so adorably charming.

"How I missed you, little Ella," he said, reaching out to smooth a golden cowlick over her brow. It sprung right back up, making Alex chuckle. "I've brought someone here to meet you, but I don't think he's ready just yet. Soon, I hope. You'll love him, Ella. You'll love him as much as I do."

Isabella went on fumbling at his buttons, one fist in her mouth as she sucked and chewed. A new tooth would soon make an appearance, a mate for the one that had come in just before he'd left for London.

"Am I foolish for needing you both?" he asked Isabella, who had discovered his watch chain and busied herself trying to find what it led to inside his fob pocket. "I am a fool, aren't I, Ella?"

His daughter simply grunted, chubby fingers rooting at the edge of his waistcoat pocket, brow furrowed in concentration. Alex sighed and pulled the watch free, offering it to her. Isabella grinned before fitting the watch into her mouth and gnawing at it with swollen gums.

Perhaps he *was* a fool to think he could win Ben back and hope he would accept that Isabella came along in the bargain. Knowing how furious he was with Alex for marrying Katherine, Ben was sure to be thoroughly disgusted by a child created of that marriage. He would have a difficult enough time explaining how Isabella had come to be, and that was only the beginning. There were still other secrets to be revealed, and Alex hardly knew where to begin now that Ben was here.

CHAPTER 8

"The Hon. Mr. L has been seen more frequently about Town of late. This author is proud of him for holding his head high after being jilted at the altar by that half-caste termagant, now known as Lady B. Perhaps the gentleman will try again to secure a bride."
-The London Gossip, 30 January 1820

When Alex returned to his bedchamber, he found Ben lounging on his bed, half-dressed with his hair still glistening from a wash. The sweet euphoria of time spent with his daughter was overwhelmed by a different sensation, one that stole the breath from his lungs. Ben wore only trousers and a shirt, which he'd left open to reveal the wide swath of his chest and that alluring mat of thick, curling blond hair. His feet were bare, and his sleeves rolled back as he lounged in casual repose, an open book laid before him.

Alex's legs were unsteady as he approached, nerves and excitement getting the best of him at once. He wanted Ben with the intensity of years of starvation and longing, but knew he walked a perilous line here. They were in danger of becoming so caught up in physical pleasures that the weight of reality was forgotten.

Clearing his throat, Alex glanced to the washroom, deciding he could at least bathe before trying to pull Ben into conversation. While soaking, perhaps he could settle on the first of many subjects to be broached between them.

He drew closer to the washroom with a frown, noticing that the water was still clear and unused. However, the washstand basin had been utilized, and several damp linens were piled in the corner.

"You could have used the tub, you know," he said, turning back to face Ben. "I would have simply used your water and called for the footmen to reheat."

"I prefer shower-baths," Ben replied without looking up from his book. "Honestly, Alex, with all the money you've inherited, one would think you might have installed one by now. Every fashionable home in London has one."

Alex wrinkled his nose. "I've tried shower-baths. The water cools too fast."

"Cold water is bracing and good for the body."

"Right," Alex muttered with a shake of his head.

Pulling the bell cord to ring for his valet, he entered the washroom to test the unused water. It was still adequately warm, so he had no need to send for fresh water. Annoyance lanced through him as he observed the linens haphazardly discarded near the washstand. He could only assume this small rebellion was yet another way for Ben to needle him. His behavior made no sense otherwise. Who didn't enjoy a hot bath?

Alex pushed the bizarre conversation out of his mind as his valet arrived to help him disrobe. Through the open door he caught sight of Ben, who had stopped reading to watch as the layers of Alex's clothes fell away. His skin broke out in gooseflesh at the slow trajectory of Ben's gaze over every inch of his skin as it was bared. Ben's eyes missed nothing, lingering in places that made Alex flush and fight not to squirm. When their gazes met, Ben's unspoken promises sent blood rushing to Alex's groin, prompting him quickly into the tub. The sooner he washed, the sooner he could climb into that bed with Ben.

With a groan, he let his head fall against the lip of the tub. He was so weak. It had only taken a lingering glance from Ben to make him forget that he'd resolved to have a conversation first.

"Is the water not to your liking, my lord?" his valet asked, hovering near the tub with a knit brow.

"The water is fine, Hammond. You may take your leave. I'll see to myself."

Hammond, who had been sweethearts with one of the footmen for the past five years, hardly batted an eyelash at leaving his naked master alone with Ben. He was fortunate to have a trustworthy staff and a place to bring Ben where they could act freely with one another. It had been his greatest wish during their university days, as he'd wearied of sneaking about to find places where they were safe to express their affections.

Alex had begun washing when the sound of Ben's footsteps signaled his approach. He held something in his hand, his eyes radiating purpose and mischief. Alex sat up straight, eyes going wide as Ben crouched, bracing his arms on the edge of the tub and holding up the shining silver object. The plug was the size and shape of a small lemon, its base wide and flat. His cock twitched as he inspected it, his anus contracting in anticipation of where Ben intended to put it.

"It has been a long time for you," Ben murmured, allowing his other hand to dip into the water. "I want you ready and relaxed."

Swallowing past the tightness of his throat, Alex nodded. "I appreciate the forethought."

Ben's hand went under the water, his fingertips skimming along Alex's belly. They trailed through the light trail of hairs leading toward Alex's groin, then brushed the length of his stiff cock.

His breaths quickening, Alex laid back and closed his eyes.

"Ben, I ... I had hoped we could talk about something important."

"Is that so?" Ben murmured, his words low and teasing as he wrapped his hand around Alex's erection. "Very well, then. Talk."

Alex thrust into Ben's tight and warm fist, the callouses on his palms abrading the soft, sensitive skin. "That isn't fair. I can hardly think when you're doing that, let alone talk."

"Hmm," Ben mumbled, releasing Alex's cock to fondle his bollocks. "Then I suppose it will have to wait. Unless ... you want me to stop?"

"Don't you dare," Alex groaned, spreading his legs as Ben's fingers crept past his balls, pressing and massaging.

Ben chuckled and did as he was bade, slowly working his way between Alex's cheeks. His first finger pressed against Alex's hole, then lightly circled with teasing strokes.

"Oil?" Ben asked.

"On the washstand," Alex choked out.

"Good. On your hands and knees."

Alex complied, limbs trembling as he maneuvered so that he knelt in the tub, the water lapping at his chest. He flinched when Ben touched him, a strong hand gripping one of his buttocks and moving it aside. The cool air of the washroom left him feeling exposed and vulnerable, Ben's gaze in his most intimate of places only exacerbating the effect. But, his cock was unbearably hard, begging for stimulation and release.

The oil was warm and slick as Ben trickled it between Alex's cheeks, and his blunt fingers followed, massaging the taut opening and offering light pressure. Alex lowered his head to the lip of the tub, staring down at the undulating beams of light cutting through the water as he did his best to open himself to the invasion. It had been so long, he'd nearly forgotten the painful pleasure of being stretched and filled, fucked toward a stunning climax. The endless nights of frigging himself to thoughts of Benedict or the images printed in his lascivious books had only ever taken the edge off. Now that he could finally have what he'd been longing for all this time, Alex wasn't certain he would last long enough to enjoy it. He was a bundle of nerve endings, exposed and raw and ready to be set off at the slightest touch.

Benedict's finger breached him, slicked with more of the oil. He was slow and patient, working the finger in and out and easing Alex into accepting him. Alex reached beneath himself to grip his cock, desperate for more and wanting it all so badly it hurt.

"No," Ben commanded, his finger going still inside Alex. "Not yet. Keep your hands at the bottom of the tub or I'll stop."

"Bugger you, Ben," Alex rasped.

"I rather thought *I* would be the one buggering *you*, and if you want that, you'll do as you're told."

Alex bit back a litany of curses and insults, knowing Ben's threat wasn't idle. If Ben stopped now, Alex was certain he would die.

He winced at the addition of a second finger, the burning sensation heightening. Still, his arousal lost none of its urgency, pulsing and swelling with need. Alex widened his legs as far as the tub allowed and raised his hips, urging Ben on. Curling his fingers in a come-hither motion, Ben found the nub of flesh within Alex that made his toes curl and his insides wind taut.

"Ben," he rasped, drowning in sensations. "God ..."

"You're almost ready for the plug, I think," Ben replied, his own voice thick and heavy with lust. "Can you take more?"

No, he wanted to say. No, he couldn't possibly take more without being torn in two. But then, Ben's cock was significantly larger than two fingers. Alex would have to grit his teeth and bear this, knowing that the payoff in the end would be well worth it.

"Yes," he ground out. "Keep going."

Ben made a low sound of approval, continuing in his teasing ministrations. He added more oil as he worked his fingers in and out of Alex while seeming to determine the right time to stretch him further. Alex swallowed a yelp of agony when the third finger intruded, but Ben's skilled strokes soon overtook the pain. The tension in Alex's back eased, and he pushed back against Ben's fingers. His hands itched to take hold of his cock, but Alex knew better than to test Ben's threat.

The torment seemed to go on forever, but before long, Ben abruptly eased his fingers free and nudged the tip of the oil-soaked plug against him. Alex followed Ben's lead, slowly pushing back to take in the plug. He held his breath as the widest part of it passed through the tight ring of his anus, then issued it on a sigh of relief as the rest of it swiftly followed. The throb of invasion dulled as the sensation of overwhelming full-ness replaced it. Ben was gone when Alex gingerly knelt up and turned—looming over the washstand and cleaning his hands.

"Take your time coming to bed," Ben said while drying with fresh linen. "Slow steps."

Alex could offer no response, too busy maneuvering himself in the tub to finish washing while trying to ignore the plug taking up place inside him. Despite Ben's directive to take his time, Alex hurried through his ablutions, eager to get on with it.

As a force of habit, he donned a dressing gown on his way to the bedroom, loosely tying it about his waist. The plug shifted and pressed against his inner walls with every step he took, and the abrasion of the fabric against his bare skin sent shivers racing through him.

Ben was seated on the edge of the bed watching Alex, amuse-ment twinkling in his eyes like chips of sapphire. "Ever fashion-able, even in the bedroom, eh?"

Alex ran a hand over the silken gold lapel of his robe and smirked. "I cannot seem to help myself."

Ben slowly came to his feet, his hands drawing Alex's eye as he began to disrobe. Alex followed those big, powerful hands as they tugged his shirt free and eased it upward, slowly revealing the whorls of hair spread over that hard, muscle-packed torso. The swells of his chest bunched and stretched as he lowered his arms and worked at his trouser buttons—his intimidating cock already showing against the fabric in a swollen outline. Alex watched with parted lips as the trousers fell away, giving him his first glimpse of Ben entirely naked in over three years.

He was more magnificent than ever, etched with grooves and sinews like a Greek statue. Of course, his prick was more impressive than those found in a museum, heavy and long and adorned with thick veins. It took everything Alex had not to drop to his knees then and there, taking that mouthwatering length to the back of his throat.

Instead, he stood completely still and let Ben come to him, his heart beating against his ribs. Ben circled behind Alex, hands wrapping around his waist to tug at the belt of the dressing gown. The robe slid off his shoulders and fell at his feet, allowing Ben's cockstand to nudge against the back of his thigh. Alex closed his eyes and eased into Ben's hold, absorbing every touch and allowing his faint memories to tangle with the present. Ben's hands skimmed up his belly and over the muscles of his chest, thumbs and forefingers tugging at his nipples. Alex groaned, swaying back into Ben's sturdy body, one hand coming up to cup his nape.

Ben nuzzled his neck, lazy flicks of his tongue and presses of his lips sending a tingle down Alex's spine. Ben flexed his hips, nudging his cock at the cleft between Alex's legs, teasing what was soon to come. Alex shuddered and tightened his hold on Ben, waiting for the traveling hands to find their way where he wanted them most. As if he'd read Alex's mind, Ben let one hand drift downward. His fingers combed through the hairs at Alex's groin, then circled the base of his cock.

Alex cried out when Ben gave his cock a long, firm stroke, his arse clenching around the plug. He threaded his fingers through the damp hair at Ben's nape, holding him tight. Ben nibbled and bit along Alex's shoulder while steadily working his cock.

Certain he wouldn't be able to stay on his feet much longer, Alex placed a hand over Ben's, stilling it.

"I can't wait," he panted, already on the edge of a climax. "I want you now."

"Be patient," Ben warned. "I don't want to hurt you."

"I don't care. Fuck me, Ben."

Apparently, it was all Ben needed to hear, because at that moment he propelled Alex to the bed. Alex went up onto the mattress, pulling a pillow toward himself and laying over it, hips up and head down. Ben followed, using a knee to nudged Alex's legs farther apart, then positioning himself so that their thighs fit together.

"Are you sure?" Ben asked. "You can just wear the plug for tonight, and we can—"

"For Christ's sake, I'm not some frightened virgin!" Alex snapped, his arousal giving way to agitation the longer he was made to wait. "It's been years. I don't intend to wait another moment. I'll be fine."

Ben said nothing in response, but he did begin to slowly pull the plug free of Alex's arse. Alex clung to his cushion, biting his lip as the hard metal stretched him again before falling free. Then, he felt the cool trickle of more oil, followed by the press of Ben's cockhead.

Panic came over Alex as he'd vastly underestimated the sheer size of Ben compared to his back passage, but he took deep, slow breaths and reminded himself that they'd done this many times before. Ben held fast to his hips, his breaths harsh as he slowly began easing into Alex. The sharp sting and flare of heat stole Alex's breath as Ben's wide head pushed through, nearly the size of the largest part of the plug. Alex clenched his jaw, pushing back on the thick length demanding invasion into his body.

"Holy Christ," Ben gasped as he nudged his way in deeper. "Fuck ... *fuck*!'

Alex might have echoed those sentiments if he hadn't been robbed of speech as well as breath. He was on fire, the pain of being invaded mingling with a distant pleasure, and the realization that this was finally happening. Ben was here, inside him, close enough to smell and touch and feel. Alex nearly wept from the poignant intensity of the moment, one he had feared might never come.

"All right?" Ben asked, pausing with about one third of his length lodged inside Alex.

"Yes," Alex ground out. "Keep going."

Ben obliged, adding more oil before pushing in further, using his grasp on Alex's hips to pull him back into the slow, forward thrust. Pulling out a little, he then pushed in a bit further, drawing a sharp yelp from Alex at the resulting burn. But Ben gained another inch, then another, and after what felt like an eternity, found his way in to the hilt. He paused, his harsh breaths mingling with Alex's short, strained ones. Alex let himself experience the feeling of fullness, marveling at the crisp rasp of Ben's leg hairs along the backs of his thighs, the strength of the hands holding him steady, the solid presence holding him together when he felt he might fall apart.

Ben's hand slid along his thigh before delving inward, finding Alex's jutting cock. Alex fought not to push into the fist clenching around him, holding perfectly still as Ben stroked him, the pleasure of it tangling with the ache in his arse until the two were indistinguishable.

"God, the way you feel," Ben murmured, his lips brushing the shell of Alex's ear. "So tight and hot. Did you miss me, Alex?"

There were equal parts a taunt and a real question in those words, and Alex decided to be honest and speak to the part of Ben that seemed to really want to know.

"So much it hurt," he whispered, his eyes prickling with sudden emotion. "Every hour of every day."

Ben didn't respond aloud, his grip tightening on Alex's cock as he rolled his hips. They groaned in unison, the stroke of Ben's rod sending waves of exquisite pleasure and a heated ache throughout Alex's entire body. Ben did it again, then again, slowly withdrawing a few inches and plunging, his hand never faltering in its rhythm around Alex's cock.

Face buried in the counterpane, Alex moved with him, rocking back to meet each thrust, then pushing his cock into the circle of Ben's fingers. Ben skillfully acted on Alex's unspoken urgings—the sharp intake of his breath, the arch of his back, his euphoric moans of pleasure. He quickened his pace when he realized Alex could take it, that he *wanted* it more than he wanted his next breath.

Ben's weight pressed Alex down into the mattress, one hand working his cock, the other braced on his shoulder. Ben's pelvis battered at him now, hard and relentless, the path eased by his careful coaxing and the lubrication of the oil. Alex was lost, utterly at Ben's mercy and never wanting it to be any other way. His climax nipped at his heels, propelled along by Ben's perfectly angled thrusts and the pulls of his hand. Alex tried to fight it off, praying for more time, but the force of it was too powerful. Alex cried out his ecstasy as release overtook him with limb-shaking intensity. It seemed to go on forever, his gut clenching and his back arching as his seed flooded from him to stain the counterpane.

Ben wasn't finished with him yet, sweat slicking between his chest and Alex's back as he chased his own finish. Alex was near collapse, unable to do anything other than accept everything Ben had to give. With a few more frantic thrusts, Ben seated himself inside Alex and spent. His growling groan of pleasure was muffled, his lips pressed against Alex's shoulder as he spilled his seed.

Ben's weight slowly eased off Alex, his softened cock slipping free. Collapsing at Alex's side, Ben freed him to do the same, letting out a relieved breath as the last bit of tension left his limbs.

For a long while, only the rhythm of their breathing could be heard as they lay back to back, each absorbed in the aftermath of his own climax. Eventually, the mattress shifted and dipped as Ben turned onto his back. Alex followed suit, but a pang through his rear had him on his side facing Ben.

Running a hand over the fleece on his chest, Ben sighed, turning his head to look Alex in the eye. Alex found himself hypnotized by the sapphire depths, fringed in those spiky, pale lashes. Ben was softer just now, more at ease. Through the haze of exhaustion and ecstasy, Alex could imagine Ben as he had been at eighteen, twenty-one, twenty-five. The furrows in his brow hadn't been so deep, and scorn didn't show at the corners of his mouth. He smiled with genuine joy and not derision. He laughed with freedom instead of sarcasm.

His heart had not yet been broken.

They stared silently at one another, but before long Ben looked away, that ever-present frown pulling on his lips.

"Ben," Alex ventured.

"Not tonight, Alex," Ben whispered, eyes squeezed shut. "I'm not stupid. I know you dragged me out of London so I would be forced to hear you out. But we just arrived, we are both exhausted and in no condition to start inviting the ghosts of the past to join us."

Alex bit his lip, not wanting to admit that Ben had a point. He was tired, and barely had the strength required to rise and wash before falling face-first back into this bed. They would both think clearer after a few hours of indolence and a good night's sleep.

"Even I like a reprieve from self-pity and anger from time to time," Ben added. "I'll give you my ear tomorrow, though I must warn you, it is only to end your ceaseless wailing. It won't change my mind, so this will simply be an exercise in futility, but one that will allow you to ease your guilt."

Alex laughed, shoulders quivering as he stared at Ben's profile. "Why can't you look at me while telling such outright lies?"

Ben snorted, but his eyelids remained lowered. "I'm only too exhausted to open my eyes right now. My God, why would you ever suggest something so ludicrous?"

Alex was trembling with laughter now, which he tried and

failed to muffle with pinched lips. "Fine, Ben. Have it your way. I will ease my guilt and you will continue on uncaring and unfazed."

"Quite right," Ben drawled.

"We are agreed."

"Indeed."

"So, we will talk tomorrow?" Alex teased. By now, he was simply enjoying being a thorn in Ben's side.

"Yes, tomorrow, as I've said already."

"Good."

"Good."

Alex chuckled as Ben heaved a sigh, turning his back on Alex and leaving the bed to go wash. Alex took his time following, still snorting and snickering at the ridiculousness of their conversation. They took turns at the washstand and then returned to the bed, clean and drowsy. Pushing aside the soiled counterpane, they flopped beside one another and promptly fell asleep within the cocoon of the lowered bed curtains.

WHEN BENEDICT ROSE AT DAWN THE NEXT MORNING, ALEX was still snoring into his pillow. He raced through his morning ablutions, then donned his worn trousers and favorite training shirt. Boots tightly laced, he made his way to the dining room within seconds before Fisher's arrival. The man had a footman on his heels, the servant carrying a silver tray with a large ale mug perched on it. Benedict's stomach quivered with dread as he was presented with his pugilists' gruel—the revolting mixture of salt, water, and raw oats. However much he may hate it, Benedict had to admit its effects were noticeable, resulting in a more svelte form, and increasing his energy. More energy equaled faster reflexes, which was of the utmost importance for men fighting in the heavyweight class.

So, he choked the concoction down without complaint, hoping to convince Fisher to take it easy on him for the first day of training in weeks. He was not as fortunate as he had hoped.

Fisher was in rare form, insisting that Benedict had gotten slow and fat and needed to be whipped into shape. So Fisher had coaxed a groom from the stables as the first light of day sent orange tendrils into the blue void. With the groom driving him alongside Benedict, Fisher yelled obscenities and aspersions on Benedict's speed. Meanwhile, Benedict ran along the uneven path, searching for the best places to plant his feet as he fought to remain abreast with Fisher's wagon. He ran Benedict until the sun beat down on them, then pushed him through a gamut of training exercises for flexibility and strength. They returned to the house long enough for Benedict to be served a breakfast of ham, eggs, and soft, buttered bread. He devoured it with enthusiasm, chasing it with black coffee.

From there, they entered the gallery, which was filled with a history of the Vautrey family told in portraits. The equipment Fisher had brought alone was waiting for them. After wrapping his hands, Fisher assisted him in several stretches. At the taut pull of his tendons, Benedict sought distraction in the art, finding they were near the section of portraits depicting Alex's immediate family. He found the previous earl's portrait first, the man resembling Alex with his high forehead, a sweep of dark brown hair speckled with gray, and those calf-like brown eyes. The portrait had been done at least ten years ago, before the decline in his health. Beside the earl was Alex's mother, who had succumbed to grief not long after her husband's death. Alex's most recent portrait hung beside his mother's, portraying him in the most surprising way. Unlike his portrait at twenty-one, showing his sense of humor and playful nature, this one characterized him as somber and stoic. His chin was too firm, his mouth too tight, his brow too heavy. Benedict felt a twisting in his gut as he took in the changes. Was this what people saw when they looked at him—the ravages of betrayal, heartbreak, and torture, aging him, dragging down his brow and curling his lips into a sneer?

His attention was stolen by the portrait beside Alex's, an ethereally beautiful woman in a gilt frame. Benedict ceased to feel the painful stretch of his inner thigh as he studied the woman, who could only be Lady Katherine Osborne, Countess of Vautrey. In juxtaposition to Alex's dour face, Katherine radiated cheer and kindness. She possessed a head full of flaxen curls, her eyes a pale and riveting blue. A soft smile revealed a dimple in one cheek, and her willowy frame was enhanced by the fluid grace of a gown that matched her eyes.

Being confronted with the specter of the countess reminded Benedict of just where he was and what he'd gotten himself into. In allowing this concession in their arrangement, Benedict had let himself be forced to occupy a space that had been meant for Alex and Katherine. The home of a man and his wife, a place to raise children and fulfill the obligations of their titles. He seethed while Fisher helped him into his practice gloves, as his mind inundated him with unwanted thoughts.

Had Alex at least consummated the union to ensure its legitimacy? When the loneliness and imposition of hiding his true nature had become too much, had Alex found solace in Katherine's bed? Had he taken pleasure from lying with a woman— more than he had with Benedict?

Benedict threw himself into the sparring session with Fisher with every ounce of his envy and frustration. The old man had gotten soft around the middle and was fond of pastries and pies —yet he kept up with Benedict with the sort of strength and endurance only an old champion could possess. He taunted Benedict over his mistakes, circling him and jabbing with fists like hammers. Despite the other man's gloves, Benedict felt every blow, absorbing the pain and allowing it to build, using it to keep him alert and reflexive. As he battered at his trainer, Benedict reminded himself that he was as in control of this situation as he had been in the beginning.

Nothing had changed. For the sake of earning the promised twenty-five thousand pounds, he would have to allow Alex to explain himself. Perhaps he could even admit curiosity over the events that had led to him marrying Katherine. Benedict had always assumed cowardice to be the reason. After all, their plans to run away to France together had been enough to frighten even the bravest of men. Benedict's mistake had been assuming that Alex's love matched his own, that he was willing to do anything for the desired outcome.

He would not make that mistake again. Alex had proven himself to be romantic and committed, but only up to a certain point. When the time came again to make that frightening leap of faith, he would surely leave Benedict behind again.

As he slumped onto a stool, accepting a drink of water from Fisher, Benedict told himself that there would be no second chance. Being stabbed in the back once had been enough, and he wasn't keen to repeat the experience.

He sat toweling the sweat from his face and neck, and trying to enjoy the few minutes left of the break Fisher had allowed, when Alex approached from the other end of the gallery. He looked refreshed after the several more hours of sleep he'd had than Benedict, dressed informally in a morning coat and loosely-tied cravat.

"I see the training is going well," Alex said as he drew near, glancing over the bits of equipment scattered about the floor.

"Well my arse," Fisher groused, tying off an enormous sack that he'd had a groom fill with oats. He'd have Benedict lifting it over his shoulders and running the length of the gallery sometime today. "He's slow and distracted. Too much drink these past months, and who the devil knows what's diverting his mind during sparring."

"It's only the first day, old man," Benedict retorted before swigging the last of his water. "I'll be my old self in a week or less."

"Yes, you will," Fisher agreed. "After a few sweating sessions to leech all that poison out of you."

Benedict stifled a groan, in no mood to be punished for a poor attitude. Alex watched, amusement lighting up his eyes.

Benedict came to his feet, shaking out his arms and cranking his neck left to right. "I'll be a few hours more, at least. Haven't you something to occupy yourself with?"

"Well, I've finished answering the correspondence that piled up while I was in London, and met with my steward to discuss estate matters. After a few hours of idleness, I've grown bored. I typically take an afternoon ride, but ... I'm not feeling up for it today."

They traded knowing glances, Benedict understanding right off why Alex wouldn't want to straddle a horse today. It lay on the tip of his tongue to tell Alex that he likely wouldn't be able to sit a horse for weeks if he had his way, but Fisher's presence forced him to hold his tongue.

"What do you say we give Fisher a break?" Alex suggested, bending down to pick up Benedict's spare gloves. "I'll spar with you."

Benedict snorted a sarcastic laugh. "Do you have a death wish?"

Shrugging one arm out of his coat, Alex switched the gloves to his other hands to free the opposite arm. "I think you'll find me to be a worthy opponent. When one lives in the country, one finds various ways to remain active. There is a boxing master in the county who specializes in training gentlemen in the sport."

Benedict raised his gloves, arching an eyebrow at Alex. "I don't fight like a gentleman."

"I wouldn't expect you to. Mr. Fisher, would you be amenable to the idea?"

"Fine by me," Fisher replied, using his teeth to begin unwinding his gloves. "You'd be in his weight class, and you have an impressive wingspan, which means a long reach. I'd be curious to see how you fare."

"No," Benedict interjected. "Leave us alone. I'll send for you when we're done."

Fisher blustered and complained, but a withering glare from Benedict kept him from protesting further. He helped Alex don the sparring gloves, then took his leave, muttering under his breath and shaking his balding head.

"Now then," Alex said, turning back to Benedict. "Are you ready?

"It's your funeral," Benedict muttered.

Alex returned his sarcasm with a teasing smile but said nothing.

"I won't go easy on you," Benedict warned as they began circling one another, taking each other's measure.

"I would never ask you to," Alex fired back, testing a swift jab with his left.

Benedict backed away, noting that Fisher had been right about Alex's reach. Those long arms gave him an advantage, while Benedict had the power of his blows to fall back on.

"I am surprised to see you wearing gloves," Alex remarked, grunting as Benedict swooped in with a right cross to his shoulder. "I thought you preferred to pound your opponents with bare knuckles."

"If I trained without gloves, Fisher and I would both be muddle-headed and broken. I'd never be able to compete. Civility matters in training, but not in the ring."

"Interesting," Alex murmured, landing a blow to Benedict's chest.

Benedict staggered back, surprised at the force behind it. They had only just begun, but Alex was proving better than Benedict expected.

Noticing Benedict's shock, Alex chuckled. "I told you, I've been training. Fisher's right ... you're slower than I know you typically are. Did your disturbed sleep make you tired?"

Benedict frowned, recalling that he'd slept like the dead all night. "I didn't awaken once the whole night."

Alex's face drew into a concerned frown as he dodged a blow aimed at his chin, knocking Benedict's glove aside with his own. "You tossed and turned, and mumbled in your sleep. You seemed to be having a terrible dream, but when I tried to rouse you, you wouldn't wake."

Benedict swore under his breath, annoyed that he couldn't remember what he'd dreamed about last night. Many mornings, he woke with a heavy weight in his chest and lethargy sapping his strength. Sometimes he remembered the terrors visiting him in the night—being immersed in ice baths and held under until he was choking on frigid water, being covered in leeches, forced to swallow purgatives so that he vomited until feeling as if his organs would be purged along with the meager contents of his stomach. However, most times, he woke only with the lingering fear those memories inspired, aware that he had dreamed but uncertain of what exactly his sleeping mind had conjured.

"I don't remember," Benedict hedged. "I apologize if it bothered you. It would be best for me to sleep alone from now on."

"I was only disturbed to see you so distressed."

"It was nothing for you to worry over."

"Just as that hole in your study wall doesn't concern me? Or how what happened to you during our separation is also nothing for me to worry over?"

"Precisely," Benedict growled, going for a vicious uppercut to Alex's middle.

Alex bowed at the waist, staggering away and protecting his stomach with his gloves. Benedict went on the offensive, but Alex recovered, coming to meet him. They locked together, grappling and trying to free themselves while avoiding one another's swinging fists.

"How much longer are you going to put yourself through this?" Alex panted, his forehead pressed to Benedict's shoulder as he squirmed to get free of his hold. "The intense training, the brutal fights? Your face is just healing, and in a few weeks you'll run out to let someone batter it all over again."

"What difference does it make to you?" Benedict challenged, easing a fist between them and bringing it up beneath Alex's jaw.

Alex fell away from him, swiping the sleeve of his shirt across his mouth. He glared at Benedict and raised his fists. "You may choose not to believe this, but I care if you go into your twilight years without your teeth, a deformed face, and a punch-drunk mind."

They danced around one another, the intensity of their sparring adding a thread of tension to the tapestry already woven between them.

"My life is my own to do what I please with," Benedict argued.

"That may be so, but there are people who would be distraught if you were truly hurt. People who love you, who wouldn't want to watch you fall apart before their eyes."

Benedict threw a jab that Alex side-stepped before delivering his own blow. Benedict registered the hit to his left shoulder, one that had been injured years ago and still pained him on occasion. It was an unpleasant reminder that he wasn't as young as he once had been.

"Don't," he warned, rolling his shoulders and resuming his stance.

"I wasn't only referring to myself. What about Aubrey and Nick? What about the other Gentleman Courtesans you call friends?"

"They have wives now, and have started making their own families. None of them needs me anymore."

"Having wives and children doesn't change the fact that they need you," Alex argued. "Do you resent them for it?"

"Of course not. I'm glad for them."

Alex edged too close, and Benedict swept his legs from under him, throwing him onto his back. Before Alex could right himself, Benedict was over him, raining blows on the arms raised to protect his face.

"If you are lonely, it is by choice," Alex managed between

grunts. "You are surrounded by people who care about you, but you keep them at a distance ... even Aubrey."

Benedict fell onto his knees over Alex, irritation spurring his actions. There were things Alex simply didn't know and could never understand.

"If you have something to say to me, let's have it," Benedict growled, batting one of Alex's arms aside and striking his cheekbone, then his chin. "But you can spare us both this drama of your own making. Our agreement says nothing of you trying to change or manage me."

Alex wrapped his legs around Benedict's waist, and one arm around his neck, leaving him scrambling for freedom. "No one is trying to manage you. I'm trying to love you, you stubborn fool."

"Nothing about that in the agreement either," Benedict huffed, pounding at Alex's ribs and trying to break his hold. His face was buried in Alex's neck, giving him a whiff of clean sweat and shaving balm. Benedict's other senses flared to life, his body responding to Alex's nearness and the tight constriction of the legs enclosing him. Alex's breaths came hard and fast, and Benedict knew it wasn't only due to the strikes he suffered to his torso.

"If you loved me, you would have never left," Benedict added. "Your words mean nothing after what you did."

"For the love of ..."

Alex turned them so he straddled Benedict, putting him in the position of power. Benedict tried to buck him off, but was subjected to several teeth-rattling blows to his face.

"I have tried and tried to tell you why I had to do it," Alex exclaimed. "I'm done with this game, Ben. If you're going to be angry with me, you will at least do so with full knowledge of what happened."

"I have no interest—"

"Your father *knew*, Ben! That's what I was trying to tell you when we left London. I wasn't referring to him knowing that we are lovers now ... but that he knew back then. He knew, and he went to my father to expose us."

They both went deathly still, Alex staring down at him while Benedict wrestled with what he'd just heard. The convergence of shock, confusion, and rage sent heat spiraling through him, and Benedict threw a vicious punch that sent Alex rolling from on top of him, one glove pressed to his eye.

Benedict came to his feet, tearing at one glove with his teeth and then shaking it off with jerky motions. "My father ... he found out about us."

"Yes," Alex said. "He had known for some time, I think."

After working off his first glove, Benedict yanked off the other before stepping forward to help Alex with his. Once done, he motioned toward a cushioned chair flanked by small, decorative statues. Alex took the chair while Benedict lowered himself onto the stool.

"Tell me everything."

CHAPTER 9

LONDON, 1816

Alex dropped the last of his books into the open trunk inside his dressing room, before promptly closing it. All around him were the few possessions he would carry with him to France. He was due to depart for Dover the moment the entire house had gone quiet for the night. Once there, he would meet Ben at the docks, where they planned to board a packet and cross the channel to Calais. They had talked of settling in Paris, but wished to tour other places before making a final decision.

All of Alex's things were packed, his passport secured inside the leather case inside his valise. He had paid his valet to keep silent, and written a sterling character letter for the man to find himself another post. Alex wanted nothing more than to be free of anything that kept him from Ben, but he didn't want to worry his family or leave his servant without a position in the process. Hamond had begged to be allowed to come along, but Alex had refused. Leaving the employ of Alex's father without a moment's notice, even if it was to follow his master to France, would besmirch his reputation as a valet beyond compare. Besides, his father paid Hamond's salary, and while Alex had money of his own, he would need it for settling in France.

After writing the character for Hamond, Alex had penned a short note to his parents. Instead of telling them that he was running away for the sake of love, Alex informed them that he didn't feel as if he were adequate enough to take his place as the earl. It pained him to lie when the formative years of his life had been spent preparing him for a responsibility he knew himself capable of carrying. However, he couldn't remain in England, where men who loved other men could lose everything, shame their families, and be brutalized in the pillory or hanged. Rather than risk putting his family through such disgrace, Alex had chosen the man he loved and the freedom of being who he truly was over upholding the Vautrey legacy. Imploring his father to turn his attentions to preparing his brother and nephew to inherit, Alex apologized for disappointing him. He had begged his mother's forgiveness and told her how much he loved her.

After that, there had been nothing left to say. Ben would meet him in Dover, the risk of them being found together driving them to travel separately. However, once aboard the packet, they would never be separated again. Traveling under the guise of being cousins, they would garner little or no suspicion. Two bachelors living and traveling together wouldn't draw notice, and France had done away with punishments for sodomy. Alex and Ben couldn't be too free and open with their affections, but the threat of exposure and disgrace was far greater in England than in France.

Alex had realized some time ago that he couldn't live without Ben. He was also weary of having to sneak about, finding places to be together for a short time before returning to the facades of their lives. Giving up the earldom had been difficult, but he would sacrifice far more for the privilege of having Ben by his side for the rest of his days.

Ben had needed very little convincing to go along with Alex's plan.

His brothers had died the year before in a terrible accident, making Ben his father's heir. However, Ben was unlike Alex in that he hadn't been prepared to inherit, nor did he wish to. His hatred for Viscount Sterling made it easy to leave without a look back.

Alex had begun to pace, anxious for the moment he could slip away with his parents none the wiser. A knock at the door interrupted his reverie, causing his heartbeat to accelerate. Alex had shared dinner with his parents earlier, and their time of quiet reading and nightcaps had ended hours ago. He'd insisted he not be disturbed, and Hamond helped ensure the rest of the staff was made aware of this.

So, who was at his door and why were they here?

A sense of foreboding made Alex's heart sink into his stomach, and his hand shook as he opened the door.

A footman gave Alex a curt bow before informing him that his father had sent for him. "He's waiting in his study and wishes to see you at once."

Swallowing the acidic bile rising in his throat, Alex kept his face free of all expression as he dismissed the footman. Running his fingers through his hair, Alex closed the door and leaned his forehead against it. He closed his eyes and took several deep breaths, telling himself that he hadn't been caught. No one but Hamond knew of his plans, and the valet was loyal to Alex and had his own secrets to keep. Alex couldn't imagine that the man would have betrayed him.

This was nothing to be worried over. His father likely wanted to speak to him about some trivial matter. Perhaps he couldn't sleep and wanted Alex to join him for a cigar. Maybe there was an estate matter he wanted Alex's opinion on.

Yes, that was it. Alex pulled away from the door and forced his feet to move—wanting to get this over with, and hoping that his father would turn in soon so he could depart. If he didn't leave tonight, Ben would be forced to wait a day or more for Alex to arrive.

Despite having convinced himself that he was still safe, Alex grew nauseous, his limbs sapped of strength. He couldn't ignore the premonition telling him that something was terribly wrong.

It was easy enough to determine why he'd been summoned once Alex entered his father's study. The earl sat behind his desk with a stack of folded papers before him, his head resting in his hands. But, it wasn't his father that drew Alex's attention, but the third person standing near the hearth, staring at Alex as if he were a pile of excrement.

His anxiety heightened when he met the gaze of Lord Malcolm Sterling. The viscount was a handsome man, having passed his looks down to Ben, as well as his Corinthian frame. The subtle difference between father and son was in the eyes. Ben had bright, clear eyes that twinkled with mischief, laughter, and secrets. By contrast, Viscount Sterling possessed the coldest, deadest eyes Alex had ever seen. And just now, they clearly radiated hatred and scorn as he looked at Alex, his lips pinched tight.

Tearing his gaze away from Ben's father, Alex faced his own. "Father? You wanted to see me?"

The earl kept his head lowered, shaking it from side to side as he murmured in a broken voice, "Not my son ... it can't be true. Where did I go wrong?"

Alex's throat constricted, and he could hardly draw breath. Yet he remained aware of Viscount Sterling's presence, and did his best not to show it outwardly.

"Father, what's wrong?" He turned back to the viscount, a sudden thought occurring to him. "Has something happened to Ben?"

Even as he asked, he knew it to be a ridiculous question. The viscount wouldn't care enough to inform Ben's closest friends of an injury or death. There was only one reason he could be here, but Alex didn't want to be the one to bring it up.

His father slowly raised his head, staring at Alex with reddened eyes and a trembling chin. "Alex ... the viscount has brought me disturbing news. I was certain it couldn't be true, but ... this is your handwriting."

Alex felt as if he'd been punched squarely in the chest as his father pushed the papers across his desk. They were unfolded, revealing his meticulous handwriting, his words. The lines swam before his unfocused eyes—words he knew by heart. The letters were deeply intimate, the revelations of his heart and mind. He and Ben had never used their names out of an abundance of caution, referring to one another as 'My dearest,' 'My darling,' or simply 'sweetheart.' The contents, however, were unmistakable. No one reading them would ever think they'd been penned from a man to a woman.

That these letters were now in his father's possession meant they had been found out. It wouldn't be difficult, in the face of such evidence, to deduce who Ben's secret lover was. They had spent nearly every break from Eton and Cambridge together, and even Sterling had to know how close they were. Perhaps the viscount had suspected them all along, and the letters merely served as proof.

Alex fumbled for words but found none. The accusation in his father's eyes and the viscount's imposing presence told him he wouldn't be believed if he tried to explain this away.

"There, you see?" Sterling said, approaching from across the room. "He doesn't deny it. My son couldn't either when I confronted him with what I had found. And it was none too soon, for I discovered that he has left the city and taken most of his possessions with him. I suspect you will find Alex's things packed in preparation for this same journey. I know very well what Benedict is up to. He has corrupted your son, turned him into a twisted, immoral sodomite!"

"That isn't true!" Alex blurted without thinking. "That wasn't the way of it. Your son isn't twisted or broken. He is a good man, and you treat him as if he is undeserving of your love. But he isn't, and if I'm the only one who can see that, then so be it!"

He closed his mouth then, realizing too late that he'd said too much. Alex hadn't been able to hold his tongue, enraged at the insinuation that he was so weak-minded that someone could warp him beyond his own nature. If anything, Alex had been the one to push and prod, to coax Ben into accepting the truth about himself.

"Something must be done," the viscount insisted. "They are our heirs and have a duty to their good names and the titles they will inherit. Benedict wasn't born my heir, but much to my distaste, fate has placed him in a position to gain everything that is mine. I won't have my estate going to a man who takes up with mollies!"

Alex's father had been silent all this time, staring unseeingly across the room, but at this assertion, he blinked and shook his head. Staring at

Alex, his grieved expression hardened into resolution, his hands clenched into fists.

"He's right," the earl said, coming to his feet. "You have been corrupted, and perhaps that failure is my own. I didn't do enough to teach you what it is to be a man, hoping that a gentleman's education would be enough. Clearly, you require further guidance. It is up to me to take you in hand."

Before Alex could argue that he was beyond the age of his majority and not required to do as his father dictated, the viscount cut in.

"What he needs is a wife ... the both of them do. I have selected someone suitable enough for Benedict, but he will not wed her if he thinks he still has a chance to ensnare your son in his plans."

Alex's mouth fell open as the two men went on discussing he and Ben as if they were children and not grown men, making plans of their own. "Have you gone mad? Neither Ben nor I will be forced into anything!"

"Yes," the earl agreed, addressing the viscount as if he hadn't heard Alex's exclamation. "Alex should marry as soon as possible. Once it is done, you would do well to keep your son away from mine."

The viscount clenched his hands, his knuckles cracking ominously as he offered a menacing smile. "I will ensure that he does. Perhaps it would be best if your son and his bride vacate London. Distance should do well enough to cool them of their sinful passions."

"I won't do it," Alex argued. "Do you hear? I will not let you plan my future as if I am some milksop!"

The viscount stepped closer, a vein in his forehead pulsing with rage. "You will marry, and you will do it willingly. If you refuse—"

"Have a care, Sterling," his father warned, rounding the desk to stand between them. "You may treat your son as you see fit, but I will not see mine threatened in his own home."

Sterling sneered at the earl. "My threat doesn't concern Alex's well-being, but if he doesn't marry the lady of your choosing, Benedict's life will be made quite unpleasant."

"You son of a—"

Alex's outburst was cut short as his father's arm shot out to hold him back just as he was about to advance on the viscount. Sterling watched him with cruel amusement twisting his lips. The man would surely have pummeled him into mincemeat, but Alex didn't care. The threat to Benedict was too real, and Alex knew the viscount was cruel enough to truly make his son suffer.

"Have you ever been to Bedlam, boy?" the viscount taunted. "Ever seen the cramped cells the insane are kept in, heard their screams of torture as they are burned and drowned and beaten?"

Alex's stomach curled at the image of Ben in such a place, desperation clawing up from the depths of his soul. He had to find a way out of this for them both. All couldn't be lost. They still had a chance. Alex had to believe that, else he might succumb to despair.

"You would never have Ben declared insane," Alex replied. "If word spread that the Sterling heir was a madman, they might speculate as to the cause. Perhaps he was born that way ... perhaps it is in his blood, passed down by his father."

"I would rather have the ton speculate over my bloodline than allow my title to pass to that deranged gomorrhean! And I'll take the Vautrey name down with me if I must!"

"No!" the earl exclaimed, panic raising the pitch of his voice. "That will not be necessary. We'll do it. Alex will be married within the next month. And you will instruct your son to stay away from mine, or there will be consequences."

"Father!" Alex cut in.

"No," his father replied, mouth firm with determination. "I have allowed you to act as you please for far too long. It is time for you to bow to the responsibilities of being my heir."

"The choice is yours," Sterling added. "Either find a respectable lady to settle down with, or I will have your lover committed to an asylum for the rest of his days, and word will spread through society that the future Earl of Vautrey is a filthy buggerer."

"That will not be necessary," the earl interjected, his voice quavering with panic. "We will do it. Give us time."

Alex's eyes began to sting with coming tears, but he held them back, refusing to give the viscount the satisfaction. He turned to walk away without a word, needing to be alone. He needed time to develop a new *plan, but it would seem he didn't have long. Alex would stay awake as long as it took; he would not lay his head down before he'd figured out a way to free both he and Ben from this trap.*

As he entered the corridor, he faintly registered the viscount's voice.

"If I do not see a betrothal notice in the papers by the end of the week, I will take that as a refusal and act accordingly."

"You dare to stand here and threaten my son—"

"A threat will seem like nothing compared to facing the hangman's noose," the viscount bellowed, cutting the earl's outburst short. "You would do well to remember that. You might outrank me, but I have the upper hand here. Do as I've demanded, and your precious son will be safe."

Alex fled to his chambers, the tears finally falling once he was alone. Hamond had made himself scarce. Perhaps word had spread among the staff of the viscount's visit, in which case his valet likely knew what was going on. Sinking to the floor, Alex leaned against his door and fought the hysteria tearing him up inside. He felt like a cornered animal, uncertain whether it was best to fight or surrender lest he be ripped to shreds. Being destroyed might not be so bad; Alex liked to think himself resilient. But Ben ... he could never allow anything bad to befall the person he loved most. If he risked defying both their fathers, Ben would suffer far more than Alex would. The viscount did not have affection for Ben as Alex's father had for him. Despite the earl's readiness to go along with Sterling's plan, Alex knew the man loved him. Fear was what drove him now.

Alex didn't allow himself to wallow in self-pity for too long. He had to get word to Ben, somehow warn him what their fathers were up to. Perhaps Ben could help come up with a solution. Regardless, he needed to feel connected to Ben in any way he could, and a letter was the best he could do tonight. He would slip it to Hamond, who had his ways of ensuring it would land in Ben's hands.

Going into the sitting room attached to his suite, Alex retrieved his writing box and began preparing to compose a letter. This was where his father found him when he entered through the bedchamber. Two large footmen flanked him, discreetly averting their eyes as the earl stood before him.

"Alex," he said, his voice gentle. "You know what must be done."

Alex shook his head, a fresh wave of tears humiliating him. "I can't. I know you don't understand me."

"You are still my son. You've simply lost your way. It happens more than you might think. Boys who attend college ... well, they ... they often toy with unnatural urges. But, a gentleman should grow out of such folly, and you are beyond the age of such choices."

Alex pushed his writing box aside and shot to his feet. "Do you think I would be this way if I had a choice? That I would want my desires to be the sort that could land me in gaol or the pillory? A man was killed last year when passersby began pelting him with bricks and rocks. His face was unrecognizable when they were finished with him. Do you honestly think a man wouldn't apply himself to the pursuit of the female sex if he knew his life depended on it? I didn't choose this any more than you chose the color of your hair and eyes."

"I don't believe that," the earl argued. "It is just as the viscount said ... his son has corrupted you, changed you."

"This is who I am! I understand what it means for the future of the earldom, but your brother and nephew ... either would make a splendid earl. And so would I. Just because I cannot produce an heir doesn't mean I wouldn't be as great an earl as you are."

"But you will *sire an heir. You will choose one of your female acquaintances, anyone who would have you. What of that Ingram girl? I assumed you had an interest in her due to the amount of time you spend talking to and dancing with her when we attend balls."*

Alex groaned. "Katherine and I are merely friends. She is one of the few people I feel comfortable dancing with, and her nearness keeps the other ladies away."

He didn't add that Katherine knew of Alex's preferences. After teasing him over staring at Ben from across the ballroom during a soirée, his silence had told Katherine all she needed to know. She had never loved him any less or treated him any differently. Alex had few close friends, and valued having Katherine in his life. He couldn't bear the thought of marrying her, ruining any chance she might have at true love.

"She would be ideal," the earl mused, stroking his chin. "She is of a

good family, and the two of you have been seen together enough that a sudden engagement will not seem suspicious. You will pay a call to her tomorrow and ask for her hand, beseech her father ... promise them whatever you must to secure the match. I will procure a special license so you can marry right away."

Alex shook his head, feeling as if a noose had begun tightening around his throat. Despite knowing he had lost, his instincts told him to fight, to rebel. It was what Ben would do when faced with this same conundrum.

"Father ... please don't make me do this. Negotiate with the viscount and think of another plan, any other plan. Just ... not this. I cannot do this."

Placing a hand on Alex's shoulder, his father gave it a hard squeeze. "You know the viscount, Alex. Do you honestly think his threat is idle? Do you truly believe he can be convinced to change his mind?"

"You're a bloody earl! Surely you have enough influence and power to silence him."

"Perhaps I could if he didn't have the evidence of your indiscretions to hold over our heads. This isn't a typical bit of blackmail. This will affect our entire family, including your mother. Would you do that to her? To us? Alex, you could be executed!"

Alex slumped back into his chair, burying his face in his hands. His father was right. With one unpalatable act, he would save his family from ruin, and Ben from life as a Bedlamite. Ben wasn't mad now, but he would be once made to languish under the cruel treatments of the asylum. Viscount Sterling was a man of his word, one who despised his son enough to follow through on his threat.

"I will allow you the night to sleep on it," his father said. "Footmen will be stationed outside any door leading into your suite. Should you decide to visit Katherine tomorrow, I will accompany you to ensure you pay a visit to her and no one else. From there, you will return to your chambers, where you will remain under guard until the wedding. I won't have you running to Benedict and plotting to rebel against us. If the footmen must stop you bodily from leaving this house, they are under my orders to do so."

Alex stared off across the room, suddenly cold and numb from head to toes. This was the kind of pain he'd never experienced before. It wasn't hot and sharp, it was heavy and cold and paralyzing.

"Make the right decision, son," his father said. "If not for the sake of your family, then for Benedict's sake. If he is sent to Bedlam, you will have to go about the rest of your life knowing you caused his fate."

With that, his father and the footmen were gone. Alex could hear the murmur of voices outside the sitting room door, then his father's footsteps carrying him away. The silence of the room was disrupted by an odd sound—guttural and tortured. Slumped forward, the tears dropped onto his hands and the legs of his breeches, and Alex realized the sounds were coming from him—uncontrolled sobs that ripped from his chest and burned his throat.

Impotence smothered what was left of his resolve, and Alex drowned in his own hopelessness.

There was nothing left to do but fall on the sword and damn he and Ben to a life apart. Alex had no weapons with which to fight this battle, not even the strength of his title, as it was only a courtesy until he inherited. No one would come to his aid; it was all up to him. As there was nothing Alex wouldn't do for Ben, he would have to spend the rest of the night coming to terms with what he had to do.

If he was destined to be miserable for the rest of his days, it would be in exchange for Ben's freedom. It was the one consolation he had to hold onto as he surrendered to the emotions tearing through him, and wept.

AFTER ALEX HAD SPILLED EVERY DETAIL OF THE FATEFUL night that had driven an immovable wedge between them, Ben hadn't said a word. He sat still and silent until the end, his face unreadable. When Alex finished, he tried to launch into an apology, but Ben would have none of it. He had simply risen from his stool and left the gallery, his steps purposeful.

Alex sat alone for a little while, allowing himself to really feel the loss of the weight that had borne down upon him. There was still more to be said, but Alex didn't think either of them could manage it just now. He was content to allow Ben his space in hopes that they would continue their conversation later.

He spent the rest of the afternoon in the nursery, enjoying every second he could spare to spend with his Ella. Her sunny disposition went a long way toward improving Alex's mood, and he'd left to dress for dinner with a smile on his face.

That smile didn't last long, as he found no sign of Ben when returning to his bedchamber. Neither Hamond nor Simmons had laid eyes on him all day. He allowed Hamond to dress and groom him, then made for the dining room. Perhaps Ben had preferred not to dress for dinner, which didn't bother Alex a whit. He simply needed to see Ben, to know that he hadn't ruined everything by finally telling the truth.

Ben wasn't in the dining room and didn't make an appearance for the meal. Fisher did join him, though he'd been a silent companion once learning that Ben had wandered off and was nowhere to be found. Alex could barely stomach a single bite, and spent the duration of mealtime pushing things about on his plate. He didn't even possess the desire to sample the cheesecake presented for dessert. Once Fisher had finished demolishing three plates full, they parted ways, with Alex trudging up to his room. Worry had him wanting to send a search party for Ben, but Alex stayed his hand. Ben was safe and would return on his own terms. Alex didn't want to make matters worse by interfering.

Shedding his coat and cravat, Alex took up a book and waited. Ben didn't appear for another three hours, washed and changed out of his training attire. He looked haggard and worn, a thick sprinkle of whiskers shadowing his jaw. Upon finding Alex awaiting him, Ben approached and took the chair beside his.

At first, neither of them spoke. Alex closed his book but remained silent, waiting for Ben to steer the conversation. As of now, Alex had no idea where they stood or where to begin.

Finally, Ben issued a deep sigh and met Alex's gaze, his mouth drawn down. "I've spent the day thinking about everything you told me, and comparing it to my side of the story. I have gone over it several times, thinking of what you might have done differently and what I might have done had the shoe been on the other foot."

"You would have been braver than I am," Alex replied. "You would have told both our fathers to go to the devil. You would have fought every footman who tried to keep you locked in your room. You would never have agreed to marry someone rather than be with me."

Ben studied him closely for a moment, slowly nodding his head. "Yes, I would have."

"I always knew you were the brave one. I wasn't strong enough to fight, Ben, and I'm so sorry. If I had to pay for my mistake for the rest of my life, it would be no more than I deserve."

"No," Ben replied, shocking Alex to his core. "You did the right thing. I would have done all the things you just said. I would have died fighting. And you would have been damned as a result of my folly. Neither of us would have gone unscathed."

Alex shook his head, uncertain he had heard Ben correctly. "You ... you aren't angry with me?"

Ben ran a hand over his face. "Not for leaving me to await you in Dover. As much as it pains me to admit it, you made the right decision. I only wished you had found some way to tell me, even after you had wed Katherine. A letter, a visit ... something."

"I didn't think you would hear me out."

"I would have."

"Would you?" Alex challenged. "I tried to pay a call after Katherine and I returned from our wedding trip. I was told you refused to see me."

Ben sat up straighter, eyebrows knitting together. "What?"

"Your father's butler turned me away and told me not to return. You didn't want to see me, ever."

Ben shook his head, then lowered it into his hands. "Goddamn it. I was never told you had come to call. My father is the one who turned you away."

Alex frowned. "Weren't you able to get word to me somehow? Even just to demand an explanation?"

Ben raised his head, a haunted expression overtaking his features. "I couldn't. You see, he didn't follow through with his threat to commit me, but when I returned from Dover, he had other plans in mind. First, the beating. He had three footmen keep me caged in so he could abuse me as he saw fit. As I lay there bleeding and aching, the footmen took me to my bedchamber. I didn't leave that room for three months."

Intuition made Alex feel sick, his skin crawling as he guessed at what Ben would reveal. "He didn't."

"He did. A mad-doctor paid to be at his beck and call meant no one had to know that I was being treated for insanity due to immoral behavior. I fought the treatments with everything I had at first. But after being half-starved and beaten until I could barely breathe, I didn't have the strength anymore. I could only muster the strength to live through each day, certain it would be my last."

"Ben," Alex whispered, grief bringing tears to his eyes. "What you must have suffered."

Ben was beyond this room now, staring into the fire and reciting the atrocities committed against him as if they hadn't happened to him, but someone else. "Purgatives to clear my body of foul spirits. Gruel and water, because a rich diet encouraged depravity and excess. All my clothes were taken away so I couldn't leave. Ice baths and near-drownings in the tub ... the water was so cold it felt like dozens of knives stabbing me in the chest. A strait-waistcoat when I grew violent ... leeches to pull the poison out of me."

A hot tear tracked down Alex's cheek, his heart aching as he was confronted with what his decision had resulted in. "How did it end?"

A soft smile curved Ben's mouth. "Aubrey and Nick. They

had visited several times after realizing they hadn't seen me about Town in a while. My father did to them what he did to you. He turned them away, telling them I was indisposed and would see no one. But they wouldn't accept it. They returned and pushed their way inside, running up to my chamber to find me shivering in an ice bath. I'd lost two stone of weight and hadn't been allowed food in days. Nick threatened to hire a magistrate if I wasn't allowed to leave. Aubrey pulled me from the tub and carried me to the bed—I was too weak to stand. He dressed me while Nick argued with my father, and in the end our friends had their way. They took me from that house and helped nurse me back to health. My father tried to retrieve me, turning up at Aubrey's townhouse to put up a fuss ... but I wasn't there. Aubrey and Nick had stashed me in the upper room over Rowland-Drake to hide me from him. Aubrey and Elizabeth's nurse fed me and kept me comfortable until I was strong enough to care for myself. I lived in that upper room for two months before returning home. By then my father had returned to Norfolk. I dismissed the entire staff and hired new servants who were loyal to me and not him. I took up training with Fisher and spent my time trying to forget you. Somehow, I never could. You haunted me in my dreams and my waking hours. It was torment."

Alex turned his chair to face Ben's, placing a hand over one of his. "I never forgot you either. I longed for you, I mourned what we could never have. But I never suffered as you did, and I will never forgive myself for it."

"There is nothing to be sorry for. I blamed you, but it was my father's choice. *He* is the one who put me through hell. I suppose for a time it was easier to blame you for all of it."

Staring at Ben's profile, Alex reached with his free hand to push back the fall of Ben's overgrown hair. The scar on his temple showed clearly, white and puckered.

"Is that how you got this scar? I'd noticed you touch it quite often, but didn't want to ask."

Ben looked at him again, making no move to push Alex's hand away. "No, my father didn't do this to me. I did it to myself."

"What do you mean?"

"I mean ... one night, I'd had enough. I didn't think I could go on any longer. I was still in so much pain, and couldn't function as I once had. I was drunk more often than not, and slept the hours away to escape the realities that awaited me."

Alex tightened his hold on Ben's hand, disbelief a stunning force. "Ben ... please tell me you didn't ..."

"I did," Ben replied without batting an eyelash. "I loaded my pistol, put it to my head, and pulled the trigger."

CHAPTER 10

*"The shocking news of the nuptials of the Hon. Mr. G—once one of
London's most notorious rakes—eventually gave way to speculation and
anticipation. How long might it take for the man to grow bored of his
new bride? Apparently, far longer than many of us supposed, as Mr. G
has not been seen about Town in months."*
-The London Gossip, 31 January 1820

Benedict supposed he had shocked Alex into a stupor. After finally revealing the truth behind the scar on his temple, Benedict had waited for the expected hysterics. There had been none. Alex only stared at him, lips parted and eyes unblinking.

There was nothing for Benedict to do but keep talking. "It was sheer luck that Aubrey happened to visit that night. He was shown into my study, where I sat with an empty brandy bottle and my pistol, trying to work up the nerve to end my life."

"Dear God," Alex whispered, his voice small and broken.

Benedict had remained steady through the recitation of his darkest moments out of necessity. He had never spoken of this to anyone, and only Nick and Aubrey knew the extent of his trauma. Only Aubrey knew the true reason his father had put him in the hands of Dr. Pruett. Now, he was cutting himself open all over again, making himself vulnerable to the person who had initially wounded him—however unintentional it had been.

"Aubrey tried to talk me down," Benedict murmured, aware that his voice had grown hoarse and that his chest was so tight he could barely breathe. "He told me that my life was still worth living. I couldn't see it then, but he promised me that I would see it for myself if I tried hard enough. But I was too distraught."

"Ben."

Benedict couldn't seem to stop now that he'd begun, all the poison and pain that had gnawed away at him pouring out in a deluge. "I told him he should let me die. I was too broken to go on, to be a good friend to him or anyone else. I didn't think I could ever love anyone as much as I loved you, and you were out of my reach. There was nothing else to live for. So ... I lifted the gun and told Aubrey to leave. I couldn't do it with him watching me. He begged, he pleaded, he threatened. In the end, I was weak ... I put my finger on the trigger. Aubrey ran across the room and dove over my desk, his fingers closing around the gun just as I pulled the trigger. He managed to wrench it far enough that when it fired, the bullet merely grazed me."

"The hole in your office wall ... I saw something shiny and round embedded inside it. That was the bullet you tried to shoot yourself with."

Benedict snorted. "Technically, I did shoot myself, and it hurt like hell. Burned my skin away and sent me toppling out of my chair. Aubrey threw the gun aside and came down beside me. He refused to leave me alone in the days following, too afraid I might decide to do it again."

"And ... did you?"

Benedict found he could no longer meet Alex's gaze. It was too penetrating and knowing, too hypnotizing in its intensity. "I wanted to," he admitted, staring down at his hands. They began to blur before his eyes, his eyes prickling. "Every year on the day of your marriage, I would sit and think of that day. You, so painfully handsome in your wedding attire. Katherine, perfect and lovely and acceptable as your match. Aubrey begged me not to attend, but I couldn't stay away if for no reason other than assuring myself that it was real. On the anniversary of the wedding, I sat in my study and stared at the safe where I kept that pistol, and contemplated taking it out. But, looking at that hole in my wall served as a reminder of my lowest point. Once my body recovered from Dr. Pruett's torture, I began putting my life back together. I had friends, and Aubrey's family became my family. I was free of my father and had made it clear he would never exert that kind of control over me again. I did have something to live for. It's why I never had the hole patched. I needed to see that bullet to remind myself how close I came to death. If I could survive that, I could survive anything."

Alex lurched from his seat, going to his knees before Benedict. With a wet sniffle, Alex threw both arms around his waist and buried his face against Benedict's chest.

"I'm so glad you survived," he said, his voice cracking. "Promise me you'll never do anything like that again. I would die if you left me that way. I wouldn't survive it."

Something within Benedict crumbled, releasing the pressure that had been building for years. He slumped against Alex, weary of fighting, needing closeness with another person when he was so raw and in such pain.

No, he didn't need to be close to just anyone. It was Alex he needed, and just now he wasn't ashamed to admit it. Laying his head atop Alex's, Benedict clung to him, allowing himself to feel the weight of all that had been said.

"There now," Benedict murmured. "My story wasn't really anything to cry over, was it? Alex, stop it."

Raising his head to look at Benedict, Alex revealed the wet streaks on his cheeks, which were flushed pink. "But Ben ... *you're* crying, too."

Benedict blinked, registering for the first time the warm

tears trickling toward his jaw. They kept coming as the pressure in his chest released, sending a wave of relief through him. His breath quickened as if he might start sobbing, but Benedict held it in, his shoulders quaking from the force of it. Alex was on his feet, pulling Benedict up and urging him into a tight embrace. Benedict couldn't have freed himself if he tried ... but then, it would be a lie to assert that he wanted to. Burying his head in Alex's neck, he allowed himself time to experience the emotional release, and the kind of closeness he hadn't allowed anyone in so long.

Alex stroked his hair and kissed his brow, before taking his hand. "Will you come to bed with me? Or I'll send for dinner?"

"I found a tavern with a decent stew and ate there. Bed sounds perfect."

He let Alex pull him along, exhausted now that all had been revealed. Benedict felt as if he'd been physically pummeled, his body aching and his head swimming. The soft mattress cradled him, and the pillow was a sweet relief to his pounding head. Alex took a few minutes to come to bed, and when he did, he wore only his breeches. Alex helped Benedict out of his shirt, then laid behind him, spooning his body in a comforting hold. His bare hand fell against Benedict's chest, fingers toying with the springy hairs. Alex nuzzled the back of his neck, pressing soft kisses along his nape.

His body began to stir in response to the stimuli, but Benedict didn't have the strength to act on it. Instead, he sank into the warmth of Alex's hold and gave himself over to sleep. The last thing he heard before falling asleep was Alex's soft whisper.

"I love you, Ben."

BENEDICT WOKE THE NEXT MORNING TO ALEX'S HAND TOYING at the fastening of his trousers. Through bleary eyes, he realized it was not yet dawn. Instead of allowing himself a few more minutes of slumber, Benedict reached for wakefulness, nudging his cock against Alex's question hand.

"Good morning," Alex's sleep-roughened voice rumbled in his ear.

Benedict murmured something in response, the pleasure of fingers stroking the length of his cock making it difficult to string words together.

Alex chuckled, the vibrations in his chest rippling across Benedict's back. "At least part of you is wide awake."

Benedict grunted when Alex gave him a squeeze, then began working him in slow, lazy motions. "It's always the first part of me to wake up."

"Hmm ... so the fact that I'm touching you has nothing to do with it?"

"Of course not, don't be ridiculous."

"Then I suppose I should stop."

Benedict caught Alex's hand before he could pull it free. Pressing it back against his cock, he rolled his hips, surging his erection against Alex's palm.

"Don't you dare."

Alex laughed again, but obliged him, his strokes becoming firmer and faster. Alex's breath quickened against Benedict's back, nibbling lips and a searching tongue finding the places along his neck and shoulder that made him shiver. Another hand worked his trousers further down, then cupped one of his buttocks and squeezed.

"God," Alex groaned. "I can't decide which part of you is my favorite, but this arse is definitely one of the most alluring."

Benedict gritted his teeth and fought off a sudden climax, wanting the euphoric haze of being pleasured before fully awake to last. "I would have thought my cock was your favorite."

"It certainly isn't anything to scoff at," Alex replied, his hand falling away before returning, a slick finger edging its way between Benedict's buttocks. "But only I know how this curls your toes."

Benedict's cock pulsed in Alex's hand as the oil-coated finger found the puckered circle of his hole. Part of him rebelled against an intimacy he hadn't experienced in years—one that only Alex had performed on him. But he was drowning in pleasure and need, the vulnerability of last night following him into the morning. His guard was down, Alex was near, and Benedict didn't want him to stop.

He groaned when Alex's finger eased through the tight ring of flesh, his hand still working Benedict's cock. Alex was slow and gentle, working his second knuckle in before withdrawing and plunging again. Benedict trembled and thrust into Alex's hand, the probing finger sending ripples of sharp and aching pleasure throughout his entire body. Alex panted against his shoulder, his own cock stone-hard and pressed against the back of Benedict's thigh. Benedict came within minutes, his seed spilling hot and fast, his arse clenching around Alex's finger.

Alex eased away, pressing a short kiss to Benedict's neck before leaving the bed for the washroom.

"Tease!" Benedict called after him, rolling onto his back and cringing at the mess coating his belly.

"We don't have time for more," Alex replied, followed by splashing at the washstand. "But if you're amenable tonight ... I'd very much like to pick up where we left off."

"I'll consider it," Benedict said, entering the washroom and nudging Alex aside so he could clean himself up.

When he finished, he turned to find Alex leaning against the door, watching him as if anxious.

Benedict wiped his hands dry on a clean bit of linen. "Please tell me you aren't going to start treating me like I'm made of glass because of what I told you last night."

Alex averted his gaze. "We exposed a lot of things last night. I don't know about you, but I'd never told anyone a word of what I confided in you last night ... except Katherine, of course."

Benedict was surprised that the familiar emotion of jealousy and hatred didn't come over him as it typically did when Alex mentioned Katherine. After last night, he'd come to see that Katherine had been just as much a pawn in the machinations of his father as Alex had been.

"The air has been cleared," Benedict insisted, even though he couldn't predict what might happen from here. "There is nothing else to say."

Alex met his gaze again, lips twisting as if he were working himself up to something. "Ben, I—"

"It's time for me to meet Fisher," Benedict cut in, a surge of resistance rolling through him. He thought he knew very well what Alex meant to say.

The final words spoken last night still echoed through his mind, heavy with meaning and a question that didn't need to be asked.

I love you, Ben.

"I really need to tell you this," Alex argued, following Benedict back into the bedroom.

"Can it wait? Fisher is already itching to tear into me after I cut my training short yesterday. Agitating him means I'll be too stiff and sore to fuck you later."

Alex perched on the bench at the foot of his bed and watched as Benedict retrieved a clean set of training clothes. "I was led to believe it would be the other way around."

Benedict smirked as he buttoned his trousers. "I think I'll keep you in suspense until this evening. We'll talk then, all right?"

Alex gave him a stern look. "Talking first, then fucking. I won't let you distract me."

"Of course you won't," Benedict teased, retrieving his worn training boots. "Try not to grow bored in my absence."

His playful mood faded away once he was out of Alex's sight, the impending conversation of the evening now occupying the entirety of his thoughts.

I love you, Ben, Alex had said, but what he hadn't asked was, *Do you still love me?*

It was a question Benedict was in no way prepared to answer. He had come here thinking to earn the money he needed and leave Alex behind when he was done. But now that he knew the entire truth, how could he turn his back? It seemed that nothing had changed for Alex despite years of separation and the mystery surrounding their parting of ways.

But what of Benedict? He had been changed so deeply by the events following their separation. Aside from the mad-doctor's torture, there had also been the unwelcome development of Cynthia Milbank—which Benedict still hadn't revealed to Alex. He wanted to and he would, perhaps even tonight. The last of their secrets would be exposed, and even as he wondered what Alex's final confession might be, Benedict also thought of what might happen next.

He still had the threats of Cynthia and his father hanging over his head, and Benedict couldn't allow himself to forget that. In a few weeks, he would be prepared to deal with Cynthia and turn his attentions to his father. He would stop at nothing to win in their battle of wills.

As he was greeted on the ground floor landing by Fisher and the footman serving up his gruel, Benedict tried to turn his mind from questions he couldn't yet answer. But, as he went about his rigorous training routine, a single question reverberated in his mind as he considered finally being free of the two people seeking to ruin him.

What then?

AFTER AN EXHAUSTING DAY OF TRAINING, BENEDICT LEFT THE gallery with sore muscles and a pounding headache. He was tired, starving, and ready for a filling meal. Fisher had promised to subject him to treatments of ice and then heat to soothe his body and prepare him for more training. Benedict didn't mind being made to sweat under piles of blankets beside a roaring fire. It was the ice that required the full force of his determination and will. Instead of allowing Fisher to lay him in a tub and cover him with ice, Benedict insisted on laying atop a pile of blankets and having the ice packed around him. Fisher had argued this point, but Benedict had insisted until the old man gave in. He had never revealed his aversion to bathtubs—even though Fisher prescribed hot baths every night after training.

He missed his shower-bath and was weary of bathing at the washstand, but had no other option. Incidentally, Benedict found he didn't miss his townhouse so much as he did the comforts of the familiar. If Alex owned a shower-bath, he might never want to leave.

Benedict nearly stumbled over his own two feet at that thought, chiding himself for being fanciful. He wasn't a young, romantic idiot and anymore, and had gotten by on stoic pragmatism long enough to know it was easier. It was also cleaner. Romantic notions had led to his downfall.

As he neared the staircase, the sight of Alex made his heart's rhythm accelerate. He was delectably dressed for dinner, making Benedict desperate to bathe and attempt to match his elegance. It seemed a near impossible feat.

At the sound of his footsteps, Alex turned, a brilliant smile lighting up his face. "Ben, there you are! Dinner will be served shortly."

"Good," he replied. "I'm starving. I won't be long dressing."

"Before you go, I should tell you ... we're having guests this evening."

Benedict halted with one foot on the bottom step, and turned just as two people emerged from the nearest salon. Dread overwhelmed him as he recognized Dominick Burke, as well as his newly-wedded wife, Calliope. They both looked sensational after an extended wedding trip, and months spent inspecting the properties Nick had inherited. Benedict was so used to seeing Nick staggering drunk and irreverent that it was difficult to believe this new version of his friend existed. He was immaculately dressed, wearing a genuine smile, and the clarity in his bright green eyes said he was completely sober. His dark brown hair was trimmed and pushed back from his forehead, his jaw smoothly shaved.

Calliope, who was of both English and Indian ancestry, was startlingly beautiful—with copper-brown skin, inky black hair, and large, dark eyes. She smiled at him as if greeting a long-lost friend. They hadn't known one another long, but had forged a friendship built on the fact that they both wanted the best for Nick.

"Nick ... Calliope," he managed, while tamping down the panic churning in his gut. "What are you doing here?"

He needed to know. If this concerned Cynthia or another of their friends, Benedict needed to deal with whatever catastrophe had occurred.

"We happened to stop through Kent on our way back to London," Nick replied, one hand rested casually at Calliope's waist. "Since I haven't seen Alex in years, I thought to pay a call and introduce them. An afternoon call turned into a tour of the house and grounds, and an invitation to stay here until we're ready to continue to London."

"It was very gracious of you, my lord," Calliope said to Alex.

"Think nothing of it," Alex replied, turning his winning smile onto Nick's wife. "And please, there need be no formalities between us. I'd like you to call me Alex."

"And you may call me Calliope ... or Callie."

"I didn't expect to find you here, Ben," Nick remarked, giving Benedict a pointed look.

There was a silent accusation in his eyes, and Benedict knew the cause. When last they had spoken of Alex, Benedict made it clear that he wanted nothing to do with their former friend. Of course, Nick didn't know the reasons behind Benedict's ambivalence, and had erroneously supposed that the reason was Katherine. He had accused Benedict of wanting Katherine and hating Alex for stealing her away.

"Alex and I have made amends," Benedict replied. "While he was in London for a brief visit, I mentioned that I needed a spacious, quiet place to train for my next match. He offered to bring me to Kent and allow me to use his home. We've only been here a few days."

Alex shifted from one foot to the other, looking away from the tense exchange as Nick eyed Benedict with suspicion. Their friend had often acted the fool in his youth, but they both knew him to be more perceptive than he let on. It would seem Benedict's paltry explanation wasn't good enough to appease his curiosity.

"I see," Nick murmured. "I seem to recall inviting you to use any one of my homes."

"Yes," Benedict said. "But I knew you and Calliope had been traveling and had no idea where you were."

Nick offered no response, and Calliope looked on with anxiety marring her features. Alex went on staring down the corridor in strained silence, seeming uncertain how to inject his customary charm into this situation.

Clearing his throat, Benedict returned to the stairs. "I will join you all shortly. I cannot subject Calliope to the sight of me after training while she eats her dinner."

Calliope giggled and called after him. "You're as devilishly handsome as always!"

Benedict trotted up the stairs, his mind racing as he thought over a plan for getting through Nick and Calliope's visit. Their presence meant he and Alex would have to practice vigilance to avoid being found out. He had no idea how Nick would react to the news that he and Alex were lovers and didn't care to find out. It would be just another thing complicating a situation that was convoluted enough.

He rushed Simmons through his toilette, frowning at himself

in the mirror once he was dressed. Benedict hadn't been paying attention to the items his valet had chosen, and had only just noticed the waistcoat he'd been buttoned into. The garment was a deep purple silk, enhanced by silver threads in a floral pattern. The buttons matched the silver threads, and the cut of the collar framed his stark white cravat and jaw to perfection.

"Simmons, this isn't my waistcoat," he said, despite noting that it fit as if it had been made for him.

"Of course it is, sir."

Benedict narrowed his eyes at Simmons, who had begun gathering his training clothes and boots. "I've never seen it before, and you've never purchased fabric like this for me."

Simmons's lips twitched as he straightened and looked Benedict in the eye. "I have not, sir. The fabric was a gift. I was instructed to visit a tailor in Canterbury to have the waistcoat made for you. It was a rush order ... arrived just this afternoon."

"Alex," Benedict grumbled, running a hand over the waistcoat and noting the fine delicacy of the fabric combined with the sturdiness of the lining. "He's behind this."

Simmons smiled. "Indeed, sir. And might I add that he was right ... you do look splendid in purple."

Once Simmons had retreated, Benedict was left with nothing to do but go down to dinner. The butler announced the meal just as Benedict reached the ground floor, and he joined the others on the short trek to the dining room. Alex and Nick were engaged in animated conversation, years of separation giving them much to catch up on.

Calliope linked her arm with his and gave him a smile. "You're looking well, Benedict. Better than I've ever seen you."

"The pure country air and my training regimen have been good for me."

"I think the company of a long-lost friend might have something to do with it, as well."

The comment was innocent enough, but it still made Benedict stiffen, his senses on high alert. Still, he had to admit—at least to himself—that Calliope was right. He had tried to fight it, but being in Alex's presence had offered him the kind of comfort and ease Benedict hadn't felt in years. Now that matters between them were better settled, Benedict supposed there was no harm in enjoying what time they had left.

Then again, he wasn't sure how much time that might be. Their arrangement was set to end in a few weeks, at which time Benedict had an important decision to make. He would need to decide what the future might hold for him, and whether that future would include Alex. After the revelations of the past few days, Benedict found it difficult to imagine that he could return to his solitary life without a look back.

As they reached the dining room, he pushed that matter to the back of his mind. There was nothing to be done about any of it now, and Benedict needed to keep his head while interacting with Alex in front of people who had no idea what they shared.

Small talk continued over the fish course. Fisher's absence from the table freed Benedict to eat and drink as he pleased, so he enjoyed his first taste of wine all week. Alex watched him with amusement in his eyes while sipping from his own goblet.

Clearing his throat, Ben sought Nick's gaze. "Did you receive Aubrey's letter?"

Nick choked on a mouthful of food, eyes watering as he followed it with a healthy swallow of wine. He looked at Benedict as if certain he'd lost his mind.

"He knows, Nick," Benedict said. "We can speak freely in front of Alex."

Nick's eyebrows lifted in surprise. "Alex ... knows. All the secrecy and sneaking about these last few years, and you see nothing wrong with letting someone else in on our secret?"

Benedict could have kicked himself for revealing the Alex knew. It was easy to forget how ambivalent he'd been when speaking of Alex in the recent past.

"He was already suspicious," Benedict hedged. "Besides, he's friend with three of us. Did you really think we could keep it hidden from him forever?"

Nick narrowed his eyes. "Indeed. And how are matters being settled with the Gossip?"

"I've uncovered her identity, if that's what you want to know. The name will be familiar to you ... Cynthia Milbank."

"Cynthia ... you mean ..." Nick followed his stammering with a gulp of wine, looking again to Alex.

Aubrey and Nick were the only ones who had known about Benedict's brief, forced engagement. Benedict gave a brief shake of his head to discourage Nick from revealing what he wanted to divulge. With Nick here, he didn't seem to have a choice. His presence would force Benedict to tell Alex the rest of what he'd been hiding

"I see," Nick said. "I assume you have a plan. You always do."

"Yes," Benedict replied.

Nick leaned in as if waiting for more, but sighed when Benedict offered nothing. "Right. I forgot. Only Aubrey is ever good enough to know what's going on in that head of yours."

Benedict's head snapped up, but Nick had busied himself with the soup course. "What was that?"

Nick shrugged. "Oh, nothing. It's just that I've finally figured out why I've been so annoyed with you these past months."

"Nick," Calliope whispered. "Now is not the time."

Benedict dropped his spoon into his bowl and sat back in his chair. "Oh, are you annoyed with me? I hadn't noticed."

Nick glowered at him, soup forgotten. "With all that has happened, you've kept almost everything close to your chest. I thought I understood it. I thought I understood *you*. Except, you don't keep it all to yourself, do you? Aubrey knows everything, and the two of you have become quite adept at shutting me out."

Alex cleared his throat. "Perhaps the two of you might want to make use of a drawing room to continue this conversation."

"Nick is the one who felt he could pick a fight with me over dinner," Benedict retorted. "Well? Go on, Nick. You are never short on things to say."

"I've said far less than I've wanted to," Nick said. "Do you think me a child, that you must coddle me and protect me from the truth? I could understand why you wouldn't want to worry Hugh or David … but me? I've known you longer than any of them, yet you treat me like an outsider."

Benedict came to his feet, hands braced on the table. "Perhaps if you didn't act like a child, I wouldn't have to treat you like one. Do you want to know why I don't tell you everything? It's because I am too busy cleaning up your messes and wiping your nose like a goddamn nursemaid! Your gambling, your drinking, your lack of care for your own well-being … I've come behind you, fixing the things you've broken as you traipse about without considering how your actions affect us all!"

"I never asked you to do any of it!" Nick roared. He was standing now, hands clenched and trembling at his sides. "I didn't need you to be my father. I only ever needed you to be my friend."

"And as your friend, I cared enough to help you. I tell Aubrey everything because of the five of us, he's the levelheaded one. He knows how to solve problems, and he can do it without panicking and making matters worse. If I never confided in you, it's because I didn't think you could handle it."

Nick snorted and shook his head. "Your overinflated opinion of yourself is astounding. You take pride in being the one to sort everyone else's problems and clean their messes, but you neglect your own! You've been falling apart for months, and we can all see it! But do go on about what a scapegrace I am. If that's what you must do to make yourself feel better, then have at it."

Before Benedict could voice the blistering retort lingering on his tongue, Calliope shot to her feet.

"Stop it, both of you," she said, a sharp command injected through her words. "Nick, we are a guest in Alex's home, and you are being unconscionably rude. You haven't seen him in years, and should take this time to grow reacquainted. Benedict, Nick has been hurt ever since that night at Boodles over the things that were said. However, he ought not have begun this conversation at the table. If the two of you wish to argue or bludgeon one another, I suggest you do so outside and leave Alex and I to our meal!"

Nick plopped down into his chair like a naughty pupil who'd just had his knuckles rapped with a ruler. His wife glared at him while taking her seat, as if to quell any lingering rebellion. Benedict followed suit, forcing himself to eat though his stomach was now in knots.

He'd had no idea Nick felt that way. Throughout their long friendship, Benedict had always been the one Nick came to with a problem. Since university, Benedict had deftly maneuvered Nick out of dangerous situations, secure in the knowledge that as long as they were friends, he would be there to continue in that way. Benedict wasn't privileged to have many friends, and for years, Alex and Nick had been the only ones. If Nick hadn't wanted his interference, he'd never said so, and he certainly had never acted as if he didn't.

The meal went on with the strained silence broken only by casual conversation between Alex and Calliope. Benedict rediscovered his appetite, his stomach begging for sustenance after the long day of training. He gorged himself on lamb and potatoes drenched in a rich sauce, pork pie with a flaky crust, and two slices of pound cake. He guzzled wine to dull the ache in his head, and did his best act as if this were a normal meal shared by friends.

When it ended, they returned to the salon, where Alex and Calliope fell into talk about fabric and gowns. Nick and Benedict sipped their port and stared at one another with silent animosity. It wasn't until Calliope approached to tell her husband she was ready to turn in for the night that Nick finally spoke.

"I won't apologize for the way I feel," he said. "But I am sorry if you felt blindsided by what I said. If we aren't friends anymore, I suppose I would understand."

Benedict laughed. "I see no reason to end our friendship over a row. It isn't as if we've never had one before."

"True enough."

"You are stuck with me, I'm afraid."

Nick took his wife's hand to lead her away. "Sooner or later, I suspect it will be *me* taking care of *you*."

Once they were alone, Alex came to sit beside him on the love seat. Their sizes pushed them tight against each other, and Alex's hand fell onto his thigh.

"I'm sorry," Benedict mumbled. "I didn't mean for that to happen."

"Think nothing of it. Nick has always had a quick temper and never knew how to hold his tongue until the right time. He baited you."

Benedict scoffed and laid his head against the back of the sofa and closed his eyes. "He does it like no one else can."

"Even me?" Alex teased.

Benedict opened one eye to peer at Alex. "Even you, though you have certainly given him competition."

With a deep sigh, Alex leaned into him, his head falling against Benedict's shoulder. Benedict laid his hand atop Alex's and took in the sweet smell of him.

"You smell like cake," he said.

Alex chuckled. "Good enough to eat?"

"Definitely. Only, I don't think I possess the energy just now. Besides, I thought you wanted to discuss something with me."

"You've had a difficult evening. It can wait. Let's go to bed."

Benedict offered no argument, his overeating at dinner having made him drowsy. His body would pay for it in the morning, but just now he didn't care.

Once alone in his bedchamber, Alex dismissed both their valets. They helped one another disrobe, hands lingering and caressing in places. Benedict had been aroused all day, rushing through his training so Alex could take him to bed and deliver on this morning's promise. However, Benedict was drained both physically and emotionally, and would likely fall asleep before Alex could even begin. All he had the strength for was a slow, lingering kiss—one filled with unspoken promises.

Then, they fell into bed together, Alex curled up against Benedict's body.

CHAPTER 11

For the next sennight, Alex watched Ben and Nick interact with one another, curiosity plaguing him. He and Ben hadn't spoken much of his life during the years they were separated, and Alex was reluctant to ask. Part of him didn't want to know about the string of men Ben had taken as lovers. Another part of him felt as if he had no right to ask when he hadn't disclosed the final development that had come of his marriage to Katherine.

However, there never seemed to be a good time to broach the subject. Ben spent his days training while Alex entertained Nick and Calliope. Alex found his friend's wife to be lovely, and her presence helped ease much of the tension between Ben and Nick. The two rarely spoke beyond a few pleasantries, and Alex constantly worried that another row would break out between them, leading to things being said that couldn't be taken back.

His nights with Ben left no time for talk, as they grew reacquainted in other ways. Ben had changed as a lover, becoming more demanding, more dominating. Alex reveled in it all, finding that his arousal was heightened by this change in Ben's demeanor. They never revisited the possibility of Alex being the one to make love to Ben. Alex had begun to suspect Ben wouldn't allow it because he didn't fully trust him yet. Alex knew what he needed to do to gain that trust, and the longer he waited, the more impatient he was to have done with it. Not just so that Ben would allow him the one intimacy he'd been denied during their arrangement, but because once Ben trusted him again, there was room for more. Alex had faith in the love of their past, knowing it could be rekindled and strengthened. His aim had always been to convince Ben to stay with him and ever leave. Seeing him walk the corridors of Vautrey Park, run the paths during his training, and sleep in Alex's bed had only increased that desire until it became all he could think about.

Aside from his own secret, Alex began to suspect he knew what Ben was keeping from both him and Nick. Now that Alex knew that the London Gossip was Cynthia Milbank, he couldn't stop thinking of that night at the duke's ball. Even from a distance, their conversation had seemed heated and volatile. Surely what Alex witnessed had been a negotiation. But what had been the terms? Why was this woman so dead set on ruining Ben and the other courtesans?

He had mentioned Cynthia to Ben only once since that disastrous dinner, only to be put off. Ben seemed as reluctant to speak of it as Nick had been. After days of wondering and being frustrated, Alex decided it couldn't hurt to do a little digging. One morning, he invited Nick to join him for his daily ride. They took a long, scenic route, alternating between bracing runs and loping trots. When they came upon a shallow creek, they dismounted to allow the horses to drink.

Doffing his hat, Alex paced toward a nearby tree and leaned back against it. "Calliope is lovely. I can tell she's been good for you."

Nick smiled, a dreamy look softening his face. "She has been. I'd never thought I would marry, you know. But my Anni ... she was simply too perfect to resist."

"Anni?" Alex prodded.

"It's her Bengali name. Her father changed it to Calliope when he brought her here from India. The only people who use that name are myself, her father, and her lady's maid."

"It's beautiful," Alex replied. "I'm glad for you."

Nick's expression grew serious. "And I am sorry for your loss. I didn't know the countess well, but she was known to be a wonderful lady."

"She was," Alex said, choking back the grief tearing through him. "I ... miss her sorely."

Nick seemed on the verge of saying something else, but Alex felt the inevitable question. He couldn't allow Nick to ask how Katherine had died; not yet.

"What happened between Ben and Cynthia Milbank?" he blurted

Nick blinked. "I ... what?"

"We know now that she's the London Gossip. Obviously, she revels in exposing people's secrets, but I read the things she wrote about Ben. They were particularly mean ... personal. Why is that?"

Nick turned away and swore under his breath. Swiping a hand over his mouth, he sighed. "I can't say."

"You can't say?" Alex exclaimed. "None of this will go away with you and Ben keeping secrets for everyone. Aubrey knows something too, I could tell when I saw him in London. This woman has been able to take you unawares at every turn because the three of you don't talk to one another. I suspect these other friends—Hugh and David—are just as much in the dark as you are, if not more so."

"Why do you care so much?" Nick fired back. "Ben was jealous of you and Katherine. He threw away your friendship for the sake of his own pride. You seem to have let him back into your life fairly easily, and now you're concerning yourself with matters that have nothing to do with you."

Alex was shocked by Nick's claim concerning Katherine. It made no sense. "Did Ben tell you he wanted Katherine?"

"No, but it was obvious enough. He attended your wedding and then refused to attend another until those closest to him began marrying. He grew irate when anyone spoke your name, and became a right ass when anyone asked him how he'd come to hate you."

Alex slumped against the tree, suddenly weary. "You cannot blame him for our falling out. I wounded him, grievously, but I cannot tell you how. It isn't my place to say."

"And it isn't my place to tell you why Cynthia is out to get him."

"Isn't it?" Alex challenged. "You said it yourself—sooner or later the time will come for you to be the friend who steps in to do something. This Gossip woman knows you all are the Gentleman Courtesans, and I assume she has proof. If we don't help him, he'll be ruined, and the rest of you along with him. Think of your wife, Nick. Think of how the scandal will affect her."

"Goddamn it," Nick muttered. "I'd forgotten that you're almost always right. I also forgot how much I hate you for it."

Alex chuckled. "You don't hate me."

"No, I don't. He's going to know I'm the one who told you."

"And he'll bluster and roar like he always does, but in the end, he'll thank you."

Nick looked uncertain, but gave in. "You know that Mr. Milbank and Viscount Sterling were friends."

"Of course. I always suspected they were trying to align their families with a marriage between Cynthia and Ben."

Nick raised an eyebrow. "Well ... they succeeded. Sort of."

"They were engaged?"

"Few people knew, and Ben refused to go through with the

marriage. He tossed her over before it could be formally announced."

Alex pushed away from the tree and began to pace. This was all news to him, but it made perfect sense. If the viscount had tried to force Ben into a betrothal, then it stood to reason it had happened after Alex had married Katherine. Had Sterling tried to punish him for running away with Alex or refusing to marry Cynthia? Alex wouldn't be surprised if it were both.

"I would imagine Cynthia was incensed to have been rejected that way," Alex mused aloud. "But no one knew. Why not seek another husband instead of becoming a spinster and wreaking havoc on Ben and the rest of the *ton*?"

"The Milbanks have been trying to claw their way into high society for years, and marriage to a future viscount might have been their best chance at cementing their place. If there is anything other than that, you'll have to ask Ben. I know nothing else."

"You've been very helpful. I think I might know of a way to end this for good, but I will need your help. Ben can't know. He'll only try to take matters into his own hands, when what he needs is help. He can't do it alone."

Nick looked at Alex as if he'd lost his mind. "This woman is dangerous, Alex. If we fail, not only will Ben kill us both, but everyone we care about will be ruined. You don't know Hugh and David yet, but they're good men. Both have wives who are expecting children—one this spring, and the other in the summer."

"I understand. The plan isn't foolproof, but it's sound."

"Are you going to treat me like Ben does and keep the details to yourself?"

With a grin, Alex placed a hand on Nick's shoulder. "Not a chance. Here's what we're going to do ..."

· · ·

ALEX RETURNED TO THE HOUSE AFTER FINALIZING HIS PLANS with Nick in high spirits. If he could pull his scheme off successfully, Ben would be free of Cynthia. Their lives could finally settle into some kind of normality with nothing else standing in their way. Tonight, he was resolved to tell Ben about Ella, leaving no further secrets between them.

Nick had gone off in search of his wife, so Alex took the steps two at a time. He would change out of his riding clothes before going to his study. He had letters to compose and invitations to send out. On the way to his bedroom, Alex drew up short before an open doorway. The small drawing room connected to his suite was occupied.

Ben lay on the ground, surrounded by small parcels. Fisher stood over him, while two footmen continued packing the bundles around Ben.

"What on Earth is going on here?" he asked.

All eyes fell to him, but Alex was watching Ben, who lay shivering beneath what he now realized was a mountain of ice.

"Rehabilitation for sore muscles," Fisher replied. "First ice, then heat."

"Hopefully, I won't freeze to death before we get to the heat," Ben remarked, voice quavering.

"If you can take a pounding in the ring, you can withstand a little ice," Fisher fired back.

"No one has *ever* pounded me in the ring. I do the pounding."

"Quiet!" Fisher admonished. "Save your energy for tomorrow's training. I know you've been eating unapproved foods. I can see it all over you. Did you think me daft?"

Ben groaned. "This would be so much easier if you were."

Muffling laughter, Alex backed out of the room. "I'll leave you to it."

"Traitor!" Ben called after him.

Alex made for his room, still chuckling as he rang for Simmons. They made quick work of his toilette, then Alex made his way to his study. After giving his steward orders regarding the invitations and who to send them to, Alex penned a letter to Aubrey and Millicent Dane. He hadn't visited Millicent while in London, but they had written to each other frequently over the years. She was one of the few people who knew the truth about him and Ben, and he had taken comfort in her letters.

Once finished, Alex left his desk, stretching his stiff neck and cracking his knuckles. Returning upstairs, he found the door to his drawing room closed, though he could still hear Ben's and Fisher's voices. Cracking the door, he flinched as a wave of unrelenting heat slapped him in the face. Ben lay under a huge pile of thick woolen blankets, while two footmen fed a roaring fire. Alex noted the sweat glistening on Ben's brow, his face flushed scarlet.

Stepping into the room he met Fisher's gaze. "Might I have a moment alone with Ben? I'll feed the fire and follow any other instructions you might have."

Fisher glared at him with clear suspicion. "Keep the fire high and hot. He's not to be let up for another half hour."

"Understood," Alex replied as Ben muttered curses under his breath.

A fireplace poker was placed in his hands, and the footmen followed Fisher from the room, closing the door behind them. Alex pulled at his cravat, the prickling heat of the room making his clothes feel too stifling.

Pulling up a chair, he sat near Ben. "Why do you allow him to put you through this?"

"Fisher's the best boxing master in England," Ben replied, his words coming out on rushed, stifled breaths. "I moan and complain, but the treatments work and his training put me in the best shape of my life."

"Fighting shape," Alex murmured.

"Of course. What else?"

Alex ran a hand over his damp brow. "Ben—"

"Don't ask me how much longer I plan to do this," Ben interjected. "I don't know, and I can't think of it now. I just ... I need to fight. Do you understand?"

"No," Alex admitted. "I don't. You walk about with bruises and a split lip. If your face isn't destroyed first, your body will succumb to the abuse. Doesn't it hurt? Don't you want some relief from the pain?"

"Pain is all I know," Ben snapped, avoiding Alex's gaze. "It makes me feel alive. It's either pain, or returning to a state of numbness, and that numbness is what drove me to try to blow my own brains out. I need something, Alex, and you may not understand it, but it's all I have."

Alex reached down and touched what he assumed was Ben's shoulder through the blankets. "It doesn't have to be all you have."

Ben turned his head away. "Don't do this now. Not while I'm ... like this. We should speak of something else."

Alex's teeth clenched and he drew his hand away. "Why?"

Ben looked at him again, his brow furrowed. "Because there are other things I must see too first. I cannot allow you to distract me from what has to be done."

"You mean the London Gossip? That's what you and Aubrey and that Lyons fellow needed to discuss, isn't it?"

"Alex, leave it. This is my mess to clean up, and I don't want you involved."

"Is it because you want to protect me, or because you didn't want me to know that you and Cynthia Milbank were once betrothed?"

Ben jolted as if he'd been stabbed, staring up at Alex in stunned horror. "Goddamn Nick, I'm going to kill him."

"Don't blame Nick. I had my suspicions, so he couldn't put me off. Why didn't you tell me?"

"Because there's more to it than even Nick knows! I was going to tell you everything when we had the chance to talk, but there never seemed to be a good time."

"Neither of us is going anywhere just now," Alex argued.

Ben pinched his lips and stared at the ceiling. He seemed determined not to give in, but Alex stared at him, willing him to speak.

Finally, Ben let out a heavy breath. "It was after you married Katherine. My father was determined that I marry since I am now his heir. I knew he'd discovered your letters, but he never let on that he knew they'd come from you. It was enough that he had uncovered my predilections, and he made it his mission to clear me of my 'unnatural proclivities.'"

"Was this before or after the mad-doctor?"

"Before. The mad-doctor was my punishment for ending the engagement. If I couldn't be coerced to put aside my desires to marry, then my father was determined to exorcise them by any means necessary."

Ben had begun to pant, the blankets undulating as he struggled for breath. Alex went to his knees beside him.

"Ben? Are you all right?"

"Get them off," Ben managed, beginning to panic as the flush in his cheeks deepened. "I can't ... can't breathe. Get them off!"

Fisher's orders be damned, Alex wouldn't sit here and watch Ben suffer. He began tearing the heavy blankets from on top of Ben. Ben struggled to get free, helping Alex push the blankets away before sitting upright, running both hands through his damp hair. Alex stood and pried open a window, the chill of the outside air easing some of the heat.

When Alex went back to Ben, he had drawn his knees up to his chest and rested his forehead atop them. He jerked away when Alex touched him, his head coming up to reveal wide, startled eyes.

"Ben," Alex whispered, afraid to further agitate him. "We don't have to speak of it if you don't want. I didn't realize ..."

"Because I haven't told you. Not even Aubrey knows what they did. I ... I was too ashamed."

When Ben didn't pull away from his touch, Alex soothed a

hand up and down his back. "You don't have to tell me. It's enough that I know what I know."

"I want you to know," Ben choked out. "I need *someone* to know."

"All right. Take your time."

Ben took a deep, shuddering breath before speaking, his words coming out low and slow. "After you and Katherine left London, my father told me what he wanted me to do. He'd always known something was wrong with me, but ... he never imagined I was ... so unnatural, so disgusting. He told me to choose a bride, but I refused. So, he began inviting Milbank and his daughter to pay calls, which turned into them staying for dinner. Cynthia did everything she could to gain my notice, but I was uninterested and determined not to bow to my father's will."

"How did the engagement come to be?"

"Our fathers made it so. They told Cynthia I wanted to wed her, and a marriage contract was drawn up. My father intended to have the betrothal announced in the papers the following week. I told him I wouldn't do it, and if he tried to force my hand I would disgrace us both by tossing her over."

Ben fell silent then, but Alex knew that couldn't be the end of it. Something else had caused Ben's visceral response, and the haunted look in his eyes told Alex it must be something horrible. He hadn't even been this rattled when speaking of the so-called treatments of the mad doctor.

"One night, I sent for a cup of tea after dinner," he whispered, his voice so low Alex had to strain to hear him. "I had just started dabbling in pugilism and had put myself on a strict diet—no spirits. The tea came, but it smelled different. Too sweet, I think ... I hardly remember. The footman who delivered it assured me the cook had made it herself, and I had no reason not to trust that."

Alex felt as if he would be sick, but stifled any outward reaction. He had a premonition about where this was going, but he needed Ben to be the one to say the words.

"He drugged me," Ben said, a tear splashing his cheek. "My father ordered opium to be put in that tea, and for a long time I had no memory of what occurred before I woke the next morning. Cynthia ... she was ... in my bed ... naked."

Alex swallowed, his belly quivering with nausea. "Ben ..."

"There was blood on the sheets ... and ... and spunk. I couldn't have. I never ... but I did. While I was drugged, she must have made me. Sometimes pieces of that night come back to me—a woman touching me, pulling me on top of her. I ... deflowered her."

"No," Alex bit out, anger making his skin flush hot. "You did no such thing. That woman, she ... she raped you."

Ben squeezed his eyes shut and shook his head. "Rape isn't something women do to men."

"Did you go to bed with her of your own free will?"

Ben made a choked sound in the back of his throat. "No."

"Were you even in your right mind and able to say yes or no?"

"No."

"Then she raped you," Alex insisted. "It doesn't matter if you went along with it when you couldn't know what you were doing."

"Alex," Ben murmured, his voice as soft as a child's. "I didn't want her, Alex. I didn't."

Alex brushed the hair back from his brow. "I know you didn't. I know ... it's all right."

Ben leaned into Alex, head falling onto his shoulder. "My father told me I was responsible for Cynthia. I had ruined her, and marrying her was the gentlemanly thing to do."

"What a despicable trick," Alex muttered, sorely wishing the viscount were here so he could pummel him.

"It was," Ben agreed. "But I wouldn't play his game. I told him and Cynthia that they both go to the devil. If they announced an engagement, I would reveal to the entire *ton* what they'd done to me."

"Good show," Alex said, pressing a kiss to Ben's crown. "It

was very brave of you."

"I thought it was ... until my father put me in the hands of Dr. Pruett. He made it clear that this wasn't just about my backward nature ... it was about Cynthia. He made me pay for it several times over."

Ben trembled in his arms, but Alex only held him tighter, gently rocking him back and forth. Ben surrendered to the comfort, clutching tight to Alex's waistcoat as he wept.

Alex waited in silence until Ben had calmed, then prompted him to sit up. "Listen to me. Cynthia will not win, and neither will your father."

"He's still trying to force me into marriage. Before we left London, he delivered an ultimatum. If I don't choose a bride, he will have Dr. Pruett testify to my insanity. I'll be committed to Bedlam."

"No," Alex insisted. "We won't let that happen. He won't touch you, and neither will Cynthia."

Ben sighed. "I'm tired, Alex. I thought I could carry it all on my own, but it's too much."

"Let me help you. Me, Aubrey, and Nick. We can help."

Ben nodded but offered no verbal response. They sat together for a long while. Alex held him without speaking, allowing Ben to experience everything he was feeling. He knew better than anyone how far a good cry could go toward purging one of grief or sadness.

Once Ben was ready, Alex helped him to his feet. "Come. You are finished with your treatments. I'm ordering you to spend the rest of the day resting and taking your mind off everything. It will all be waiting for us tomorrow."

"*Ordering* me?"

Alex smiled. "What good is this title unless I can throw my weight around a bit? I'm the earl, this is my house, and my word is law."

"Fine," Ben grumbled. "But you made me a promise yesterday. Tonight, I demand you deliver."

Alex tugged on Ben's sodden shirt, pulling him close. "Why wait until tonight?"

Ben's gaze fell to Alex's lips. "I need to wash. I'm drenched in sweat."

Alex backed toward the door, pulling Ben along with him. "I'll wait."

They made a beeline for Alex's chambers. Once inside, Alex dismissed Hamond, who was busy tidying the room. While Ben made use of the washstand, Alex made quick work of his clothes, the loose fit of his casual morning coat making it easy to achieve the task without help. By the time Ben emerged from the washroom, nude and smelling of sandalwood soap, Alex was lying in bed with a bottle of oil waiting conveniently at his side.

Ben's cock was already erect, standing high and bobbing with every step as he approached. Alex took himself in hand and stroked, simply enjoying the sight of Ben and anticipating what was to come. Ben came onto the bed and prowled toward him, arms caging Alex in. Their lips met in a slow, hypnotizing dance, tongues gently pushing and probing, soft pants racing between them. Ben laid between his legs, nudging his cock against Alex's and sending a moan through his chest. He arched into Ben, one hand slipping down to cup a taut, firm bottom cheek to urge him closer.

Ben released his lips, kissing his way down Alex's neck, then back up to his ear. Alex's eyes rolled back into his head as Ben nibbled and licked, finding the places that made his cock twitch and strain with need.

In a move so fast it took Alex's breath away, Ben rolled, reversing their position so that he lay on his back. Alex stared down at Ben as he reached for the oil and placed it in his hands.

"Ben," Alex whispered with a shake of his head. "Are you sure? I ... I still haven't told you the last of it. There's something—"

"I don't care," Ben protested. "I've laid myself bare, and no matter what happens between us, I won't regret it. Aubrey became my confidant after you left, but only because I trusted him. He was there when no one else was."

"When *I* wasn't there," Alex lamented.

"That doesn't matter either, not anymore. You were always the person I trusted most, and despite all that's happened, I still do. I trust you with the parts of me I could never give to anyone else—and I don't only mean physically."

Alex felt a rush of acute euphoria. Ben was saying all the things he'd wanted to hear. Even if he hadn't yet spoken those three, sweet words, Alex would accept what he was given. It was enough for now.

He leaned down to kiss Ben's cheek, then opened the vial of oil. Ben widened his legs and lifted his knees as Alex gripped his cock in one hand and used the other to explore the crevice of his arse. Ben stiffened when Alex's finger pressed against his anus, gaining less than an inch through the tight sphincter.

"Keep going," Ben said when Alex paused. "It's been a long time, but I want this. I'm ready."

"Not yet," Alex chided. "But you will be."

Ben took a deep breath, the rigidity of his body easing as Alex pushed deeper. He took his time, just as Ben had with him, sinking one finger as deep as possible and working Ben's cock to keep him relaxed enough to take a second. Ben groaned, his hand joining Alex's on his cock. They stroked together, the preliminary leak of Ben's seed trickling down their knuckles.

"More," Ben demanded as Alex thrust and curled the two fingers, reluctant to give too much. "Now, Alex. Give me more."

"Careful," Alex murmured, slowly adding a third finger. "I don't want to hurt you."

"Fuck," Ben groaned as Alex added more oil, pushing his fingers deeper and finding his pleasure spot. "Nothing about this hurts. It's ... Christ, that's good."

Alex's lips twitched with a smile. "That's good to hear."

"Shut up and give me your cock."

"Not yet."

"Yes. Now."

Alex paused, giving Ben a quelling look. "Impatience will make this harder."

"If I were any harder, I'd explode."

Alex wanted to laugh, but the urgency of Ben's need only increased his own.

He oiled his cock and added more to Ben's pucker, nudging his legs wider. Ben obliged, using one foot to nudge Alex closer. Alex braced himself over Ben, trembling from the intensity he found in those fiery blue eyes. Ben barely blinked, watching Alex with heated anticipation and naked desire.

Alex nudged against Ben's opening, easing his head through and pausing. Ben had tensed, but quickly relaxed, allowing Alex to raise a leg and take it over his shoulder. Ben took hold of his own cock, grunting and groaning while Alex worked his way deeper in careful thrusts. His head spun from the pleasure, the tight grip and heat surrounding him.

Ben gripped the back of his neck, holding tight as Alex withdrew and pressed further in, their foreheads coming together. He nuzzled Ben's nose with his and smiled, and was rewarded with a fiery kiss. Ben's other hand gripped his buttocks, pulling Alex closer while consuming his lips. Alex gained the last few inches with a final thrust, he and Benedict moaning as they came together, connected by more than the physical.

Alex could hardly breathe through the sensations of being so close to Benedict, being inside him, lying face to face in the bright light of day. Alex rocked into him, joining his hands with Ben's to help pump his cock.

"Alex," Ben rasped. "God ... Alex, yes."

"Ben," Alex whispered in return. "I missed you. I missed you so much."

Ben responded with a guttural moan, his hand urging Alex's faster on his cock. His breaths quickened and became harsh, his arse clenching around Alex's prick as the telltale signs of an impending climax showed on his face. Alex thrust faster, his own finish looming near. Ben clenched his teeth around a roar as his cock jerked and spilled, streams of mettle coating his belly. His hand fell away as he took Alex's frenzied thrusts, writhing and moaning through his climax. Alex never let up, pumping Ben through his climax, then collapsing atop him as his own tore through him with toe-curling force.

They lay together in the aftermath, limbs entangled, lips nuzzling along bared skin. Eventually, Alex disentangled himself and staggered to the washroom. Soaking two linens and lathering them with soap, he used one on himself, then offered the other to Ben—who had yet to move a muscle. Ben fumbled with the linen, his eyes drooping with fatigue.

"How do you feel?" Alex asked.

Ben snorted and peered at him from beneath his lashes. "Fine. Wondering why I made you wait so long. Christ, that was perfect. I'd forgotten."

"I know the feeling."

Ben offered no reply, for he had dozed off, the linen discarded at his side. Alex retrieved and did away with it, as well as his own. He had turned down the counterpane before climbing into bed, and was now able to pull it up to Ben's chest. He was far too restless to sleep now, and had plans to make. Nick was scheduled to leave in the morning and would carry his letters to London for Aubrey and Millicent. His invitations would land in the right hands within the week.

Everything was coming together just as he'd hoped, and Alex looked forward to watching it all unfold.

He took another lingering look at Ben, so charming in his sleep. Alex could see the boy he had befriended, the young man he had loved so dearly, and it made his heart blossom with a pleasant and poignant ache.

Running his fingers through the tousled blond hair, Alex murmured, "I love you, Ben. I always will."

Ben, issuing a sigh and rolling onto his side mumbled a startling response. "I love you too, Alex."

CHAPTER 12

"This author has received a most coveted invitation for a dinner party in the home of the Earl of V. Rumor has it, the loftiest of peers are to be in attendance—making this event one of the most exclusive of the year thus far. This author cannot wait to report to you the goings on of the occasion."
-The London Gossip, 15 January 1820

Benedict stared at Alex's back as he was led up the staircase to the third floor. He had made an offhand comment over dinner that despite Alex's claim of a renovation, there were no sounds of work being done, no workmen coming or going. Alex had been elusive in his response, but promised to show him after their meal.

"The renovation was lie, then?" Benedict asked as they walked the darkened corridor, Alex's lamp shining on pristine floors and charming wainscoting.

"Forgive me," Alex replied. "I needed you to stay downstairs until I could show you. If it makes you feel any better, this floor was renovated earlier this year."

"Noted," Benedict said grudgingly. "As you said, this is the last secret you have to share. I don't fault you for lying to protect it."

Alex paused near a door, his expression somber as he faced Benedict. "I think you should reserve that judgment until I explain."

Benedict frowned. "Explain what? What are you hiding in here—a dead body? A trove of pirate treasure? A man you want to share with me?"

Alex pulled a face. "I am not the sharing type. *This* is what I have to explain."

The door swung open and Benedict followed Alex inside. A fire crackled in the hearth, and tapers scattered through the room illuminated soft of yellow and pink décor. Benedict didn't understand what he was seeing at first, his mind jarred as he gazed over shelves neatly arranged with toys, another chest brimming with more of them, and a rocking horse adorned with yellow ribbon. A small, mousy woman sat in a chair near the fire, knitting needles clicking as she worked.

The woman gazed up at them with an uncertain smile. She stood, set her knitting aside and curtsied. "Good evening, my lord. She's been fed and is right cheery this evening. Have you come to put her to bed?"

"Yes," Alex replied, casting a nervous glance at Benedict. "But first, I wanted to introduce her to my guest ... and you as well. Rosalind, this is my dearest friend, Mr. Benedict Sterling. Ben, this is Rosalind, the nursemaid."

It was that final word that rattled through Benedict's mind, and the reality of what Alex wanted to show him became clear.

Not what ... but *who*.

Rosalind had uttered a greeting, followed by something else directed at Alex. Benedict heard none of it as he watched the nursemaid cross the room and reached down into a polished oak cradle. She stood upright presenting a child small enough not to be able to walk, but too big to be swaddled. The baby held a delicate rattle in one chubby fists, and alternated between shaking it and drooling on it as the woman approached and handed the babe to Alex.

Benedict stared with disbelieving eyes as Alex held the child close to his chest, running a hand over glossy blonde curls. The infant ignored its father in favor of Benedict, a one-toothed smile and bit of drool making part of him violently rebel and another part surge with curiosity.

"Ben ... this is Lady Isabella Harriette Obsborne."

The girl gurgled and sputtered as she again went at the rattle with her gums. Benedict could feel Alex's gaze on him, wary and pleading.

"She ... she's your ..."

"My daughter," Alex filled in. "Yes. She is six months of age."

Benedict did a quick calculation, remembering when he'd read the news of Katherine's death. By then she had been dead for a few months already.

"Katherine died in childbirth," he said.

"A few days after," Alex replied. His voice had taken on a low, reverent quality, as if holding his daughter and speaking of his dead wife required a certain recognition. "Something went wrong ... she was weak from losing too much blood and never recovered."

Benedict glanced about, finding that the nursemaid had left them. Still, he lowered his voice just in case. "How did you ... I mean, I know *how*, but ..."

"It was difficult," Alex said, lightly stroking Isabella's back. "I had resolved years ago that I would never be a father. I couldn't do what was required to make one. Or so I thought. It was Katherine who convinced me—not because she wanted me in that way. Our friendship was too pure, and she knew that I preferred men. But she wanted a child. I owed her as much, didn't I? She had married me knowing she would never have passion or real love, only the material comforts of being a count-ess. She was a wonderful woman—brilliant and sweet and nurtur-ing. Katherine deserved someone to love."

"So did you," Benedict said, finding that the words weren't simply a banal reassurance. Benedict had spent their separation lonely and nursing an ache deep in his soul. He had been alone, with no one to love or love him. He had never stopped to think that Alex's life might have been weighed down with the same excruciating isolation.

"Perhaps," Alex said with a shrug. "But I was willing to try for Katherine's sake. I wanted ... I felt it was my duty to ensure that she, at least, enjoyed it, but she asked me not to. She didn't want to learn what it was like to take pleasure from the act, when she knew it wouldn't continue after she'd conceived. I visited her night after night, hating myself for being unable to muster at least an ounce of interest. The relief I felt when she was conceived ... it was due more to knowing we might never have to do it again. Neither of us particularly cared for it, and we were ready to forget and move on. But then ... Ella was born and ... and Katherine ..."

Benedict grasped Alex's shoulder and squeezed. "Little Isabella survived. She's the last piece of Katherine you have left."

Alex turned tear-filled eyes on him. "Then you understand. I know you have every reason to hate Katherine—"

"I don't hate her. I barely knew her. It was you I hated for leaving me, but even that hatred was misplaced. I cannot pretend to be happy that you married her, but I also cannot begrudge you finding whatever happiness you could—whether it be as Katherine's friend, or Isabella's father."

Alex's shoulders slumped with relief, and he smiled as Ella presented the rattle to him. She giggled when he took it from her small hand.

"She looks like you," Benedict observed. "She has Katherine's hair, but your eyes and your smile."

Alex gave him a puzzled look. "She doesn't have enough teeth for us to know who's smile she has."

Benedict raised an eyebrow. "I know your smile when I see it."

Alex bounced Isabella at his side, angling her toward Benedict. "Ella, this is Ben. We love him ... yes we do."

Benedict offered a finger, which the girl took into her grasp and squeezed. "Hello Lady Ella. Lovely to make your acquaintance."

The babe offered him a smile, showcasing the single tooth protruding from her bottom gums—which were reddened and swollen, indicating a mate was on the way.

"Would you like to hold her?" Alex asked.

Benedict stiffened, uncertainty welling up in him. "I ... I don't think I should."

Alex looked disappointed but didn't argue. "I understand."

"It isn't that I don't want to. I love babies, it's just ... I think we need to talk about ... everything."

Benedict's face flushed at his ineloquent flustering. This felt like tricky territory and he hardly knew where to begin.

"You don't have to explain," Alex said, steadily bouncing Ella as he went to a nearby rocking chair.

"There's still Cynthia and my father to consider. I cannot risk bringing scrutiny upon you, or your daughter."

"Ben," Alex murmured, arranging the baby so that she lay against his chest. "When it's all over we will talk. So long as you know that Ella is the only person I could claim to love more than you. She is a part of me. Where I go, she goes. I think you should consider whether or not you can accept that."

Alex then diverted his attention to Ella, who still seemed to want to play. She toyed with her rattle and babbled, but Alex held her tight and began to rock while whispering to her, words Benedict couldn't make out. With nothing left to do or say, Benedict took up the chair the nanny had abandoned, taking in the sight of father and daughter.

His mind still wrestled with the idea of Alex as a papa, but the scene before him made it all-too real. Instead of the revulsion Benedict might have expected to feel, he was riveted to the picture they made—Ella's innocence framed perfectly by the strong but gentle hold of Alex.

Could he accept that Alex came along with a child? Could he live with that should they choose to recommit themselves to one another?

As Ella drifted off to sleep with Alex's hand firm at her back, Benedict found his answer.

Yes, he certainly could live with this.

ANOTHER FORTNIGHT PASSED BENEDICT BY IN A FLURRY OF training as his impending match loomed closer. When Fisher wasn't putting him through his paces, he was in the company of Alex and Ella—who had been let out of hiding now that Benedict knew of her existence. While he wasn't ready to let himself bond with the girl just yet, Benedict found himself watching her often, noticing that even as a baby she possessed her father's natural charm. Alex was like a child himself when playing with her, rolling on the rug, bouncing toys across the floor, and producing a range of noises that made Ella laugh every time.

Before Benedict could allow himself to imagine what life might be like with the two of them always underfoot, making him smile and laugh, he needed to know what the future might bring.

The nights were theirs together, and Benedict found their lovemaking was enhanced by freedom from mystery and strife. They lay together talking until they fell asleep, speaking of everything and nothing at all. Despite knowing he would soon have to face Cynthia and his father, Benedict was too happy, too at peace to allow himself to think of it.

"I cannot wait until we return to London for your match," Alex said.

"We?" Benedict teased.

"You didn't think you could be rid of me that easily, did you?" Alex replied.

Benedict was content to let matters lie for the time being. A letter had arrived days ago from Aubrey, who had assured him that all was well and quiet in London. The note had been rather short, but Benedict supposed his friend had enough to juggle with a business, a family, and the task he had been entrusted with.

Two nights before they were to set out for London, he and Alex dressed together for dinner. Simmons and Hamond took inordinate care with their attire, with Simmons stuffing Benedict into another colorful waistcoat. This one was a brilliant gold with black trimmings and gleaming buttons, a black cravat serving as a backdrop for a brilliant diamond tiepin. His coat was burgundy worsted, fitting taut through the shoulders due to the muscle he'd packed on these past weeks.

"Perfect," Alex said as he inspected Benedict from head to toe. "Though ... I do wish you'd allow Simmons to trim your hair. You look thoroughly villainous wearing those clothes with that hair. Like a Gothic novel villain."

"No one is touching my hair," Benedict said, brushing a small piece of lint off Alex's shoulder. "And you seem to know more about Gothic novels than any man of my acquaintance."

Alex sniffed. "Say what you will, they are riveting pieces of art. I'm particularly fond of a new author who has only become popular in the past two years or so. Perhaps you've heard of E. Whiswich?"

Benedict barked a laugh, not certain whether it was funnier to reveal that one of his friends was married to this author, or to keep Alex in the dark until he could meet Evelyn Radcliffe. Hugh's wife had made quite a name for herself—with a *nom de plume*, of course.

"I have a passing acquaintance with the woman."

Alex's eyes grew wide as saucers. "Please say you aren't bamming me."

Benedict shrugged. "Perhaps I could arrange an introduction."

Alex grabbed his arm, his grip unyielding. "I'll do anything."

Benedict allowed a wicked grin to spread across his face. "Anything?"

Alex pulled him by his arm until their chests bumped, pressing a soft kiss to Benedict's lips. "Absolutely *anything*."

"I will hold you to that. Now, are you going to tell me why I had to dress like this just to eat dinner with you and Fisher?"

Placing a hand over his heart, Alex gasped in mock horror. "The company of an earl and a boxing master aren't good enough for you?"

"Of course not," Benedict said with a laugh. "And I do enjoy the sight of you in that coat. I thank you for not wearing the one that matched mine—I still haven't forgiven you for having them made behind my back."

Alex smoothed both hands over the lapels of his royal purple coat, the splash of his signature yellow cravat contrasting in a unique way. "I didn't want to upstage you, so I chose the violet. I will reveal to you the reason for your elegant attire in a moment. First, I have a proposition for you."

Following Alex's indication for him to sit on the bench, Benedict smirked. "A proposition. And here I thought that was my job."

Remaining serious, Alex reached into his breast pocket. "This time, it's my job. I believe this belongs to you."

A block of ice settled in Benedict's chest as he unfolded a bank draft, signed over to him in the amount of twenty-five thousand pounds. Suddenly, acting as Alex's courtesan felt sordid and wrong. He'd begun the arrangement for a reason, but now regretted it sorely.

"Alex—"

"Just hear me out," Alex said, not accepting the draft as Benedict tried to give it back. "I am placing an important decision in your hands. Your first choice will be easy. Take the money and use it to silence Cynthia—yes, I know that's why you needed it. I didn't need you tell me; it was plain enough when you insisted you had a plan. Your plan seemed dependent on earning this money from me ... and earn it you did."

"I can find another way. I don't want your money. What we did here, together ... you cannot buy that. Second chances aren't a commodity."

The beaming smile Alex gave him warmed the icy block away, and Benedict felt as if he could breathe again.

"Then make the better choice," Alex said. "Your second option is to let *me* deal with Cynthia and your father myself. Before you say anything ... Nick and I developed a plan to end this, tonight. All is in place, but we won't act without your leave. If you say no, this dinner will be just that. If you say yes, you will trust me to execute the plan without interfering."

Benedict's mind screamed that he would be a fool to entrust this task to anyone else. His heart told him that he'd done it all alone for too long, and his weariness was a problem of his own making. He was more than ready to leave this phase of his life behind and start something new—perhaps with Alex and Ella in tow. Alex could have come back to him with six children and a basket full of puppies, and Benedict would still have taken him back. He knew what he wanted, but he needed the obstacles of Cynthia and the viscount out of the way before he could claim it. It seemed Alex was willing to fight alongside him to make the dreams of their youthful love into a reality.

Benedict had thought him weak all this time—a coward for walking away instead of choosing to stay and fight. But there was much to be said for the power of hindsight. Knowing what he did now, Benedict could see how wrong he had been. It had taken incredible strength of will to do what was necessary, and while Alex had already proved that once, he seemed prepared to do so again.

"Will you at least tell me what the plan is?" he pressed.

"No," Alex insisted. "If you say yes, I will take it as you placing your faith in me and letting someone else take the lead for a change. I'm a terrible leader on the dance floor, but I promise you that I am prepared to end this threat to you and your friends effectively and efficiently. So, I suppose there is only one question left to ask. Do you trust me?"

Benedict stood, allowing the bank draft to flutter to the floor. He had a feeling that taking Alex's money would open another rift between them. Now was the time to prove that he could be the man Alex deserved.

"Yes," he said without hesitation. "I trust you."

Alex smiled, pulling Benedict into a quick embrace. Then, taking his hand, he guided Benedict from the bedchamber. "Remember, no interference."

"I'll be as silent as a fly on the wall. I must admit, I'm looking forward to watching this mysterious plan unfold."

They released one another's hands as they reached the stairs, falling silent. A heavy sense of finality fell over Benedict, but he reminded himself why he had agreed to Alex's offer. He had something to prove, and he would not to let Alex down. The murmur of voices reached out to them from the open doors of the dining room—so many voices, Benedict couldn't distinguish them all.

"A dinner party?" he whispered as they drew closer, ripples of laughter and the high and low pitches of conversation reaching out to them.

"Like none you have ever attended."

The murmurs died away once they entered the room, the butler's voice intoning their names. Dozens of pairs of eyes landed on them, speculative and questioning. Among those seated down the length of the table, Benedict spotted his dearest friend. Hugh sat with a very pregnant Evelyn at his side; their dark heads bent together as he whispered something in her ear. Beside them sat Aubrey in Lucinda, then David and his wife, Regina. David's wife was only just beginning to show her condition, and her ethereal beauty was the perfect complement to her husband's swarthy good looks. Dominick and Calliope sat across from them, with Millicent and Celeste together on Dominick's left. Millicent raised her wineglass and gave Benedict a slow nod, as if to reassure him that all was well because she was here.

The presence of the people he considered his family offered some relief from his apprehension, but his attention was soon stolen by the other occupants of the room. His father sat to the left of the head chair, dour and imposing, his mouth fixed in a dark scowl. Other members of the nobility filled in the other seats—one duke, three earls, two viscounts, and a baron. Some had come with their wives, others were alone, but all were prominent, well-known members of the *ton*.

Ignoring his questioning glance, Alex spread his arms like a master of ceremonies and flashed his magnetic smile. "My lords and ladies, thank you for joining me this evening. Many of you are familiar with my good friend from university, Mr. Benedict Sterling. His father is here with us, as well. Viscount Sterling, it is a pleasure to see you again."

The sharp bite of his words clearly said Alex was not pleased in the least to have Benedict's father in his home. The viscount's expression showed that the feeling was mutual.

"Ben, if you would, take your place at the end of the table," Alex coaxed.

Benedict wanted to rebel, but fought past it to do what he was told. Aubrey's steady gaze bolstered him as it always did, steeling his resolve. Once Benedict was in his place—seated as far from his father as possible, he looked to Alex and waited.

"As stated in your invitations, this dinner is more than an opportunity for us to gather and socialize. It is also a chance for us to combine our collective power as peers of the realm to deal with the scourge plaguing us. I speak, of course, of the London Gossip."

Voices raised in a clamor, many cursing the elusive gossip columnist, others whispering to one another as if to protect their secrets.

Alex raised his voice to be heard above the din. "Please! Remain calm and hear me. As one with a vested interest in the end of that vicious scandal sheet, I have decided that it is time to take action. I know there are others, but my investigation of recent columns has revealed to me that each of you has been slandered by this woman's pen. Together, we are influential enough to put an end to her reign."

"How?" asked one of the barons, one who Benedict knew had three mistresses stashed throughout London, out of view of his wife. "No one knows who she is."

Alex met Ben's gaze and winked, seeming to enjoy his place as the center of attention. "My lord, before I address your question, I must introduce the guest of honor. Hodge, please show her in."

The butler moved to open the door to the antechamber, standing aside as a woman thundered through, hands planted on her hips. It was Cynthia Milbank, dressed to the nines and fuming.

"What is the meaning of this?" she hissed, descending on Alex with an accusing finger pointed in his direction. "You invite me here, and then proceed to lock me in that room and leave me to languish?"

Alex took gentle hold of Cynthia's arm, turning her to face the other guests. Benedict stifled a chuckle as her roughed mouth parted into a circle of shock. In her anger, she hadn't even noticed that the others had been seated for dinner. She met Benedict's gaze, and he couldn't resist taunting her with a little wave.

"Miss Milbank, I do apologize for the wait," Alex crooned. "But I had to ensure that everything was in readiness for your big entrance. You see, all these people have gathered here to meet you."

Cynthia's sharp gaze pierced Alex, her diminutive height doing nothing to decrease her presence. She whispered something that Benedict couldn't hear, but whatever it was made Alex laugh.

"All will be revealed in time, Miss Milbank. Please, sit here at the head of the table. I saved this seat just for you."

By now, some of the guests had caught on to what Alex was about to reveal. Their spiteful glances in Cynthia's direction spoke volumes, though no one seemed to want to interrupt Alex. With footmen stationed at every door leading from the room, and the eyes of the nobility upon her, Cynthia had no choice but to sit.

"Now," Alex said, hands braced on the back of Cynthia's chair. "My lords and ladies, may I present to you Cynthia Milbank ... the infamous London Gossip herself."

The philandering baron was on his feet, spittle flying as he raged at Cynthia. "You scheming little tart! You ... you unconscionable snake!"

"I second that," drawled the Earl of Hartmoor from his place at Benedict's left side. The man was known for his Scottish brogue and a head of hair that trailed down his back—as well as a slew of scandalous acts that had led to him being dubbed 'Hartless'. No one dared speak the insult to his face. "My name has appeared in your pitiful little column one too many times. Even if it was well-deserved."

A few nervous laughs went up, but most of the guests seemed paralyzed by this news. Benedict was enthralled, now completely invested in watching the spectacle play out. His father looked as if he wanted to stand and pummel Alex with his fists—which Benedict wouldn't take sitting down. If Alex wanted a spectacle, Benedict was ready to oblige him.

"You have no proof," Cynthia blustered, head held high. "This is an outrageous accusation. I should have you prosecuted for defamation!"

"And every man in this room will return the favor by seeing you imprisoned for libel," Alex shot back. "Sit down, Miss Milbank!"

Cynthia had been halfway out of her chair, but Alex's raised voice startled her back onto her backside. She was practically snorting with rage, shoulders heaving as she speared Benedict with a murderous gaze. "You're behind this, I know it."

Before Benedict could reply, Alex chimed in. "Oh, Mr. Sterling had no idea what I had planned for this evening. I invited him because out of every person in this room, his is the name you have dragged most thoroughly through the mud. He deserves a seat at this table as much as the rest of us."

"Hear, hear!" David called out, raising his glass.

"Now," Alex continued. "As to your assertion that I have no proof ... Hodge, please show Mr. Lyons in."

The door to the corridor was opened by a footman, and Warin Lyons stepped through. In his hands, he carried several sheaves of documents. With an acknowledging nod at Benedict, he silently began making his way around the room, offering everyone a bundle of papers. He saved Benedict for last, his stoic face belying the amusement in his eyes.

"Mr. Sterling," he murmured as he dropped a sheaf before Benedict. "Consider this my thanks for all you've done for me."

Benedict stared down at the papers as Lyons melted into a corner of the dining room, stunned by what he found. He and the others flipped through the pages as Alex spoke.

"Each of you has been given a different collection of documents, which you should feel free to pass around to peruse. But what you will find are records of payments made from Miss Milbank to a printer in Whitechapel and one in Marylebone—both responsible for producing the copies of *The London Gossip* that are distributed through the city and beyond. There are also written accounts of the lords who have been extorted of funds to escape being skewered in Miss Milbank's column—signed before witnesses. I would like to thank Mr. Graham, Mr. Burke, and Mr. Radcliffe for collecting these statements and acting as those witnesses. Each statement has been paired with banking records that show the deposit of funds for every man who caved to Miss Milbank's outrageous demands."

One of the earls slammed a fist atop his set of documents,

nostrils flared and eyes wide with fury as he stared at Cynthia. "I want her tried and punished for her crimes! Slander! Extortion! Blackmail! This cannot be allowed to stand!"

A few voices raised in agreement, the baron with three mistresses the loudest of all. Another man seated beside Benedict's father came to his feet, bringing the entire room to a standstill.

Camden Rycroft, His Grace the Duke of Avonleah, had remained silent through the entire meeting, his sharp blue gaze missing nothing. That everyone quieted when he stood was a testament to his well-earned position as one of the most powerful peers of the realm.

"I agree, my lord, it cannot stand," he said. "However, I must remind you all that a public trial will bring our scandals to light. Some of us have secrets that are more dangerous than the others, and we still have not uncovered the extent of what else she is privy to."

"Quite right, Your Grace," Alex replied. "Which is why I will appreciate the help of yourself and everyone here to ensure that the poison of this woman's vitriol spreads no further. In the process, we will preserve our reputations and keep our secrets."

Cynthia shot to her feet, her chair pushing back against Alex's middle. She was in a lather, fists clenched as she whirled manically, as if to set her cold eyes on every one of them.

"This is preposterous! You all cannot be daft enough to believe these claims! Those documents are a fabrication, and Lord Vautrey's vendetta against me is nothing more than an attempt to cover his own disgusting secrets!"

"Be very careful with your next words, Miss Milbank," Alex said, his low voice heavy with warning. "I am prepared to be gracious toward you, but only if you do not push your luck. I will not tolerate accusations against my good name under my own roof. Now sit down, and shut your mouth."

"No!" she roared, backing away from the table, one hand

falling over her bosom. "No! This isn't right! This isn't how it was supposed to happen!"

"Ah, I see," Alex said. "You expected Mr. Sterling to cater to your whims. How much did you attempt to extort from him to keep his secrets?"

"The man has been running a prostitution ring right under all your noses!" she bellowed, waving a wild hand in Benedict's direction. "*He* is the proprietor of The Gentleman Courtesans, a scheming bawd who sought to prey on the vulnerable women of London by peddling the sexual favors of several men. Many of them are here tonight. Mr. Drake, Mr. Burke, Mr. Graham, and Mr. Radcliffe! They were all willing participants in the sordid enterprise!"

One could have heard a pin drop in the explosive silence following Cynthia's tirade. Every muscle in Benedict's body clenched, his hands itching to strangle the woman where she stood. But, as the others looked curiously at his friends, not one of them flinched. David's lips quivered as if he were laughing at a private joke, and Nick looked as if he might burst with the words lingering on his tongue.

Alex remained as cool as ever. "Mr. Burke, would you care to address this ridiculous allegation?"

Nick gave Cynthia a coy smirk as he stood to his feet. "My lords and ladies, despite the deranged ramblings of this woman—who is a proven liar and schemer—I am here to assure you that no such agency exists. There are no gentleman courtesans."

"You lie!" Cynthia cried. "I have proof! The testimony of a woman who swore to me that you warmed her bed for almost a year. A dress shop was used as a secret meeting place. Your calling-cards—"

"Only spelled out the initials of the real agency that myself and my friends took part in creating. The Gentleman Courters; an agency dedicated to reforming men with scandalous reputations in preparation for marriage, as well as matching potential brides with men seeking wives."

Benedict goggled at Nick, unable to fathom what he was hearing. Had it always been this simple—disguising a courtesan endeavor as a matchmaking one?

"Any man who has been taken under the tutelage of Mr. Sterling can tell you that he has an uncanny skill for reading people," Nick continued. "With that skill, he was able to match myself and my friends with the perfect companions. I stand here today a man reformed, in love, and happier than ever, thanks to Benedict pairing me with my beautiful wife."

"I second that," Hugh put in, joining Nick on his feet. "If it weren't for The Gentleman Courters, I would never have been matched with my dear Evie, who is the light of my life. I would not be expecting my first child, or achieving such greatness in my art."

David laid a hand atop Regina's on the table, giving her a glance filled with affection. "I think everyone in this room knows I would have never stood a chance with a woman such as this, had not Mr. Sterling shaped me into the man I am today ... a man worthy of a woman like my darling Regina."

Aubrey kissed his wife's gloved knuckles and grinned. "I cannot reiterate what my friends have already said to eloquently. We all have Mr. Sterling to thank for our happiness. He has done nothing wrong, and Miss Milbank has made it her mission to twist the true spirit of the agency to paint Mr. Sterling as a villain."

"Perhaps her own state of spinsterhood is to blame," Nick muttered while taking his seat.

David snorted a laugh, nearly spewing wine across the table, while Aubrey shook his head at both him and Nick. Benedict couldn't decide how he felt, his head spinning as he absorbed the masterful orchestration of Alex's plan as it played out before him. He would never have imagined his friends might come together to put the talk of The Gentleman Courtesans to rest for good. It drove home just how much he had underestimated them all, how much he had taken on alone unnecessarily.

"Now then," Alex said, looking to a deflated and defeated Cynthia. "Are you ready to admit the truth? I warn you, if you continue to lie to us, my good humor will wane, and I will be forced to deal harshly with you."

Cynthia stared down at the rug, her slumped shoulders and wet, reddened cheeks speaking of her helplessness. "All right ... yes. Yes, I am the London Gossip." Her head snapped up, her tear-filled face nearly purple as she resumed her rebellious posturing. "But I only became the Gossip to prove that you lords with your titles and the fortunes you haven't earned are no better than the rest of us. You're only men—disgusting animals and the whores you consort with!"

"I resent that remark," Celeste said with puckered lips.

"Hell, I resemble that remark," Millicent quipped, sending both women leaning into one another in a fit of giggles.

"Nothing wrong with being a whore," added the Earl of Hartmoor. "It's good honest work."

"Don't you dare mock me!" Cynthia railed. "I held your secrets in the palm of my hand, your livelihoods, your futures! I destroyed who I wished with the stroke of my pen, and I could take every one of you down any time I liked. I am not some insignificant merchant's daughter. I have proven that I am better than you, smarter than you! I made myself from the ground up, and not one of you can claim to have done the same! I have made myself more powerful than all of you!"

"Not anymore," Alex said. "Henceforth, all your writings will cease, under the name of the London Gossip or any other pseudonym."

"Hang you," Cynthia ground out, tears steadily streaming down her cheeks. "Hang you all!"

"Miss Milbank, I have long run out of patience with you," Alex retorted. "You will be silent and listen! Your time as the London Gossip is over, and with the help of the people gathered here, I will ensure that you can never hurt another person. Firstly, every printer in London has been made to understand that producing any materials written by you will result in dire consequences. Their business will dry up, and they will be destitute—we will see to it ourselves."

"I damned sure will," Hartmoor grumbled.

"Secondly, with the help of Mr. Lyons, I have procured the names of all the men in your employ. They will be paid handsomely to never lift a finger on your behalf again. Try intimidating anyone without your thugs for reinforcement."

"I will personally finance that endeavor myself," Hartmoor said. "Gladly."

"And I will help him," added the baron.

"I thank you, my lords," Alex replied. "Thirdly, the young boys you used to distribute your papers have been compensated for their paltry wages and the cruelty you subjected them to. Their families will live in comfort, and they will spread the word to all in their neighborhoods that they would do well to avoid accepting any further work from you."

"With the help of my Ladies' Charitable Society, I will ensure that no one who lives in need will come crawling to you," said Margaret Rycroft, the Duchess of Avonleah. The woman was quiet and poised, her soft voice holding a biting edge as she glared at Cynthia. "The power of a woman isn't in how well she can tear others down, but at how passionate they are about building others up."

"Oh, I like her," Celeste whispered to Millicent—or rather, she tried to whisper, but too much wine had taken hold of her senses.

"She's an absolute darling," Millicent replied. "Remind me to introduce you to her later."

"Finally," Alex went on. "You will leave London immediately. I don't care where you go or what you choose to do with the rest of your life, but any inkling that you are up to your old tricks, and I will circulate pamphlets as far as I can reach, outing you as The London Gossip. I imagine there are any number of lords who would wish to know who you really are, and they will not let you off as lightly as I have."

"And Miss Milbank," said the duke. "I wouldn't suggest refusing to heed these demands. I intend to ensure that Lord Vautrey's pamphlets number in the thousands and are distributed to the furthest edges of England. You will be welcomed nowhere."

Cynthia ground her teeth and shook her head. "No. I won't do it."

"You will, or we will involve the law. With all the evidence we've compiled, no court in England will show you sympathy. No one will believe the lies you've tried to spread about Mr. Sterling once your true character is exposed. You will rot in prison ... perhaps even the one your family shares a name with. I can see it now ... Cynthia Milbank, a prisoner of the Milbank Prison. A joke, a disgraced has-been. It would be a just reward for what you've done."

"As an alternative ...I have a remote Scottish castle that would be perfect for imprisonment," Hartmooor purred.

Cynthia's face went white in the face of Hartmoor's threatening gaze.

Hartmoor grinned and waved a dismissive hand. "I'm only joking ... though you would be wise to heed His Lordship. The offer is better than the one I might have given."

Cynthia's throat bobbed as she swallowed. "Very well. It seems you have left me no choice."

"There is one other matter to be handled privately between us," Alex said. "If you cooperate, I will consider our bargain sealed. If not, the deal is off."

Benedict noted the cut of Alex's eyes toward his father, and the relief he felt was overtaken by another wave of dread. Alex had hinted that he intended to deal with Cynthia and the viscount in one bold stroke. Wondering what else he had up his sleeve put Benedict on the edge of his seat.

"Agreed," Cynthia bit out, avoiding the gazes of those seated at the table.

"Excellent decision," Alex said. "Hodge, escort Miss Milbank back to the antechamber. I will join her momentarily. As for the rest of you, I am pleased to announce that dinner is served. Eat, drink, and enjoy the spoils of victory."

The entire dining room erupted at once, people coming to their feet and toasting with their glasses, shaking hands and smiling. Benedict headed straight for Alex, but was waylaid by his father stepping into his path.

"What in God's name do you think you're doing?" the viscount demanded. "What did you think to achieve with this tasteless display?"

"Now, now, Lord Sterling," Alex crooned, coming up behind the viscount. "I cannot allow Ben to take credit for what was all my doing. A full explanation is in order, I think. If you would join Ben, myself, and Miss Milbank in the antechamber?"

As Alex came to his side, the viscount faced him with defiance hardening his jaw. "I will not take orders from you or anyone else."

Edging close and lowering his voice so that only they could hear, Alex returned the viscount's defiant stare. "You will accompany us now, or I will make another announcement concerning Miss Milbank and her involvement in a scheme of your design."

Benedict's father blanched, a vein in his temple pulsing. "You wouldn't."

"I just exposed a gossip peddler in my own dining room. I wouldn't suggest testing me."

Benedict thoroughly enjoyed his father's defeat, as the man was left with no choice but to obey. He shouldered his way through the other guests, blowing through the door without a look back.

Benedict took Alex's arm before he could follow, feeling as if he might burst. "I could kiss you right now."

Alex smiled. "You could, but I wouldn't recommend it. Save it for later. We aren't done yet."

CHAPTER 13

Alex stood back as Ben and his father entered the antechamber and noticed the final person he had invited to join them. He wouldn't let himself feel relief until this final piece had fallen into place. Without it, Ben would never be free to move on with his life.

"Dr. Pruett," Ben choked out, taking a step away from the wizened man rising from an armchair in the corner. He was frail, stooped and gray-haired with cloudy eyes. From what Alex had gathered, the man relied on burly footmen to restrain his patients so he could administer his barbaric treatments.

Alex had found that the mad doctor wasn't purposely malicious, but simply a man whose methods were fading out of practice. He was a relic of a dying generation of doctors, his brutal methods the only thing he knew.

"Pruett!" Viscount Sterling exploded. "What the devil are you doing here? You have been handsomely compensated to adhere to *my* commands, and I gave you strict instructions to stand by in London and wait for me to send word!"

Clapping the viscount on the shoulder, Alex shoved him down into the nearest chair. "That was true until a few days ago when Dr. Pruett's response to my letter arrived in the post. You see, the good doctor here wishes to retire, but finds that torturing people at the behest of their family members too lucrative to quit. His livelihood depends on it."

Dr. Pruett raised a bony finger. "See here, my lord … as I have explained, my methods are scientific in nature and not meant to harm the body but to purge it—"

"Yes, yes, and I'm the bloody queen of England," Alex groused. "Do let me finish."

"Of course, my lord. My apologies, my lord."

"As I was saying," Alex said, turning back to the viscount. "I have offered to grant Dr. Pruett his wish, purchasing a cottage in the county where his daughter and grandchildren live, and paying a generous settlement for enjoying his twilight years. However, my generosity has a condition, one that the doctor is willing to fulfill. This agreement is only binding if Miss Milbank can be convinced to do her part."

Ben had drawn closer, his initial shock at seeing the mad-doctor abated. He looked as if he were taking in a riveting play at the theater.

Cynthia stood with her arms crossed defensively over her chest. "What more do you want from me? You've taken every-thing else."

"Just this final thing." He gestured toward the final remaining chair, upon which sat a writing box and a fresh sheet of paper. "You will sit here, with the four of us as your witnesses, and offer written testimony of the events that led to you sneaking into Ben's bed while he was drugged and using him without his consent."

Ben flinched at his side, but Alex stayed him with a steady hand. Cynthia looked to the viscount, who appeared to be on the verge of spontaneous combustion.

"You said he wouldn't remember!" Cynthia accused. "The opium was supposed to make him forget."

"I could never forget that I wouldn't willingly touch you if my life depended on it," Ben snapped. "The rest came back to me eventually."

"It was for your own good," the viscount growled. "Marriage could have changed you, stoked your natural urges. But you were too content to wallow in vice and sin. Too busy chasing this one's arse cheeks all over London instead of shaping yourself into the son I deserved!"

"You deserved nothing!" Ben roared, lunging at his father until they stood almost nose-to-nose. "You had everything a man could want—the perfect wife, three healthy sons, more money than you could possibly spend in your lifetime. And still, it wasn't enough! Mother wasn't good enough, so you broke her spirit. I wasn't good enough, so you beat me, berated me, and treated me like a dog! Yet you wonder why I hate you so much it has become like poison in my veins ... but no more. I was done wanting you to love me and accept me years ago, but now, I've decided I'm done allowing you to occupy space inside my mind, to haunt me from a distance, and force me to live in fear. As of this moment, you are dead to me."

As if to drive the point home, Ben went to the other end of the room and turned his back.

The viscount tried to follow, but Alex impeded him, pushing a firm hand against his chest.

"You are as much a fool as I always thought if you ever believed I could love a worthless, twisted creature like you," the viscount spat. "What a sight the pair of you make—a deranged sodomite and his foppish mollycot."

Alex reacted before he could think, sending his fist flying at Sterling's jaw. The man staggered against the wall, then slid to the floor, dazed and bleeding from the corner of his lip. Alex felt the eyes of the others on him, but spared them no mind as he loomed over the person who had tried to destroy the man he loved.

"You don't have to love him, because I do," he said, shaking his aching left hand. "And I will continue to love him in a way you never did, starting right now. Miss Milbank—"

"I'm nearly finished," she called out, much to Alex's surprise.

Alex hadn't noticed that during the exchange, she had already sat to begin composing her statement. He turned back to Sterling. "My lord, did you know it only takes the word of two physicians to declare a man insane and have him committed? Considering what you did to Ben, I assume you do. You see, it has occurred to me that only a madman would arrange for his son's rape. No sane man would do such a thing to his own flesh and blood. Why ... I do think that would make you a prime candidate for Bedlam.

"You sniveling little—"

The viscount's outburst and attempt to rise was quelled by Alex's foot against his chest. He pinned Sterling down, not bothering to stifle the primal urge to inflict pain. The viscount grunted and squirmed beneath his shoe, but was unable to free himself.

"I may be a fop and a molly, but I will break every bone in your face for what you've done to Ben," Alex rasped. "Now pay very close attention. If you so much as sneeze in Ben's direction, I will inform anyone and everyone of influence the contents of Miss Milbank's letter. I might not be able to have you prosecuted for such a foul act, but I can ensure that no one of society will see you as a gentleman ever again. No decent home will be open to you, and what little power you possess will evaporate in an instant."

The viscount sneered, his eyes dancing with mocking amusement. "Have you forgotten that I have insurance of my own? A certain collection of letters that would prove the ruination of not only Benedict, but yourself."

Alex rolled his eyes at the predictable threat. Reaching into his breast pocket, he came out with the bundle of old, wrinkled pages tied together with twine. "Are you referring to these letters?" At the viscount's grunts and rumblings of outrage, Alex laughed. "You aren't the only one who knows how to throw his weight around as a peer, and in case you have forgotten, the Vautrey earldom and Osborne name are older and more esteemed than your own. If I was able to convince and pay someone to steal these letters from your home, what else might I be capable of?"

"I don't need the damned letters," the viscount growled, all traces of his amusement gone. "The mere whisper of your nature into the right person's ear would be enough."

Alex inclined his head toward Dr. Pruett, who had watched this entire exchange in curious silence. "That's where Dr. Pruett and his colleague come in. If you breathe a word about Ben or myself to anyone, I will call upon them to declare you insane. You will be left to suffer a slow and painful death in Bedlam, where you will find no sympathy or mercy. If you value your freedom as well as your life, I suggest you return to Norfolk and never show your face in London or Kent again. I will take it as a personal threat if you do, and I've been known to act irrationally when threatened."

"I'm finished," Cynthia said from her corner of the room.

"Very good, miss," Dr. Pruett replied, retrieving a seal from within the satchel hanging from his arm. "If you would be so kind as to retrieve that taper, we will seal it properly."

As they set about that task, Ben remained stony and silent, leaving Alex to finish off the viscount. "Am I understood, Sterling?"

The viscount refused to answer at first, glowering at Alex as if contemplating murder. Alex pressed his full weight on Sterling's chest, producing gurgles and panicked flailing.

"All right," the viscount managed between wheezes. "All right, goddamn you! I agree!"

Alex backed away just as the doctor approached.

"It is done, my lord."

"Good," Alex replied. "Now get out of my sight. I will send word when your new lodgings are prepared. Hodge, see Miss

Milbank to the room I selected for her. She is not permitted to leave until I escort her off my property in the morning."

Pruett and the butler left with a silent Cynthia in tow. Alex stooped to take Sterling by his lapels and yank him to his feet. The man's feet scrabbled on the slick tiles as he fought to get free, to no avail. Alex wrenched open the door to the corridor and threw Sterling over the threshold. Two of his biggest, strongest footmen awaited his orders.

"See the viscount off Vautrey lands immediately. He is not permitted within a mile of the gates."

Alex slammed the door just as the men each took hold of Sterling's arms, dragging him to the entrance hall. When he turned, Alex collided with Ben, who was upon him with a strong grip and a guttural growl. Alex found himself pinned to the nearest wall, with Ben's mouth assaulting him in a feverish kiss.

Ben's hands braced his jaw, his lips devouring and his tongue plunging as he went at Alex as if starving for the kiss. Alex was breathless when they pulled apart, Ben's eyes bright and burning with a dozen different emotions.

"You ridiculous, daring, beautiful man," Ben said with a shocked laugh. "How did you ... when did you ... I have so many questions."

Alex stroked Ben's cheek, now dizzy from his sensual assault. "Impressed, are you?"

"Impressed is too mild a word, but it will have to do. When I get you to bed, I'm going to show you just how impressed I am."

Alex laughed as Ben kissed his neck, his day's worth of whiskers tickling the tender skin. "It doesn't matter how or when. It only matters that it's over. You're safe now, and so are your friends."

Ben pulled him close, his head rested on Alex's shoulder. "I can never thank you enough. Everything good that has happened this past month has been because of you. I was dying, slowly and painfully. You brought me back to life."

"You fought for it all on your own," Alex insisted. "I couldn't do it all alone. You were always the strong one, Ben. I think, for a time, you simply forgot that."

Ben leaned back so they were eye-to-eye, one hand bracing Alex's cheek. "I love you. I haven't said that to you in so long, and I almost missed my chance to say it again. I love you, Alex and I always will."

Alex leaned into Ben's touch, absorbing it along with those sweet words. Ben had mumbled them while half-asleep and drugged from the aftermath of lust. This was different somehow, more real.

"And I love you," he replied. "Whatever comes next, I want you to experience it with me. I don't want ever want to be away from you again. I know we cannot have the same sort of life as those who love one another and can legally wed and freely share their devotion. But if none of that matters to you, it doesn't matter to me. I just want you and Ella, and a long life devoid of all the hurt and destruction our past has given us."

"Yes," Ben replied, giving Alex a short, soft kiss. "I want that, too. Now that you've offered me the world, you'll never be rid of me. You'll be stuck with me when I'm old and fat and curmudgeonly."

Alex laughed and poked at Ben's hard, flat stomach. "You will never be fat, and you're already an insufferable curmudgeon."

Ben gave Alex a playful push, then patted his belly. "Just wait until you've lived with me long enough. I only have two states—hard as a marble statue, or soft as a buttered roll."

"Fortunately for you, I happen to adore buttered rolls. And I think I will enjoy feeding you desserts and watching you grow portly and gray."

Ben took his hand and led him back to the door of the dining room. "And I shall enjoy watching you, skinny and balding, still traipsing about in your banyans."

"Perhaps I'll add a turban to the ensemble once I begin to age. I think they look rather dignified."

Alex squeezed Ben's hand, enjoying the moment of intimacy

before they had to hide their true affection from their guests. It didn't matter that only a select few would know what they shared. Alex was grateful that they could be who they really were, free from prying eyes and judgment when they were alone. They could become what they were always meant to be.

"Whatever you're wearing," Ben said just before they opened the door. "I will love you in it ... and take joy in stripping it off you and throwing it to the floor."

AFTER THE PARTY GUESTS HAD BEEN SHOWN TO THEIR ROOMS for the night, Benedict, Alex, and the original four courtesans and their wives gathered in the drawing room for drinks. With Aubrey leading, they toasted to the defeat of the London Gossip and the permanent departure of Viscount Sterling. Port and sherry flowed as Benedict introduced Alex to Hugh and David and their wives. Hugh drew Alex into an absorbing conversation about painting, while Aubrey and Nick played at cards. Calliope sat at the piano to play for them, while Lucinda lingered nearby to chat with her. Regina and Evelyn sat side by side on the loveseat, shoes removed and pregnant bellies cradled by loving hands.

Benedict stood back and watched them all with a deep sense of satisfaction settling over him. Just before they'd entered the drawing room, Nick had draped an arm over his shoulders and given him a little jostle.

"Did you like that Gentleman Courters bit? Came up with it myself."

Benedict had laughed. "Of course, I ought to have known. Only you could have cooked up something so outlandish."

Nick had shrugged. "If you truly think about it, for all the times you insisted that we weren't a matchmaking agency, it's exactly how we ended up. You were just too damned good at your job, Ben. You found the perfect women for us and changed our lives. We owe you so much more than we gave tonight."

"Nonsense. I did it because you are all dear to me. No thanks are needed."

He smiled now as he thought of Nick's comment regarding matchmaking. Apparently, that had been Benedict's true talent all along—he simply hadn't realized it.

As his gaze fell on Alex, he was seized with the need to share what he had gained. The others would know who he really was, and what Alex meant to him. His earlier fears over being accepted had been shed the moment Benedict had killed the viscount in his mind. He didn't wish true death on his father; he was simply content to live, pretending that the man was no longer walking this earth.

Interrupting Alex's talk with Hugh, Benedict took his arm and led him into full view of the room. "A moment, if you please," he called out.

Calliope ceased her playing, and Nick and Aubrey set down their cards.

"What are you doing?" Alex hissed as Benedict's hand snaked lower so he could intertwine their fingers.

"Having done with the last of our secrets," Benedict replied. "Do you trust me?"

"With my life. I know you wouldn't tell anyone who shouldn't know."

Acknowledging the shocked and puzzled gazes of his friends, Benedict clung tight to Alex's hand. "I could never repay you all for what you did for me tonight. I know your own families were at stake, but the lengths you went to ... it showed me that we are all more than friends. We are a family, and families don't keep secrets. I cannot express how sorry I am for feeling as if I couldn't trust you with my own secret. For so long, I couldn't rely on anyone, not even my own father ... not my own self. But you four—my closest friends—and the women you've taken to wife ... you're the only family I ever had, and I want you to know who I really am."

Raising his and Alex's joined hands, Benedict opened his

mouth to deliver the rest when David's voice floated from the other side of the room.

"My God, he's a molly!"

Several pairs of narrowed eyes pinned David to the spot, and he winced, giving Alex an apologetic look.

Alex took it in stride without missing a beat. "It's true, I am. Oh, and so is Ben."

David was on his feet, disbelief morphing his features. Behind him, Aubrey watched from his chair while Nick slowly stood, his brow furrowed. Hugh remained silent, looking on with his typical perceptive gaze.

"But ... that can't be!" David blurted. "When we were all bachelors, he ... I mean ... he ran through more Haymarket whores than any of us!"

"There is also Celeste," Nick offered. "I refuse to believe that any red-blooded man with sense would decline to—"

"Dominick Burke, if you finish that sentence, I will murder you with my bare hands," Calliope called from her place at the piano.

"I wasn't speaking of myself, Anni," Nick replied with a sheepish grin. "I simply meant—"

"That Lady Browning is a prime article," David finished, failing to notice that his wife was glaring daggers at him. "Though she doesn't hold a candle to my Regina."

The wife in question beamed and rubbed her belly, her ire soothed.

"I won't believe it," David went on. "Benedict Sterling, notorious rake is a ... a ..."

"A man who prefers other men," Benedict filled in. "Believe it, because it's true. Alex and I have a deep, long history, and I love him. We are more than friends, more than lovers. I do not think a word exists that could adequately describe it. But my life is with him now. I know this may come as a shock, but I cannot live in the dark anymore—not among my family."

"Soul-mates," Lucinda offered. "I believe that's the word

you're looking for. In Plato's *Symposium*, two halves are betrayed as having once been a whole. When the halves find one another, they cling together, searching for wholeness and love. That is what the two of you are, and I am happy for you both, but especially you, Ben. After all you've done for Aubrey and I, you deserve to be happy."

"Hear, hear," Hugh said, breaking his silence. "And for the record, I knew all along."

David thrust his elbow into Hugh's ribs. "You did not, you filthy liar."

Hugh shoved David aside. "I did, but I never said anything because I couldn't be certain and it wasn't my place. Perhaps the rest of you were too drunk to notice that while Ben always brought whores back to wherever we decided to flop for the night, he never used them. Not once."

"Goddamn it, you're right," Nick said, pushing a hand through his hair. "I thought it was because he was too particular for his own good. I never imagined ..."

"You are still the man I know and admire," Hugh said, offering Benedict his hand. "This changes nothing for me."

"Or me," David quickly put in. "I cannot pretend to understand it, but you've changed, Ben. I suppose you are responsible, Alex?"

Alex lowered his gaze as if suddenly shy of all the attention. "I cannot take all the credit."

"Yes, you can," Benedict argued.

David offered Alex his hand, giving it a hearty shake. "Then you are part of this family, too. If Benedict loves you, you are one of us now. Watch out for Nick, he cheats at cards."

Expecting a swift denial, Benedict glanced up to find Nick had detached from the group to stand near the window. As the others gathered around Alex to offer their support and acceptance, Benedict moved toward him, disheartened by Nick's silence and withdrawal.

Aubrey met him in the center of the room. "He's hurt Ben.

He asked me if I already knew, but he didn't have to. He already realized that I knew."

Benedict sighed. "I never meant to hurt him. I only ever wanted to protect him."

"Tell him that," Aubrey urged, giving Benedict a gentle push in Nick's direction.

Trepidation curled in his gut as Benedict braced himself for what might occur. Nick might be disgusted by him, or angry that he'd been kept in the dark. Perhaps their bond really was ruined now.

He stood beside Nick, who braced an arm on the frame and stared out into the night. The sky was clearer in the country, offering a stunning view of a full moon and blanket of stars over the landscape. Benedict watched Nick from the corner of his eye, uncertain whether he should speak first.

Fortunately, Nick took that decision out of his hands. "How long?"

"Since we realized we loved each other? It happened at Cambridge, though looking back, I realize I always felt something more than friendship toward him. Nick, we never meant to shut you out, but you have to understand ... Alex and I could have lost everything by allowing too many people to know."

"And I suppose you thought I couldn't keep quiet. Aside from being a drunk and a gambler, I also don't know how to hold my tongue."

"Nick—"

"Why Aubrey? Just tell me that much. I was with him when he stormed your house to free you from that mad-doctor. While he pulled you from that tub, *I* was the one who held your father back. Aubrey took you to that room above his shop, but *I* fetched the doctor and sat with you until you awakened. I visited with your favorite foods and coaxed you to eat. I did my damnedest to make sure you survived because you were more than my friend, you were my brother ... and you were half-dead, but I needed you. And when all was said and done, Aubrey was the one you credited with saving your life. Am I so insignificant to you?"

Benedict felt the blow of each accusation, momentarily struck dumb by the truth in them. While Nick looked on, he struggled for words until only two fell out of his mouth.

"Thank you."

Nick scoffed. "I don't need you to placate me with thanks."

"No, but you do need to know a few things. Someday, I will tell you why I've always said that Aubrey was the one who saved my life. I see you as my brother, just as you see me. It's also the way I feel about him. He and I always shared a bond because we both inhabit a world where there are few men like us. At least I can hide my differences. Aubrey can never shed his skin, not that he'd ever want to. It was enough to make us rely on each other when it felt like we had no one else. But you and I ... we shared a bond too, though I don't think I ever told you why."

"What do you mean?"

"Haven't you ever wondered why I treated you differently than the others? Why I was so invested in you securing your future, settling down, and managing your funds?"

"Well ... no. You were always like a mother hen. You kept us all in line."

"Yes, but you were a special case. I saw you drowning your-self in drink and gorging on women and gambling, and I worried. You were on a destructive path, one very much like my own. You listened to me, you came to me often for advice, and I felt responsible for you. We were both essentially fatherless, the castoff sons. We both made our own way while thumbing our noses at those who derided us. If I was harsher with you than the others, or more concerned, it was because I knew you could take it. I knew that because we are the same. I saw myself in you. Perhaps I was wrong to keep secrets and not to trust you as I did Aubrey, because the truth is ... he might have saved my life, but so did you—and not just by nursing me back to health. You, Aubrey, Hugh, and David became my family, and I needed that more than anything. People to care for, to love ... to, I hoped, love me back in some way, in *any* way. I was that desperate for it, and when I felt I was losing you all one by one, I became—"

"A right bastard," Nick cut in. "But we all knew you were suffering. None of us knew how to reach you but Aubrey."

"Now, you do too. The one thing I haven't told you must wait. Tonight is a happy occasion, and I don't want to spoil it. I just wanted to know that we will be all right—you and I."

Nick took Benedict's offered hand, then drew him in closer for an embrace. Benedict clutched him back in shock, never remembering a time Nick had ever been so free with affection.

"We will always be all right. Like you said, we're family. Families fight, but they make up and they move on. If you and Alex are happy together, then that is enough for me. What you prefer otherwise is none of my business."

Benedict clapped Nick's shoulder as they pulled apart, then they went to join the others, accepting fresh glasses of port from Hugh.

"A final toast," Aubrey said, raising his glass. "To Ben, the greatest matchmaker in all of England. You always said you weren't arranging marriages, but you knew us well and too easily recognized our perfect counterparts. Perhaps you ought to go into a new line of business."

Drawing Alex into his side, Benedict lifted his own port. "As of this moment, I am officially retired—from both matchmaking and boxing."

Stunned looks greeted him, along with Nick and David's protests—but none of them were as shocked as Alex.

"I thought you said you needed pugilism," he said. "I would never have tried to force you to stop."

"I know," Benedict replied. "By the way, I didn't say I needed pugilism ... I said I needed the pain, to feel something, to have a purpose. What need do I have of boxing when I have you? You give me joy and love, and it has proven enough to cure me of my need for pain. After this final match, I'm finished. You are all I will ever need."

They shared a quick kiss before everyone else joined in on the toast, glasses raised high. Their voices echoed from the high ceilings as one chorus.

"To Ben!"

EPILOGUE

Benedict leaned back against the supportive weight at his back, still marveling as he had all those years ago that Alex's chest was as smooth as his was hirsute. A wet hand trailed through the wiry curls, a pair of soft lips grazing the back of his neck.

"Someone seems to be enjoying his bath," Alex teased, his other hand splashing in the steaming water lapping at Benedict's belly.

"That's because I have a pleasant diversion. How we both managed to squeeze into it is beyond me. How the devil are we going to get out?"

Alex nipped at his ear, and Benedict's cock responded as his mind was taken off the near-crippling fear of being immersed in a bathtub. He had promised Alex he would try it, not knowing that his darling would include himself—naked and wet—as part of the bargain.

"Getting out is half the fun," Alex murmured, his hand sliding down Benedict's stomach.

"Hmm," Benedict mumbled. "I think I like baths now. I'll like them even better if you move that hand a little lower."

Alex withdrew his hand and turned Ben's head to inspect his face. "I think not. Fisher's orders were strict—you are to rest and avoid overexerting yourself for at least a sennight."

Benedict winced as water from his wet hair leaked into the split skin over one eyebrow. It was one of a dozen small injuries sustained during his final match—one hard fought and hard won. His opponent—a leviathan named Bruno with more strength than sense—had given Benedict quite a walloping before finally succumbing to a brutal uppercut. Benedict wouldn't be surprised to learn that the man would have to drink his meals for the next fortnight or so.

After the match, he and Benedict had retreated to Alex's townhouse, where they closeted themselves away for time alone.

"What if I lie really still?" Benedict pleaded. His blood was always feverish after a fight, and just now it was rushing straight to his cock. "You could stroke me off right here in the tub. Or ... if I lift up just enough, I could ride your cock until you—"

"Enough, you brazen slut," Alex chided. "There will be plenty of time for that. You're officially retired, and we are free to do as we please. The moment your sennight of rest is over, I will fuck you until you are unable to sit."

"Not if I get to you first," Benedict grumbled. "But then ... what will we do now? As you said, we have the world before us and nothing but time and each other, and Ella."

Alex toyed with a lock of Benedict's hair with a wistful sigh. "You know, I always regretted that we never made it to France. What do you think of a continental tour? Ella would love the shopping in Paris."

Benedict rolled his eyes. "Ella isn't old enough to understand the intricacies of shopping with you."

"She's her father's daughter," Alex said with a sniff. "Her taste is exquisite, and she will love it."

With a laugh, Benedict reached back and patted Alex's neck. "If it's Paris you want, then you shall have it. Let's take the first packet we can find leaving Dover. We will travel and introduce Ella to the wonders of France, and when we're done, we'll take her to Italy, then Greece. She'll be more cultured than any lady her age in no time."

Wrapping both arms around him, Alex kissed Benedict's temple. "Thank you."

"For what? I wanted to go to France, too."

"For accepting Ella. You've been so wonderful to her, and I think she's under your spell."

"The sneaky little lamb has learned that I'm the best at rocking her to sleep, and I know better than you what to do when her gums are sore."

A brandy-soaked rag had earned him Ella's favor, and from the moment he'd first held her—trying to soothe her cries as she rubbed her fist against sore gums—Benedict had been her willing slave. The girl was most certainly her father's daughter—charming, beautiful, and capable of wrapping Benedict around her chubby finger. He'd been doing a fine job of spoiling her rotten, even when Alex insisted she not be held constantly, or that Benedict was too rough when they played. Ella always had a smile for him, and screamed with delight when he tossed her—carefully and mindfully—about.

"There is nothing to thank me for," Benedict replied. "Ella is a part of you, so how could I not want to make her happy?"

"You have made us *both* ridiculously happy."

"Does that mean you've changed your mind about letting me ride your cock?"

Alex issued a low groan. "No, but if you hold very, very still …"

Benedict sucked in a sharp breath and did what he was told as Alex's hand closed around his erection, teasing and toying with him.

"Oh, God, that's perfect," he moaned, closing his eyes and submitting to bliss.

"Yes, it is," Alex whispered. "And so are you, my love."

LONDON, *1820*

One month later …

To my dear friend, Benedict,

I hope this letter finds you in the best of health and spirits, and that you and His Lordship are enjoying your time abroad. I am writing to inform you that I have followed your instructions regarding the remaining Gentleman Courtesans, with one important exception. I hope you will forgive me for acting against your dictates, but as you left the matter in my hands, I could only proceed as I saw fit.

When you hired me, I was lost and searching for purpose. I saw a kindred spirit in you, one that I clung to for the simple fact that you were the sort of man I wanted to be. You have molded and shaped me until I have developed a mind like yours for the intimidating task of managing courtesans and the women who hire them.

As well, in my conversations with our remaining gentlemen, I have found that many of them do not wish to be cut loose with the settlements you promised. With Cynthia Milbank tucked away in some far-flung place, they feel more confident than ever that their business can go on as before.

And so, it falls to me to guide them, to help them as you did me and all the others. Do not despair for our safety. Thanks to Lord Vautrey, we may now develop a new operation—one that will keep us hidden from prying eyes and wagging tongues.

Thank you again for all that you have taught me, and I hope you will understand why I decided as I did. The other gentlemen and yourself may not have known it at the time, but you were all searching for something and were fortunate to find it. While I am certain that what I'm searching for isn't as intangible as love or companionship, I cannot deny that I share such a need to go out and find what is waiting for me. Any gentleman who feels such a compulsion will be afforded that same chance.

I have destroyed the bank drafts you sent, as it did not feel right to use the funds you meant as retirement pensions for the gentlemen for my own means. However, with smart management and savings, I have accumulated enough of my own money to invest in this renewed enterprise.

Please give my regard to Lord Vautrey and thank him for the Parisian truffles he sent with your last letter. I know only he would have a taste for such fine sweets, which I will savor for as long as I can.

Faithfully yours,

Warin Lyons

AUTHOR'S NOTE

THE GENTLEMAN COURTESANS WILL CONTINUE...

With the mysterious Warin Lyons at the forefront, a new crop of gentleman courtesans are ready to take over London—seducing ladies (and gentlemen), and losing their hearts in the process.

Look for the 6th installment of The Gentleman Courtesans in the future.

THE GENTLEMAN COURTESANS
SERIES READING ORDER

Now Available:

Tempting the Bluestocking (prequel novella)

Portrait of a Lady

What a Courtesan Wants

Making of a Scandal

Taming of the Rake

Chasing Benedict

ABOUT THE AUTHOR

Sexy heroes ... sassy heroines ... electrifying erotic romance.
Victoria Vale has written over two dozen Romance and Young
Adult novels under various pseudonyms. As a lover of erotic
romance, she enjoys nothing more than a sexy hero paired with a
sassy heroine, flavored with a dash of spice and lots of heat. A
wife and mother of three, she enjoys reading (of course),
cooking, sewing ... and other activities that aren't appropriate for
inclusion in a biography.